About the Author

Peyton Hoyal lives in Charlottesville, VA with his family. An English Major while attending Berry College, he was a classroom teacher for several years in Boone, NC before shifting careers. Peyton writes in his spare time, usually at night, amid a busy work and family life. He is an accomplished distance runner, avid fan of good movies, and ardent whiskey connoisseur.

Ebon Shades

Peyton Hoyal

Ebon Shades

Vanguard Press

VANGUARD PAPERBACK

© Copyright 2024
Peyton Hoyal

The right of Peyton Hoyal to be identified as author of
this work has been asserted by him in accordance with the
Copyright, Designs and Patents Act 1988.

All Rights Reserved

No reproduction, copy or transmission of this publication
may be made without written permission.
No paragraph of this publication may be reproduced,
copied or transmitted save with the written permission of the
publisher, or in accordance with the provisions
of the Copyright Act 1956 (as amended).

Any person who commits any unauthorised act in relation to
this publication may be liable to criminal
prosecution and civil claims for damages.

A CIP catalogue record for this title is
available from the British Library.

ISBN 978 1 83794 077 6

*Vanguard Press is an imprint of
Pegasus Elliot Mackenzie Publishers Ltd.*
www.pegasuspublishers.com

This is a work of fiction. Names, characters, businesses, places, events and
incidents are either the product of the author's imagination or used in a
fictitious manner. Any resemblance to actual persons, living or dead, or actual
events is purely coincidental.

First Published in 2024

**Vanguard Press
Sheraton House Castle Park
Cambridge England**

Printed & Bound in Great Britain

For my wife and daughter

Part I:

Autumn

Elsa Privette

Sometimes a deer would ease cautiously out of the trees surrounding the small clearing above the even smaller house below. It would timidly step from the shadowed safety of the wood, ears twitching, eyes flickering, and then enter the field with its head down. If she saw one, she would always pretend to take a picture with her hands cupped into the general outline of a disposable camera. With one eye closed, she would raise her index finger and make a clicking sound as the animal entered her field of vision. She had a real camera once, got it for her birthday, but the nineteen pictures it produced were gone in an afternoon. That was a happy day.

Today, however, was not.

The collar of her faded T-shirt was still damp from a mix of tears and sweat. Her small hands trembled, and each breath wheezed in and out like a chain smoker's. She rocked almost imperceptibly on the time-smoothed stone wall where she sat, her legs not yet long enough to touch the ground. From a distance, her hand-me-down Converses looked suspended in air, her legs being little more than spindly thread above their black tongue.

Most kids looked forward to the summer break from school, but not Elsa Privette. She dreaded the pause between school years. Too much time at home. Too much time on her little trembling hands. During school, between classes, band practice, and the occasional blessed weekend spent at a friend's house, time passed on a different spectrum altogether. The summer's long days stretched on, like a cicada's song, amplified to a distorted and disquieting pitch. Only a few more days before she could return to the safety net of school's ritual. There was a quiet solace in each nuance, the off-tune national anthem, the smell of hand sanitizer before lunch, the cool velvet of the water fountain caressing her lips.

She looked down the hill to where she could see the diminutive outline of her house. The empty dog cage in the backyard looked like a vacant grave plot from this vantage; the tiny roof with its disheveled shingles looked like a pool of black tar. The tire swing hung on the big oak like a medallion. It swung almost imperceptibly, even on a windy day, and today was eerily still. She pictured her sister swinging happily against the warm rubber of the open circle. Her smile brightened her dark eyes, perhaps a dandelion in her hand and a ribbon situated in her chestnut hair. If she concentrated hard enough, she could capture that image, too, in her make-believe Polaroid.

Click.

There, a happy photo to remain as infinite as the tire's perfectly circular geometry. Pictures really do last forever if you care for them. She would keep that one for herself to have close at hand on days like this. She needed as many small comforts as she could extract from the world. Pictures, her cat Scruffy, and, perhaps most importantly, the little red pillow her grandmother had made for her by hand. These things were her world, at least inside her mind.

Someone yelled below. He yelled her name, then an ugly word. Then another, louder this time. She jumped just a bit, and then hurried off down the hill back towards the tiny house below. Her legs flashed through the summer grass like little scythe blades.

It wouldn't be long now. One way or another, the summer was bound to end.

Rylan

The highway had already begun its serpentine ascent when my thoughts were quiet enough for me to take stock of where I was. Almost another two hours of driving remained. I was just hitting the first of the Asheville exits. My family and I used to retreat into these hills for holiday vacations when I was a kid. Excitement would envelope me as we neared the North Carolina line and begin the long, slow climb to our favorite little tourist towns. Now, I was retreating into the same mountains as a young man for very different reasons. The joy they once incited was replaced with despondent resignation, and my body felt preternaturally tired. Listless and dull.

    This was not a holiday, and I was not on vacation. All of the belongings that I cared to bring were layered to the roof of my SUV. Even the passenger seat was occupied with trinkets and boxes. The evening sun shone bright in the west over the ridge, peaking at odd intervals to blind my sight from the black ribbon ahead. The radio was on low, advertising the end of summer events at Maggie Valley, but it might as well have been white noise. I wished that I could also fill my head with static, but the recording in my mind continued to play loud and clear. It was like watching the same rerun of an old tv show over and over. You knew every line, every black and white moment, yet you chose to keep watching for reasons unknown. I was in such a loop, and I was beginning to think that I preferred it that way.

I left Atlanta earlier that day, expecting the drive ahead to gradually make me feel better as I went. Space would help me heal, or some trite thought. On the contrary, my brooding had only worsened with each passing mile. The cityscape had given way to suburbs; the suburbs had faded to an infinite row of trees, and eventually the exits grew farther apart. Climbing into Appalachia, roadside stands offered fresh vegetables and boiled peanuts. The rolling hills became ever steeper, and the first billboards advertising ski resorts and mountain lakes had appeared like obelisks in the distance.

The further I got from home, the more I began to feel like a fated, lone astronaut departing the Earth. A one-way mission to find a hospitable new planet, drifting into Oblivion. To report back on my findings, save the world via radio transmission. And in so doing, I was also expected to die. Charlton Heston came to mind, but with a twist. Simple Laika, too. Even though the world was doomed to destroy itself in some fiery holocaust, I would regret not sharing the fate of everyone I knew. I had become Paradox in that way, so the only path was forward.

And away.

The gravel crunching under my wheels brought me back to a tepid kind of reality. My GPS would otherwise have announced, in a vaguely robotic British accent, that I had arrived, but we were far beyond the efficacy of satellites to find the way. All around were trees; in the distance only mountains. It had begun to rain some time back, and now my aunt and uncle's house rested in a heavy mist. All the lights were on inside, illuminating the twilight after my headlights had faded. The coziness and quaint aspect of the place was just as I remembered. Their house had always been a welcome sight, but now it was also a sanctuary.

I sighed deeply, gathered myself for conversation, and stepped out of my car into the night. My uncle's deep voice called out as I was sifting through all of my crap to find my suitcase in the backseat. Uncle Ray appeared on the front porch, looking robust and healthy, even in the shadows.

"Hey, honey! Rylan's here."

"Okay! Tell him I'll be right outside! I'm just checking the turkey in the oven."

My aunt's voice came wafting through the kitchen, crackling like the embers of a Tennessee bonfire. I had almost forgotten that unmistakable accent. Most of my family spoke with a rolling Southern undercurrent, but Aunt Linda had a true *twang*. It had texture and taste, like honey and lemon.

My uncle cleared the yard in a few careful steps, following a little stone-step path with grass growing just over the edges. He had the look of exactly what he was, in his corduroy slacks and loafers: an almost-retired college professor with years of leisure time ahead of him.

"Rylan! How was the drive, kiddo?"

"It wasn't too bad, Uncle Ray. I made good time."

"Good! What can I grab for you? Give me some bags, load me down."

"Oh, I don't have too much that I need to get tonight. Just my suitcase and this backpack should do. Thanks, though."

We hugged at my car while the door was still open. He smelled like expensive aftershave with a hint of good Scotch below its astringent bite. He was almost exactly my height, which wasn't remarkable, and his arms felt warm and reassuring as they wrapped around me tightly. I took after Uncle Ray, that's for sure. And it wasn't a bad thing, I thought.

"Come on inside. I know your aunt's dying to see you."

After exchanging all the niceties with Aunt Linda, and getting my things settled in the adjacent guest house, we all sat around their dining-room table in a post-dinner glow.

"That was delicious, Aunt Linda. Wow, you really didn't have to go to the trouble just for me."

"Oh, stop. Yes, I did, sugar! We were so excited to have you coming up to stay with us, I couldn't help but cook you a good meal! Ray and I have been looking forward to it all week."

She laid her soft hand on top of mine on the table to illustrate the point. The white tablecloth and long candles made this feel like Thanksgiving, although it was only August. Linda's eyes were sleepy and blue. She had a wonderful bone structure, despite her age, and I always thought she must have been a dish when she was younger.

"Well, thank you both again for letting me come stay for a while. It really means a lot."

"You're welcome, son. It's our pleasure, really. Now, tell us about this new job? I know we talked about it on the phone, but we want to hear the details."

Uncle Ray had stood briefly, as he spoke, to open a curio cabinet in the corner of the room which held an extensive whisky collection. He helped himself to another pour of Lagavulin and offered the bottle to me with a dramatic gesture.

"Sure, I'll take a dram. As they say."

Linda and I had been having a little wine with dinner. I was starting to relax a bit. I could feel the piano wire tension from my drive and the last few weeks starting to temporarily uncoil. It was the blood buzz of familiarity. It was laughing with close family. It was a pleasant medicine.

"And I'll get dessert, while you boys have a toast." Aunt Linda offered.

Our glasses clinked once he returned to the table. The first sip of whisky went down smooth and rounded. My mouth felt alive and pampered as a gentle burn rose from the back of my throat. Suddenly a peach cobbler and Breyers vanilla ice cream appeared. We were all settled. They were both now awaiting my answer.

"So, the job... You remember my friend Kevin from college, who still lives up here, right? I think you guys might have met him a few times."

They both nodded. Uncle Ray wiped an errand drip of ice cream from his stubble with the clumsy stroke of a napkin.

"Well, he's teaching at the high school now. Coaching baseball, too, I believe. He said there was a last-minute opening at one of the elementary schools outside of town. Way out, apparently. Near the lake on the Tennessee border. A teacher out there had decided to retire over the summer, and they were desperate to fill the role. English and Literature, sixth through eighth grade. He put in a good word, the principal called me early last week, and sort of interviewed me over the phone. We hit it off, and here I am!"

"That's great, son! I'm glad that it worked out so well. Is that Cades Creek Elementary? That is way out there, for sure. You'll be able to see Banner Lake on your way to work every day, at least."

"Yeah, that's it. I think it's the smallest school in the county. The principal, Tony Davis? Does that ring a bell? He used to do IT at the college, Uncle Ray. I thought you might know him. He seemed like a cool guy. From up north – Vermont, maybe? We talked music and movies more than work stuff, really. Kevin had already sent him my resumé and all that. I'm going over to meet him tomorrow and get all of my HR stuff completed."

"No, I don't think we've met. The college is much bigger now than when you were in school. Probably double the student size. You may not recognize campus."

We talked on for a while, and it was starting to get pretty late. We helped Aunt Linda clean the kitchen, with much protesting on her part, and she retired shortly thereafter. Uncle Ray and I poured a nightcap and went outside to the porch. He left the door open, and the Tom Waits record that had been playing in the living room wafted out into the night air. Other than that, just a chorus of summer insects humming their own tune. Off in the distance, I could hear the slow lull of the river not far away.

"Cheers, son."

Our glasses clinked, as glasses do. I rocked gently in my chair and the soft glow of the porch light seemed to move, too, as I reclined and shifted forward in slow oscillation.

"Hey. . . Um, you want to talk about anything? You doing okay? I can tell you're a little down: your eyes look tired. Thanks for faking it tonight in front of your aunt."

Uncle Ray spoke cautiously, but his tone was genuine. He wasn't expecting a dramatic retelling of events, but really wanted to make sure that I was doing okay.

"Oh, yeah. No, I'm fine. Just. . . Trying to move on and get my mind off things."

"Want to tell me what happened? I mean, you mentioned the gist of it over the phone. . . Your dad said it was a pretty ugly break-up."

I took a long sip of my whisky and stopped rocking in the chair. I couldn't remember if I had told anyone the whole, sad story yet or not. I was a very private person, and I didn't handle embarrassment very well. I looked at Ray, and his soft eyes seemed to welcome my elaboration without judgment. I sighed audibly before speaking.

Fuck it. . . Guess I'll spill my beans.

"Well, you know Teresa and I had been together since college? You met her enough to know her basic personality, right? She was a smart girl, liked to have fun, but God, was she *conceited to the core.* . . Her dad had some money, and she felt pretty entitled in just about any scenario. She could be really hard to be around unless you were totally used to her antics. I don't think I realized much of this before we got engaged last year."

Uncle Ray nodded quietly as I went on, swirling his drink to occupy his hands.

"You know we taught at the same school in Atlanta, and she was getting her Leadership certificate to be an administrator in the next few years? She wanted to be the *big boss,* of course. Well, she started spending a lot of time with our principal. Young guy, related to the superintendent, only taught two years before they deemed a huge promotion appropriate. You know the type. . . He was her 'field mentor' or whatever, and they started meeting up every day after school while I was coaching track. Eventually, these afternoon mentoring sessions started leading to drinks, and then dinner, and getting home at almost midnight. I didn't immediately call her out on it because I thought there were other people at these social gatherings, but eventually curiosity got the best of me. Some things she said didn't add-up, and I just started getting uneasy. So, one night, I went through her phone–"

"Oh, no. . . You never go through the phone! Rule number one!" Ray said, half-laughing to lighten the mood.

"I know! Big mistake, I guess. Or not, considering. . . She had been guarding that phone like the Holy Grail for a while, and I started to notice. Every time she left the room, she took the phone. She wouldn't even take the damn dog outside without snatching it up first. Except once, and it was an accident. . . She left it on the kitchen table, face down, one night while we were eating dinner, just to go to the restroom. I had to figure out her password and all that. It was her birthday. . . How stupid, right? She wasn't gone but a minute or two, but I saw enough."

"Uh-oh."

"There were texts, and pictures…"

"Oh…"

"And meet-up details and all that. But the worst was how she had been completely disregarding me every time he asked *if I was suspicious, or should we tell him, or what if he finds out*? She was acting like I didn't matter, like I was utterly oblivious and frankly too dumb to suspect anything. It was pretty terrible. She came back from the bathroom, and I was still scrolling through the messages. One by one by one. She flipped, obviously. My hands were shaking, I was so hurt and so furious all at once.

"I held the phone up out of reach while she jumped like a puppy after a treat again and again. She hit me twice, *in the face*, trying to get it back. It took everything I had not to retaliate, Uncle Ray. You can imagine. I've never been so upset. She really thought she could get away with the whole thing. And the worst part was– Her anger was purely from being caught, not cheating on her fiancé in the first place. She even had the brass to say, *how dare you go through my phone!* We didn't fight much after that. I threw the phone against the wall and just left. Slept in my car that night. Didn't go to work the next day, or the next."

"That sounds awful, son. I'm so sorry."

"It's fine. I guess."

I was exhausted from retelling my poor, pitiful account. Waving my hands every few sentences for emphasis and reliving the whole thing.

"What happened after that?"

"I got my stuff from the apartment that weekend and stayed with Mom and Dad for a few weeks, like a kicked dog. She took over the lease, no questions asked. I'm sure her dad could afford it. . . I went back to school the next week, didn't say anything to the principal the first day. Or the second day. He was obviously avoiding me like the plague, and he was still technically my boss, which was even more infuriating. Hearing his voice over the intercom, seeing his name appear on a mass email. . . It was like being trapped in a nightmare. I literally didn't sleep for two weeks, save for a fitful hour here and there.

"On the third day, right before the end of the year, I bumped into him in the teachers' lounge. Just us, nowhere to hide. He just stood there with his stupid coffee and stupid school-mascot tie when I came in. . . I walked right up to him, stared him down. I had practiced this moment in my mind. We both knew it would come. He just studied the floor, his shiny shoes. And he said, *Rylan, I'm very sorry about all this...*

"I had rehearsed some really nasty phrases and retorts, but they didn't come. His *I'm sorry* spiel put me over the edge. All I could do was knock the coffee mug out of his hand and point an angry finger at him. . . I couldn't make any words come out. Never touched him. I know my face was probably distorted into some awful expression and beet red. Not nearly as fierce as I would have wanted in that instant. The floor was carpeted, so the damn mug didn't even break. The coffee spilled on him, sure, but not enough to even matter. The whole thing was just too embarrassing. He didn't speak, either, after that, which may have been a silver lining. He just stood with his head down, blinking at nothing. I walked out and went back to my classroom. Believe me, my students watched movies for the rest of the day. I was pretty useless after that.

"The next morning, I went into his office and quit. Told him that I expected a glowing reference and my full last month's pay. He didn't argue. He didn't ask me to even finish the week. I slammed his door when I left, which got a few cross-wise stares, but that was the long and short of my *big revenge*."

"Geez, Rylan. Wow. That's quite a story. Hey, if I may, these things do happen quite a lot. I've heard some doozies and I've even had my share of break-ups in another life. Your boss, though. . . Oh, that takes the cake in recent memory. Have you talked to Teresa at all? Did you at least get the ring back? I know you talked about it being pretty expensive."

"We've had a few text-message exchanges. Nothing more than a few words and very business-like about the apartment and whatnot. She did give me the ring back, but she never really apologized. Not that it matters."

"What are you going to do with the ring? Do you have it here?"

"Yeah, it's upstairs in my suitcase."

I paused for a moment, finished my whisky, and then answered his other question.

"Uncle Ray, I'm going to sell the shit out of it, first chance I get."

Our laughter echoed off into the distance. The night accepted our mirth with indifference. In the dark, everything around us was now still.

On a boat, and the sunset. She was there, like she always was. And a few estranged high-school friends that I hadn't seen in almost a decade. We were on that vacation to Jamaica again, bathing in the too-bright sun. Someone out of sight kept repeating, 'Where are the Wild Things? Where are the Wild Things?' over and over and over like a skipping record. And a big Caribbean pelican, with a face that looked more like our dog, kept flying too close to the boat. She leaned in close. I could smell her hair, that perfume. She smiled, eyes hidden by oversized sunglasses, her gently freckled face starting to tan and she looked beautiful.

Back inside, a flip of the page, walking up the stairs in my childhood home to the wide landing up top. It was dark. For some reason, I couldn't make any sound. I kept reaching for lights to no avail. I was enveloped in the dark, and it seemed like the air no longer satisfied my craving to breathe. I turned to the left at the top of the stairs like I had a thousand times before. My bedroom door was closed, and I could hear the formation of sound emerging from within. I had to process the noise. It was desperate and primal, a man and woman. She made a cry like an injured deer, then a deep moan. I could hear rustling and a knocking as I leaned my ear to the door, all shrouded in darkness. There seemed to be the almost imperceptible glimmer of candle light inside the room. The man then made a noise. There was a finality to it that made me feel sick. Nausea swept over me like the waves lapping on the boat I was just aboard.

And then, I heard her voice so clearly. It was Teresa. She laughed with all the potency of shattering glass.

He'll never know. We'll never let him. This will only exist in total darkness.

Then, I was overcome by panic. I was at the bottom of a well and the last shimmer of sunlight was dissipating above me. I could no longer breathe, and I succumbed to the impenetrable embrace of Inevitability. There was a solace in the acceptance of pain.

And then I was awake. Not with a start and not covered in cold sweat. I awoke to an emptiness, and a kind of paranoid energy. I was used to this, to these dreams. To be haunted. It happened almost every night as I balanced upon the beam of asleep and awake. Sometimes they came at two a.m., or three. I checked the clock. Today, the bad dreams had come at 4:11 a.m. Regardless, I was always wide awake after their visit. Sleep was no longer restful, so I ultimately planned to abolish my need for it, if at all possible. It was doing me no favors.

I sat up at the edge of the bed, ran my hands through my hair, and glanced over at my phone. No green light flashing. For weeks, I had spent whole hours at night staring at that phone. Looking into its dark face and hoping that I would see that little green light flashing. That indicated that I had a new text, and that meant someone was thinking of me. I always hoped to see a message from Teresa. Especially late at night, or very early in the morning. That might mean she was alone, and that she was still thinking of me.

That little green flash of light. . . A sort of religion. I prayed for it, and to it. I felt like Gatsby staring across the water, watching a distant orb flicker and fade. A brief flicker of hope, a wish, and then it was gone. And like Gatsby's fated love for a specter named Daisy, no text ever came. At least, not at a time when it might have mattered. When it wasn't about the power bill or what our password was to pay the rent.

That green light was evil, I thought, and then I got out of bed in my little room in the guesthouse, adjacent to my uncle's home. I was alone, it was early, and a strong cup of black coffee was my only solace.

Looking around in the dim, the guesthouse was cozy enough. Very familiar in its own way. I had spent many a night up here in my formative years, which weren't too far in the rear-view mirror. I really hadn't brought too much of my own into this space. I had a few trinkets here and there. Enough clothes and little creature comforts to last me a while, until I could get my own place. A big trunk was the highlight of my effects that rested at the foot of the little bed, just as it had in my childhood room, and my college dorm, and in our closet in Atlanta. Collecting dust, rarely open, but within it held a vastness of memories and memorabilia that ultimately shaped my being.

Good thing was, I was establishing a routine. That was important, so we are told. I had always been the type of person who floundered into a deep existentialism without the neat confines of a daily routine. And even then, what was the point of it all? It made slightly more sense when one created a *point for it all*, but the questions that remained could never be answered.

Who am I? What is my purpose? Does anything make a difference? Are we simply floating on a very lucky rock, spinning about the sun, awaiting an asteroid named God to make his acquaintance with us and set the slate clean?

Those were the questions. And to pique such nihilistic thoughts, I even had a hobby. A best friend in the purest sense that went way back for me. After my coffee, I would lace up a pair of reasonably worn-down shoes, perform a series of meaningless exercises, and go out into the waiting darkness for a run. It was the ritual, and it would be done. The hobby had eventually evolved into a sport. A sport then provided me with hundreds of trophies, a good scholarship, and even prize money, when I had really needed it. Like any good friend, it was patient, and it provided comfort when there wasn't much else.

Stepping outside into the cool mountain air, turning on a headlamp, and venturing into Kubrick's *real country dark* to run at a not-slow speed was exhilarating in its own right. The trees passed in the dim light like gray ghosts, occasionally a set of predatory eyes would appear from within their bosom. Green, like the evil light on my phone. And below on my opposite side, the specter of an old mountain river floated past. Its gentle roar was like a Siren's song in the dark. In the gloom, it was the idea of a river and nothing else. The smooth stones it drowned and caressed every minute of every day rested in its rushing waves, wrinkled like linens, patiently carving its way into the marrow of this place, like the veins that run up and down our own bodies.

Despite the empty feeling that burrowed through my middle, something was starting to shift. Being up here, in these protective hills, *starting over*, running the roads I loved as a younger man, I was starting to feel at home. My paranoia and dread still coursed through me like live wire, but that was okay. I could deal with that. The important thing was to keep moving forward. To relish this time. Enjoy it all, like a Machiavellian prince who has inherited the earth. The cog wheels were definitely turning within the machine that guides our lives, and it was imperative that one followed their lead.

The gravel crunched gently with every footfall, and I was left with only the rhythm of my breathing and the stirring of my thoughts out in the deep, loving darkness.

Elsa Privette

The fair-skinned, freckled, young girl with the tangle of blonde hair was awake before the sun. Before any alarm could disturb her quiet sleep. She had dreamed of something in the night but couldn't recall the substance of her slumbering pictures. The ones she could remember always seemed to be important. Sometimes, they even seemed to come true. Not exactly as she dreamed them, but as a physical shade of her nocturnal ruminations. Formed, but not fulfilled. Like clay figures before the kiln. Things always changed slightly, but you still had your figure after the fire.

It was the first day of school, and Elsa was excited. It was the end of a boring summer for her. She didn't have to sit at home all day, listening to her mom argue with her bespoke stepfather (they weren't married, which bothered Elsa). Every third day or so, when too much liquor was consumed, those arguments turned into full-blown fights. Someone would get hurt, someone would end-up with bruises, and it was rarely him.

Elsa was not immune to getting caught up in the fray, and neither was her older sister, Jenny. More often than not, their fights would somehow drag them in, as well. Like an irresistible gravity. Like drowning.

But school always seemed to fix things. For nine months of the year or so, she felt more protected. School gave her purpose, and she was an excellent student. When her grandmom was still alive, summer hadn't been so bad. She could escape up the road and spend a few nights with her whenever she liked. Her mom barely noticed she wasn't around. Sometimes Jenny would come with her, sometimes she wouldn't. She was getting older, in high school now, and didn't seem to like Elsa as much anymore. She was more interested in cigarettes and boys. One of her friends even had a car, so she was barely around at all this summer.

Elsa looked at the clock on her little bedside table. It read 5:58 a.m. in red block numbers. The bus was still thirty minutes from arriving. No one else stirred in the house, and she was already dressed, with backpack ready. She thought she'd better wake Jenny. Down the narrow hall, on the right. She tip-toed so she didn't wake her stepdad. He would yell. He always yelled when you woke him up. His head always hurt him in the morning, and you couldn't be loud.

Ever.

Elsa knocked quietly on Jenny's locked door. She didn't used to lock her door, but she did now. No answer, so she knocked a little louder.

"Okay, okay! I'm getting up."

An angry voice within. Jenny sounded so much like their mom, it startled her sometimes.

"Sorry, Jenny. I didn't want you to miss the bus."

"I ain't missing no bus. I said okay."

Elsa nodded to the closed door and walked further down the hall into the living room. The old furniture sat unremarkably in a stark arrangement before the blank-eyed television deity mounted on its tiny pulpit in the corner. They worshipped it nightly, if no one was fighting, as they ate microwaved dinners or cheap hotdogs. The god demanded that flickering images of campy violence, lying politicians, and fake newscasts starring well-dressed media zealots be shown throughout the evening.

Elsa hated television. She preferred to read and loved all of her books like kindred family. She could get lost in them, but they weren't just for diversion. She was a realist, after all. She didn't live in a fantasy world within the pages like some sappy Austen character. They were, however, for her *education* and for her entertainment in an otherwise bleak little life.

Another small hallway led to her mom and Randall's bedroom. The door was cracked. She peaked in, although she knew she shouldn't. The room smelled musty. Lingering cigarette smoke, menthol from a bad muscle rub, and a deep dampness from the window being open. Morning humidity crept in like a specter. In the dim, a pile of dirty clothes appeared on the floor beside the bed. Empty beer cans, Dr Enuf bottles, Little Debbie wrappers, and some other discarded cardboard littered the room. It grossed her out in their bedroom, and she hated being asked to clean it by her mom.

Elsa was a good kid. She was obedient to adults. She had impeccable manners, despite never being taught them by anyone but her grandmother. However, she also had her own thoughts. They often ran contrary to the pile of filth in this bedroom and her mom's tenth-grade education.

Two heaps in the vague shape of a man and woman were thinly disguised under the covers. They both snored. Her mom let out a grunt and her beau, Randall, scratched his leg under the sheets. Elsa made a disgusted face, and carefully crept away from that animal pen and back towards the kitchen. No sense waking her mom. She and Jenny had been self-reliant since they could walk.

When Jenny finally emerged with her hair tossed unkemptly, wearing too much eye-liner and glittered lip gloss, Elsa already had two sandwiches made for their lunch, chips in Ziplocs, and cereal in bowls awaiting a milky shower. Captain Crunch this week. One of Elsa's favorites. Jenny said she wasn't hungry, so Elsa carefully poured hers back in the box. Only one hit the stained linoleum, and then it was time to walk up the driveway to catch the bus.

Another year was upon the two girls. One, the younger, tip-toeing the minefield of middle school; the older, high school, with all the attitude of her mother and the disdain for the world of their derelict father. Wherever he may be. If he even still *was*.

Elsa boarded the bus with a smile, greeted the driver Mr. McHenry, and took a seat near the front beside her friend, Gerald.

This was the happiest moment of Elsa's summer.

Rylan

I got to work every day just before the buses: between 6:59 a.m. and 7:02 a.m. was safe. I could sneak into my classroom through the side door unnoticed. I was enjoying my co-teachers at the little elementary school, but not this early. They may try to engage me in conversation. There was the loveable religious zealot with, like, nine kids. There was the 'I should have retired by now' bitchy math teacher, of course. She was really fun at parties, I bet. There was the doe-eyed first-year, fresh out of a tiny college nestled in these hills, and then you had the eccentric music teacher. He liked to corner me to converse with too-high diction in the afternoon, when I was trying to leave. And then there was me. Automatically the odd-man-out, but faking it so well.

I somehow fit in among educators and academics. That might be a stretch out here in God's country, but this was all good. I was about to get my first paycheck at a new school, in a new school system, and I was the cool new guy teaching the mountain kids all about the Queen's English. The children had never seen a teacher in a sports coat and dark jeans before, and it was such little things that young people find captivating. I had no discipline problems in my classroom. I was a great actor and had *presence* with every lesson. My time on the stage each day afforded me nearly forty thousand dollars a year and almost three months of paid vacation every summer.

Who could possibly complain? I wasn't much for material things. Those never seem to last, after all. The dead have no use for their earthly trappings, or so I hoped.

And, at the same time, it was all utterly exhausting. My dark eyes beguiled no evidence to the contrary. Less than a month in, and I was a veritable automaton going through similar motions each day. As I fumbled with the key to get into my classroom, balancing notebooks and a breakfast wrapped in a paper towel, my head was starting to throb. On top of it all, I was probably drinking too much. Whether at home with Uncle Ray or out in town at one of two decent bars that weren't piled to the ceiling with college kids, I had been knocking them back lately.

Cathartic? Sure.

Relaxing? I guess.

I had even made out with a hippie chick outside the oddly good sushi bar the other night. Her hair had smelled like lavender and weed. She had a nose ring. Her name was Amanda. Or Ashley? I didn't bother getting her number, and I hadn't driven her home. I don't expect she remembered much of me either, after the last round of six at the bar.

Jesus Christ. . . Or had it been Ansley?

All to say, it was taking two strong coffees, an hour of running, and a gallon of water to get me back to one hundred percent in the mornings. The fluorescent lights in my classroom didn't help matters, but this was all a self-imposed Hell.

I had just enough time to review my first lesson, write three 'essential questions' on the marker board (I had some essential questions of my own, ironically), one for each pre-teen grade level, and take a seat at my desk to pretend to look busy in case anyone cared to come check in on young Mr. Wilder at this early hour.

No one came today. After too brief a silence, the bell rang like a fire alarm in the deepest stage of sleep. Soon, a swarm of adolescent bees would descend upon me and I would be expected to perform. A State-paid puppet for their entertainment and closely-monitored education. Don't stray from the curriculum, avoid any contentious topics, be attentive, and make sure they all feel special. Easy enough, I supposed. I rose with a smile to greet the first rush of sixth-graders.

It was 7:25 a.m., and they all smelled like syrup and kerosene.

———

A few days later – or over a week, I'm not really sure – it was after lunch, and I had taken my 'more-advanced' seventh-grade class to the media center to complete their end-of-unit project in the computer lab. The lab was really just a row of old computers at the back of the library, and this was my nod to the mandate of "introducing technology into key lessons". Their assignment: research an author from early American literature and share their most important works (or something). Ultimately, it gave me a rather peaceful hour to pace around the library and not be the pivotal source of entertainment for a classroom full of kids. Not dissimilar to a hired clown at a birthday party, minus the promise of cake and the possibility of a big tip if my balloon animals were especially on point that day.

I had made a quick round to check on everyone's progress, made sure none of the boys had deviated to deer-hunting websites (or worse), and was then pondering a large mural painted on the back wall of the open space. Invoking Milton, best guess. The Garden spanned wide across with its lush flowers and beautiful shades of green. Adam and Eve were pleasantly absent from this rendering. That, and there was a Milton quote across the bottom of the painting. Perhaps that gave it away.

The quote read (and it was not from 'Paradise Lost'):

"Where Darkness spreads his jealous wings, And the Night Raven sings; There, under ebon shades and low-browed rocks, as ragged as thy locks, in dark Cimmerian desert dwell."

That's mighty fine.

I caught myself unconsciously stroking my beard as I poured over the lines and pictured myself sitting upon the Tree of Knowledge as Serpent, awaiting sweet Eve to come sample my forbidden fruit. I felt a presence behind me, and I turned instinctively. And there she was.

"A bit heavy for an elementary-school library, right?"

Blonde, elfin, everything...

Staff name tag. Lacy Elridge. I had seen her only in passing, but now I could actually *see* her, standing so close.

"Very. And I love the explicit nod to the whole 'Church and State' thing."

"Were you under the impression this was a secular little school?"

"Not at all. I love the romance of old-time religion."

"Somehow, I doubt that."

"What makes you think that?"

"Let's see. Everything. Nothing. I don't know... You have a look."

"Thank you, I think."

I extended my hand.

"Rylan. Or, Mr. Wilder, I guess."

"Lacy. Or, Miss Elridge. *I know*."

She laughed. It was like candy to my ears. She had none of the typical awkwardness inherent in young, bookish educators. She was smart, I could tell, but not weird. No herd of cats marauding through her house or anything. Quick glance: devil-may-care button-down shirt, untucked, nice dress jeans, red nails. They were short and well-tended. I hated long nails, especially the fake ones. And down two inches from the manicured nail on her left ring finger, no diamond, no band.

Fantastic. Hope springs eternal, or something. My mood might shift into one less dour, after all.

"Nice to meet you, Ms. Elridge."

"You, as well."

One or two of my students were looking our way. Our conversation continued, lots of muffled laughter and leaning against various pieces of furniture. I could feel their little eyes absorbing every motion, every nuance of our posture. How else were they supposed to learn about human courtship? We were *teaching*, even then. This was the important stuff. Their project about some dead guy's bullshit poem or another just illustrated the framework that binds the day. We were all that young, once. How much do we remember from school, really? Try to recall a single academic lesson in its entirety. . . But, that first love note passed in class, or the day the boy broke his arm on the playground? That's the glue that binds our memories from page to page in the flip book of reminiscence.

I wanted to remember this. That look in her eye. The librarian, of all people. Cliché in movies, but not in real life.

And Hope was a terrible, wonderful, dreadful thing.

And it is all we have.

A few days later, in the teacher's lounge, I asked Lacy out while I was checking my mailbox and she was getting a Coke out of the vending machine. I was not especially smooth, but I was direct and reasonably confident.

It's best to never beat around the bush in such moments, I've found.

"Hey. Want to have dinner with me this week?"

She glanced over at me. Opened her Coke with a dramatic snap and fizz. Paused only for the briefest, longest moment.

"Yes. Sure. Say 'when' and I'll be ready."

And that was enough.

Eliza Stone

Some time ago...

The burning of sage was said to rid spaces of past evils, malevolent spirits, and cleanse the aura of a home before new inhabitants arrived. It was an old practice, popularized again by New Agers and self-described Mystics of the modern era. Eliza Stone was neither, but she did believe in the Ancient Ways. The traditions of days-gone-by were all she had left, and she cleansed every new home she entered with a thorough sweep of the burning herb. Tradition and ritual might help keep the demons at bay, after all.

Religion had long left her personal belief set, although she had been a devout church-goer when her daughter was born. She had tried to get her life-together, set the record straight, and start over anew when she retreated to the mountains. There was a safety in the hills. The city had too many distractions, too many bad choices down too many dark alleys. Her daughter was everything to her. Her rock and her anchor. Her reason to stay clean and walk the straight line. She was beautiful and innocent, like a spring flower.

Little Lilly Stone had elevated her young mother from derelict drug addict to marginally successful real-estate agent. A bright girl and quick study, getting licensed had been easy enough while she worked odd jobs at Goodwill and the Super Eight off HWY 105. Lilly would sit on the floor with her teddy as her mother cleaned motel toilets, sorted clothes that smelled of moth balls, and changed the stained sheets of hurried one-night stands.

She had a set of VHS training tapes, grainy and dated, that she would play in practically every room she cleaned. She had found these tapes at a pawn shop while looking for a cheap, toddler car seat to fit her taped-together Honda Accord. She purchased them at a steal, thinking that God was giving her a sign. Through the film of dust and grit on their paper sleeve, she saw a possible future emerging. Tea leaves and divination, or perhaps the zealous hand of Providence? Who could say for sure, as they were ultimately one and the same.

On the tapes, a portly old man with a pronounced beer belly detailed the specifics of obtaining one's real estate license between chords of inappropriately enthusiastic 90s music, trailing away in the background. She would watch the four-part training series over and over until she could recite every line. People probably thought she was crazy, straightening clothes on the family-store racks, bouncing a two-year old on her hip and silently mouthing the tenets of realty to herself as she worked.

The baby never interfered with her work, and she might have even enhanced it. Liza liked having her as a little audience, and Lilly didn't know any better but to follow Mama along. She never made much of a fuss, even when teething, and seemed content as long as Eliza was within sight. So, her two employers turned a blind eye to the appendage Eliza brought to work with her each day. The appendage was very cute and sweet after all, her bouncy curls and rosy cheeks good for business, on the whole.

Despite a criminal record flagging on her background check, Eliza's positive references and top percentile score on the real estate exam eventually landed her a job. A *good* job, too. Not at one of the big agencies, but at a local business called Mountain Realty that served the area's vacation-home community. At her interview, she had managed to charm the two brothers who owned the company, and they put her on a three-month draw plan until she got her feet under her. This was her break, her one chance, and she didn't intend to screw it up. Her dingy t-shirts and sweatpants were replaced by a few (cheap) pantsuits and uncomfortable heels. She might be going places, after all.

It took a few days for her to manage not to look like a gelding pony in the new shoes. It took a few days for her to figure out the right way to wear her hair. How to paint her nails. How to talk to a different crowd than her previous co-workers who, like herself, were on food stamps and on a separate latitude altogether than her soon-to-be vacation rental clients. When Eliza Stone looked at herself in the smeared mirror of their tiny apartment, after her first weeks of work, she started to like what she saw. Donning her make-up with special care, she was almost pretty. Some days. In the right light. When she was able to smile.

Four years later and doing very well for herself, Eliza and Lilly had moved to a newer, much nicer apartment. It had a fireplace and patio. Big garden tub in the master bath. Lilly loved playing with her yellow duck in the bubbles while Eliza read to her. They even got a discount from Mountain Realty on the two-bedroom condo. Her pantsuits were no longer cheap, her heels were now made of real leather. She was clean, and sober, and feeling quite well.

Lilly, who still rarely left Eliza's side, was being homeschooled and was a sharp student, like her mama. She came along to every showing, and was probably the reason Eliza had closed a few hard sales lately. No one could resist the charm of the single-mother out working hard. And Lilly's curls were pretty irresistible, too.

And that's where they were going one day last winter: to a house showing. She had tried to cancel with the prospective buyers due to weather, but they had flown all the way from Boca Raton to see the property. They wanted the house before summer, they had said. Money wasn't an issue, they claimed.

The taped-together Honda Accord did not fare well in the snow, and it was practically a blizzard outside. When Eliza and Lilly began the descent from their condo out to the highway, the brakes simply couldn't hold against the snow and underlayer of thick ice. Panic enveloped Eliza like a vice, as they slid, entering the highway unencumbered. She turned one last time to see Lilly in her pawn-shop car seat, playing with a doll and seemingly unalarmed by the slide.

Eliza frantically turned again to the highway ahead. The shape of another vehicle speeding towards them, unable to slow down to even the slightest degree. Across the road, a field draped in white. A corpse covered in a bleached sheet. And upon that perfectly pale canvas, a figure stood. Caught her eye distinctly, despite the horror of the moment.

A wolf? Impossible. A dog? No, something else. Something lonelier and more wild.

A single coyote bore witness to the incident. Stared right into Eliza's eyes as through a rifle's scope. She focused on the shape. Could make out every color of its coat, every follicle of hair bristling on its cold back. She felt a kindred fondness for the creature for no reason at all. His sad eyes were her own. He, too, felt her impending sorrow.

And that was that. When the truck hit the little sedan, all was white as snow. Then, the cold came like ice. Eliza felt like she was floating, as her thoughts began to settle. Darkness came like a welcome blanket on a winter's day. Like the beckoning of a cozy dream, luring her into what would become a nightmare. Pulling her down into a blackness without respite.

For Eliza Stone, there would be no more reasoning down in the dark. That part of her would be long gone, like the scent of burning sage in an open space. Vacant absence was all there was left, and she had long neglected the light.

Sheriff Carlton Scott

His knee ached as he pressed the gas pedal, nudging the truck forward up the steep dirt road. Four-wheel drive engaged, the innumerable switchbacks were navigated skillfully with quick transitions of his rough hands on the steering wheel. Left, right, left. Taking him back to his days as a patrolman. But that was a long time ago. He was much older now, as everyone is. Even a baby two days old is double his starting age. Toddlers were antique relics of their former selves, and Sheriff Scott was beginning to feel that he might belong best in a museum.

With the deep green of the trees all around and the occasional mountain vista peeking through the foliage, this drive would be considered *scenic* by non-natives. For him, this drive was frustrating, at best. A nuisance, and terrible for his new truck's transmission. His whole body bounced with each bump, but his mind began to instinctively focus as he got closer to his destination.

He had received a call earlier that afternoon about a weird smell coming from an abandoned house near the top of the mountain. Something akin to cat piss and rotten eggs, the guy had said. He had been out scouting some lease land to place a deer stand, and said the smell was pretty awful. Burned his eyes and all. There was a reputation for some homecooked meth out this way, so Carl let his deputies finish their cheeseburgers at the station and decided to take a drive. It was a Saturday, after all. He didn't like to stay cooped-up on the weekends, when he was working.

He knew the landmarks that the hunter had mentioned pretty well up here.

Beyond the cattle gate and the old REPENT sign, about a mile further, there's a shack back in the woods a bit. Hard to see from the road.

That was the description, or pretty close to it. The further you got outside of town, up into the area locals knew as Pelt Camp (it was some sort of Daniel Boone reference), things could get a little hairy. The few houses up here, the people up here... Well, they were pretty damn *rough*. Backwoods, lawless, not a high-school degree among them for miles. This was not the sort of place you wanted to find yourself in need of help, but it was the sort of place you might want to cook some bathtub crystal.

Sheriff Scott remembered when the worst thing up here was finding the occasional moonshine still. Maybe you'd arrest some poor bastard for manufacturing a 150-proof batch, but it did little good except to get the adrenaline pumping. There were always fifty more stills to bust, and he considered those days as the *good ones*. Sure, there was plenty of white lightning still being made up here, but the drugs were far worse. The teeth, the skin, the hair...He'd locked up twenty-five-year-olds who looked older than him. Hooked on the stuff. Violent, erratic. Always dangerous when they were high.

He just didn't get it. He had done little more than sip on a few too many Buds when the occasional wild moon had shown in his day, so the concept of methamphetamines was just that – an abstraction, a concept, a really bad dream. Sheriff Scott benefited from seeing the world in black and white, for the most part, but there would always be exceptions to the dominant colors in his preferred palette. He called those *gray areas*, and gray was not a favorite color of his.

Speaking of gray, he had just passed the almost invisible driveway, where one of his deputies had been killed two years prior. Young guy, barely on the cusp of manhood, and from a good family in the area. Sheriff Scott had been asleep when the call came, his wife turned on the lamp as he wrestled with the phone beside their bed. The digital clock read 1:13 a.m., and he was more than a little groggy.

A hurried voice shook and rattled on the other end of the line; another one of his guys obviously on the verge of shock. Said they had responded to a domestic disturbance call up on the ridge, Pelt Camp. Approached the front door, heard fighting inside, and then a blast... A bright flash and wood panels splintering everywhere. Scorched ozone.

"Danny's dead, Sheriff. Bastard killed him and then his wife before I could return fire. Double-barrel twelve-gauge. Got him in the side of the head as he was knocking on the door. We had the blue lights on, Sheriff. He knew we were police. Should have turned them off…It's so awful, my god. I have his brains all over me… Danny, Sheriff!"

The old man with the disheveled gray hair sat up in bed. He knew what he had heard but looked over at his wife to make sure he wasn't still dreaming. She covered her mouth, and it only confirmed the reality of his wakefulness. This one would have the whole town up in arms, he knew it. He could picture Danny Hagler's bright eyes and boyish face vividly in his mind as he spoke with the deputy. Got the details together, hung up, and then dressed to head down to the station. His wife had him a to-go coffee ready as he was pulling on his boots at the kitchen table. It was pitch black outside, when he got in his truck. The radio came on with an old Whelan Jennings song. His headlights illuminated the darkness, but their scope was too narrow to matter. It was all so dark.

And that was already two years ago, he realized. Seemed both impossibly long ago and like it happened last week, all at once. The toxicology reports came back flagged red for meth and fentanyl, both the man and his wife. He remembered pulling back the sheet at the morgue. Loosely recognized him from a few priors, despite the blackened quarter-sized crater in his face where the deputy had taken him down. Six rounds of ten from the bottom of the stairs, through the gaping hole in the front door. Dumb luck and four years on the Army pistol team expressed in ten loud claps echoing off the despondent hills.

Not bad, and good riddance, the Sheriff had thought.

A day late and a dollar short, he also thought.

The problem with hiring these by-the-book military kids was this... On another slab in the same cold morgue, lay a young deputy who had yet to begin his life. The sheriff preferred his country instincts and good sense to protocol, and he ardently wished he had responded to the call that night. Maybe, just maybe, two lives would have been saved.

Who could ever know for sure?

A little further up the road, the sheriff could make out a figure rounding a tight turn a few hundred meters ahead. The bright red shorts caught his eye first through the trees, and then a whip-cord thin man appeared on the downhill straightaway. No shirt, sunglasses on despite the cloudy day. *Moving along, quite fast.* Efficient despite the rough road. He looked very out of place up here.

The sheriff slowed down as the runner approached his truck. Let his window down and waved a hand for him to stop. There wasn't quite enough room for him to pass without turning to the side on the narrow stretch of dirt road, so the younger man stopped his watch and looked a bit flustered. He gave a shrug of his shoulders and lifted his hands. A *'what the fuck?'* gesture he had seen a few times before in his day.

Feisty, the sheriff thought.

The runner approached the truck on the driver's side, still looking a bit pissed. He was vaguely familiar-looking. Muscular and veiny. His expression changed somewhat when he recognized the sheriff. He had probably seen a billboard or pamphlet with him on it. Or the giant star with Tanawah County Sheriff emblem emblazoned on the side of his Ford. Maybe that gave it away.

"Oh, hey Sheriff. Sorry, I thought you were. . . well, not you."

"Uh-huh. What are you doing running up here? What's your name?"

"I run up here a lot. Is there a problem? My aunt and uncle live down the road and just across the river. I'm Rylan Wilder. Teach out at Cades Creek? We met a few weeks back at the high school. The planning day luncheon?"

"Oh, right. I thought you looked familiar. No, no problem. It's just we don't get many runners up here. It's not a great place to – um – exercise. Or anything, really. These people aren't very friendly."

"I've noticed that. That's why I looked a bit. . . terse, when I saw you stopping. I've already had a few cross words with the locals."

"I bet. Thing is, though, I'm serious. I wouldn't be running up here. Or ever coming up here at all. I promise, you really don't want to mess with the people out here."

Speak of the devil, as just then an ancient, rusted sports car pulled into view at the next turn. Some shady character or another barely visible through the trees. Cigarette smoke drifting from an open window. Revved the engine lightly to signal his presence on the narrow road. To move the sheriff and the runner expediently out of his way.

The sheriff nodded in that direction. Rylan turned to see what he was motioning towards, heard the engine rev. Nodded in silent understanding.

"Got it. I will take that to mind, Sheriff. Thank you."

"Uh-huh. Hey, question. Did you smell anything weird up the road a ways? I got a call a while ago about a very strange smell."

"Yeah, something's dead or rotten up there. I thought it might be a deer carcass or something. Smelled like rotten eggs and cat piss."

"That would be the smell. Thanks. Be careful getting down the mountain. I'll get out of your way."

"Thanks, Sheriff. Good talking to you."

"Likewise."

And with that, the runner slipped along the side of his truck, tapped the bumper to let him know that he had passed, and the quickly disappeared around the next bend.

Odd birds, those hyper Type As, the sheriff thought as he proceeded up the road.

Rylan Wilder. He repeated his name a few times, devoting it to memory for some reason. The younger man was already out of sight in his rear-view mirror.

The sheriff stopped at the appointed place his deer-hunting caller had described. Getting out of his truck, he could already smell whatever it was cooking off in the woods. He already *knew* what it was. No mystery there.

Elsa

She had known the big kid they called *Geronimo* since she was in kindergarten. He was full-blooded Cherokee, while the real Geronimo was most assuredly not, but the boy never seemed to mind the moniker. He appreciated the familiarity, like an inside joke that had followed him like a shadow since birth. Teachers, his football coach, everybody always called him that. Everyone except Elsa. It didn't feel quite right to her, so she just called him Gerald. They were also neighbors, of sorts, and she hated feeling impolite.

He was almost six-feet tall in the seventh grade, a good bit taller than Mr. Wilder, and much taller than their stumpy gym teacher, Mr. Rhoades. But where Mr. Wilder had a sharp look about him and mannerisms resembling something akin to a cautious fox, Geronimo was clumsy and seemed to move in a kind of slow motion. Regardless, Elsa had always looked forward to Gerald's jokes and good humor in class. She had even let him look over at her paper during tests to help him pass an exam here and there. He was a happy boy with a droopy smile and floppy, jet-black hair. But, on this particular Saturday, he was neither happy nor in good humor.

He had loved his grandmother very much, and she had passed away the day before.

Elsa could relate, and walked with her head down behind her mom and sister as they trod up the road towards the Yona household to pay their respects. Elsa's mom April had begrudgingly put together two covered dishes to take up to the old house. Some kind of casserole with soggy French fried onions on top, and a Kraft macaroni and cheese with too many breadcrumbs baked into it for a homemade effect. The dishes they presently jiggled within had been her own grandmother's, after all. Elsa stared into the one containing the casserole as she walked. It sweated beneath the glass top, and was ultimately too depressing to keep her attention. Elsa wondered if her grandchildren would one day use the same flower-decorated ceramic for holidays and special occasions. Maybe they would make something better than this for her own wake, but that was likely many, many years in the future. They would probably just use something plastic.

She had known Gerald's grandmother really well, actually. She used to watch them while Gerald's mom was running errands and her mom was– well, off doing something else. She had only called her *Mrs. Yona*, but surely she had a first name. It made her sad to think that she hadn't ever asked what it might be. Elsa assumed that she had to be at least eighty years old, because that was a good age for grandparents and she definitely looked every day of it. Her raven-black hair streaked with silver, the wrinkles, the liver spots, the deep gray of her eyes all spoke of many years and of a full life. She lived with Gerald and his mother in the old, white house that seemed to lean a bit to the side. Its weathered roof, screened doors, and creaky porch all resembled her own. They had an attic, though. She and Gerald used to play up there with the grandmom all the time.

She remembered rainy days in the summer where the elder Mrs. Yonah would bake them cookies and bring up Kool-Aid for them as they went through old trunks, and boxes, and photo albums from their family. She was never a particularly warm woman. Her face was hardened like a statue, she was quiet, she didn't smile, but there was a concealed kindness that beguiled all evidence to the contrary. At least when it came to kids, and to her and Gerald in particular. She watched them play and make-believe with the curiosity of a first time zoo-goer. Everything they did seemed to infinitely hold her attention.

Elsa tried very hard to conjure another memory, but that was where her mind kept going when she was intrinsically trying to tell Mrs. Yona goodbye inside her head. That attic, with the rain coming down, and the old lady's hands folded across a homespun dress with a hard look embossed across her dark face. Under that look, who could tell? Perhaps an infinite kindness, an abyss of warmth.

Smoke wafted back from her mom's cigarette, bringing her back to the moment and away from her thoughts. She had handed-off the casserole dishes to free her hands to smoke. They had arrived at Gerald's and were almost at the steps of the house. A man with long, black hair rocked in a chair on the porch. White paint peeled off of everything it was smeared upon, and there was a vague smell of wood rot in the air. The grass in the untidy lawn was long and overgrown in patches, but they had a Billy goat which kept things reasonably tame. His name was Chester, and he was nowhere to be seen on this gray, late summer afternoon.

The man on the porch stood as April took the steps and greeted him. He was unfamiliar, heavy-set, and spoke in a deep, muddled tone that Elsa could hardly understand. After a brief exchange to make sure it was okay that they come inside, the man somewhat hesitantly nodded and opened the screen door for us to enter the house. Elsa looked him right in the face as she passed into the living room. He was definitely a Yona. Apparently only Gerald knew how to smile in that family. But, then, he winked at her and that made her smile.

The family was gathered on sofas and seats and aluminum chairs in the living room. The tv was on, but the volume was turned down to an inaudible level. A big guy in a baggy suit was touting the benefits of a Chevrolet truck on a local dealership commercial on the screen. No one seemed to care. Everyone looked up briefly as they entered the house, and then their eyes reverted back to the floor or off in the distance. Elsa remembered her own grandmother's wake, and visitation, and funeral. It had been noisy and impersonal. This, however, felt very intimate. She suddenly wondered if they should even be here. It was the right thing to do, she supposed, to bring food and pay your respects, but she also felt like she was privy to something that was maybe only meant for *this* family.

April spoke to Gerald's mom in the kitchen and motioned to Elsa and Jenny behind her. The girls set the casserole and macaroni on the counter amid a myriad of other covered dishes. They didn't seem to be touched, and no one seemed to be eating. At her grandmom's gathering, Elsa remembered everyone eating plate after plate, like it was Thanksgiving Day. One of their uncles even skipped her in line to scoop out mashed potatoes, and pour gravy, and take two biscuits on his second trip to the table. These people, what few there were, all seemed to be too grief-stricken to eat, or move. Or, really, blink. She recognized very few of the Yona family members gathered in the next room and asked Gerald's mom where her friend was, so that she could see him. The mother, who looked ten years older than she was, said he was outside helping with the "arrangements" for the afternoon. Whatever that meant.

Jenny turned around and whispered to Elsa. "Go to the bathroom with me. These people are giving me the creeps."

Elsa nodded, and off they went down the familiar hallway, which led to two small bedrooms and an even smaller bathroom. Unlike in their house, where a cluster of aging family photos lined the hallway in their haphazard frames, these walls were bare. In fact, the whole house was sparsely decorated. There was far more tucked away in old boxes upstairs in the attic than there was down on the main level. It was like when the grandmother had passed, the house was again an empty shell waiting for the next generation to inhabit. Gerald, and his mother, and perhaps a few of the other family members mourning in the living room, would seamlessly slip into this humble dwelling and so it would go.

Elsa thought about this for a moment while her sister used the bathroom and she waited in the hallway. This may have been the first time she understood the concept of generational passage. A person was born. A person met a mate. A person had children. A person aged while the children grew, and then eventually a person's expiration invited family to take their place. Everything in the middle might only be details, she thought, and those details might end up in an attic. In a dusty box. The playthings of grandchildren.

Just then the toilet flushed, and Elsa's sister reappeared.

"Did you need to go?"

"No. I just came back here with you."

"Oh. Thanks. I was freaking out in there. It's so quiet. I was afraid to breathe."

"I know. It's weird."

"Where's your friend? The big kid."

"They said he's outside doing something."

"Let's go see."

"Okay. Just for a second, so we don't get in trouble with Mom. There's a screen door in the back bedroom that leads outside."

The girls walked down the hallway together. As they left the sunlight of the main room behind, the shadows grew and it was practically dark. The door to the bedroom was almost closed, and the girls pushed it open gently as they made their way outside.

When the door swung open and the room came into view, it took Elsa several long seconds to realize what she was seeing before her. In the room, on the old bed, a figure lay very still. It was the silhouette of a person. Then, Elsa recognized its clothing and shape. And then, her face and hair. Gerald's grandmother, or the form she once inhabited, lay on the bed in the quiet room. Her skin looked soft, but at once gray and lifeless. Two coins rested on her eyes, numbing the humanity of her form more than one could imagine. In the corner of the room, a similar-looking old woman rocked slowly in a chair. It creaked lightly as she moved, and Elsa felt her sister's hand reaching desperately for hers as they stood in the doorway.

The living old woman seemed fixated on the dead one. She only gave the slightest nod to the girls in the doorway, then her eyes returned to the corpse neatly displayed on the top covers of the bed. Elsa and Jenny were frozen in places for what seemed like an eternity, then they backed up slowly into the safety and half-light of the hallway.

As they made a very slow and tense retreat, a voice came from the room. It cracked like the old woman had not spoken for ages.

"Mind you close the door, child. I'd like a quiet moment with my sister."

At that, Jenny could no longer contain herself. Her scream escaped through cupped hands, and she ran back into the light of the main room. Elsa, torn and frightened by what she had seen, conscientiously closed the door before making her own escape back down the hallway.

She liked to respect her elders, as it were.

Several hours passed, and now the party had moved to the back yard. The 'arrangements' were to take place soon. The women and girls were given seats, the men and boys all stood around on the shabby back lawn. Most had their hands deeply burrowed into blue-jeaned pockets. The sky showed its respects by crying big raindrop tears that fell at odd intervals.

When the girls freaked out earlier at seeing the grandmother's body, their mom had hurriedly dragged them off into a little drawing room out of embarrassment. She apologized fervently as Jenny made weird, stifled shrieking noises as they passed the family.

In the dusty drawing room that only housed a sewing machine and a few stacks of books, April knelt in front of the girls. She implored them both to calm down, covering Jenny's mouth at one point.

"Shut up, both of you. Look, I don't know what's going on exactly, or what you just saw, but apparently the funeral is *today*. The women in the kitchen just told me, before you two snooped off and decided to spy on a dead woman. These people are different... They don't do things like we do. The wake, the *whatever*, and the burial are all happening *today*. Like, in just a little while. So, go back out there and keep quiet. Do you understand? We'll go home as soon as we can. I'm sorry you had to see that, but Jesus... Keep your voices down. It's like a tomb out there."

And so now Jenny, Elsa, and April sat amongst the family in a crooked row of chairs on the back lawn of the Yona house. Awaiting the *arrangements*. Elsa had only seen Gerald once since she arrived, and he had only given her a quick wave and a half smile. His eyes were red and swollen like he had spent most of the day crying. He probably hadn't wanted Elsa to see him like that.

A few meters in front of the small assortment of family, the deep green grass gave way to a sudden shade of murky brown, where the hole had been dug. It did not appear to be a full six feet and seemed to yawn towards the mourners as it was dug on a gentle slope, which grew steeper as the yard surrendered to the tree line. Three shovels rested on a large oak tree, which a gray-haired man leaned against, as well. Just as still as the muddy implements. He wore all black, kind of like a preacher, but different somehow.

I've dreamed of this, Elsa thought. She was certain. It was more than déjà vu and she was prone to such gray areas between her reality and her dreams. Sometimes, they tended to collide. Always in unexpected ways, and she could never put her finger on the specifics until they manifested right in front of her.

"Mom, what's going on?"

Jenny was getting restless. She whispered in April's ear, but it was almost not a whisper.

"They're getting ready for the burial, I guess. The women said that she had no birth record, so this all off the books. We're not supposed to talk about it. We're just *guests*."

Elsa thought about that. *We were guests*. She understood what that meant in this case. This was outside the norm. She had never seen a corpse lying with coins on its eyes, about to be buried in a backyard by the family. But she also thought that this was special in its own way.

When her grandmother had passed away, there was a plasticity about the whole process. It wasn't organic. They took her body to a funeral home, she was embalmed and stuffed like the taxidermized deer in their living room, and then a preacher who had never really met her went on and on at the funeral. He seemed so sure that Jesus loved her, and that she was a good Christian woman, and she would be missed. Elsa thought that these sentiments fell flat. She wanted to talk about her grandmother's stories, and how she used to knit them all kinds of things, and her chocolate pie.

The preacher seemed preoccupied by heaven and the Ever After, but what about how she really was? Right here, during her life. What about how her hand felt when she caressed her cheek? What about the chicken soup she cooked when she was sick?

This actually all made sense. She was happy for Gerald in that way. This was better.

After a few more long minutes, the screen door from the back bedroom swung open. Once was a false start. It closed with a loud clap; no echo. Then several men and Gerald appeared carrying a figure wrapped in a cream-colored sheet. Their steps were slow and measured, but still the figure bounced awkwardly in their arms as they walked. All around, everyone turned to face the house. As soon as the men appeared, the darkly-dressed gray man began to wail and chant in a language far older than their own. A human language, primal and reverent. A mourning, full of respect and true empathy.

Jenny covered her mouth. April studied her nicotine-stained fingers. Elsa looked on with an awestruck expression. She was absorbed with the *arrangements* now unfolding before her. She had goosebumps on her arms and thought the old man's song was beautiful. It was desperate, and personal, and painted a perfect picture of longing. The rain picked up, and the sheet got wet. She could see the lines in the old woman's face start to emerge. She could see her hair. The outline of her bosom and her thin, frail limbs. Elsa felt tears streaming down her face before she reconciled the emotion. It was all too much, like bagpipes and Cohen's 'Hallelujah' all at once.

The men fumbled with the heavier-than-it-looked burden as they lowered her into the shallow grave. They laid her head downhill upon their first attempt, there was some arguing amongst them, and then they righted her so that her head would rest on the incline of the gentle slope. Despite the rough-handling, the old woman looked at peace to Elsa. Almost smiling under her rain-dampened sheet.

My boys, she might have thought as they laid her down. *They are trying so hard. . .*

Elsa could feel the spirit of the elder Mrs. Yonah all around as they begin to shovel the soil on top of her remains. She also felt her own grandmother close by. As the gray old man chanted and melted everyone with his archaic song, and her friend Gerald cried and cried, and her mother studied her fingers, Elsa almost wanted to laugh. This was all so real. And so perfect. And she couldn't wait to hug Gerald and tell him that everything would be okay.

Because, in the end, it would be. In the welcoming soil, surrounded by our loved ones, feeling the bliss of whatever awaited us after this part was finished, everything would always be okay.

And that was very beautiful to Elsa, in that moment, and in this place, and with her family.

Rylan

I had broken out my purposefully distressed leather jacket for my walk around town. Dark sweater underneath, and it was the perfect fall afternoon. Busy out today. I could barely find parking. Students scurried everywhere, some in groups, some had their eyes fixed on little computers in their hand.

Friday afternoon reprieve from work, and the weekend stretched ahead. I had plans, first in a while, and they included a hip librarian that I was fascinated with, apparently.

Captivated? Intrigued, even?

Probably, but it was a nice place to let my thoughts rest in the sun, when they had been so accustomed to darker shades. She had picked a beer fest just outside of town, and then a "whatever we want to do next" for our second outing together. I liked the spontaneity, and just then my own little computer buzzed in my pocket. Her name appeared in a small box of text above the clock on its screen, and I smiled, in spite of myself, when I read,

"What are you doing?! I'm leaving work in ten, and bored. And hope you aren't out on some three-hour run so you can text me back."

I would definitely text her back, but I had an errand to run first. Beside the phone in my pocket, there was another curious object riding shotgun at my side. It sat in a velvet box, and it simply had to go. I had expected this to be some monumental event, getting rid of this engagement ring, but that was perhaps melodramatic. It was just the selling of a rock: it had no significance, it was over and done. Time to close a door.

I walked past the college campus. Nostalgia ran through me in slow, shifting waves like the leaves falling from the maple trees that lined the street. There was the arts complex with its huge theater, where we all used to watch the BANF film festival when it would come to town. The football stadium, where football games were held (I had been to two games in four years, not really my cup of tea). And then, there was the unnamed-but-decidedly-Daniel Boone-inspired statue right on the corner. A bronzed and fury-stricken pioneer stood with arms raised, hat asunder, and seemingly ready to brawl. He had been neutered since I was here last, as the whiskey bottle which once adorned his left hand and the lever-action rifle which had graced his right had been removed. There were no battles remaining that necessitated such effects, apparently.

The only remaining frontier rested tightly in the clutches of each passing college kid's portable black mirror. Not even space held such mystique, nor danger.

And I caught a glimpse of myself as I passed the pawn-shop mirrors, one street up from campus. I was older than I had been when I used to walk these streets on the daily. I looked younger than I felt, but age knows no bounds and is a fluid bird, forever in flight.

When I opened the door to the store, I knew that I was leaving one part of me out on the street, while another stepped inside to barter over pressure-cooked carbon. Such a strange symbol for love, the diamond. Expensive, but worthless. Plentiful in its natural form, yet relatively rare above the den within which it rested. Timeless, sure, but time is lethal. Even to diamonds.

I thought that love was better portrayed by the simple exposure of flesh, as I spoke with the shop keep. Flesh, fallible and temporary, yet warm and welcoming, was all you needed for love to blossom. To take a chance in the cold earth, and sprout seed, and it was ours to tend or lest the flower die before fully realized.

My words to the man, I don't remember. The price he offered was much less than I paid, so I pressed a bit, and I ultimately got what I expected. A small fortune for me at the time, and worth nothing in the long run. But, when I left the store, bereft of a heavy weight, I felt better.

Better – a vague concept, but I was smiling in spite of myself as the cool, fall afternoon met me at the door. I reached into my pocket. Pulled out my own little black mirror. I texted Lacy. Told her I was free. Come and get me. Come walk around town and reminisce with me on this fine autumn afternoon.

And I hoped that my black dreams would abate. I wanted things to be better, and I wanted my mind to be free as each passing leaf in the soft breeze.

Randall Lightner

The screen door slammed as he swore under his breath, stepping into the cold. Bitch was yelling in the kitchen, goddamn kids everywhere.

Didn't they have school? *Well, it's Saturday, you dumb fuck. They'll be here all day...*

He opened the door to his old truck and took the familiar big step into its cabin. It cranked without hesitation, and the familiar Cash tape came on to clear his head. In his rearview mirror, the woman was standing in the yard yelling something. Shot him a bird. No bother. He just turned the volume up and started backing up. She could move. Or not. He couldn't care less. They fought all the time. He'd get fed up. Hit her. She'd bitch some more, hit him back, and eventually he'd just leave the house. Otherwise, he'd kill her. And her annoying kids.

The gravel crunched under his tires, and she did eventually move. Still screaming at him in a dirty house coat. Old concert T-shirt beneath it peeking through, just panties below that. If she didn't put out so much in the sack, he would have left a long time ago. Just like her husband did.

That guy, Randall thought, had been a genius.

Just up and leave. Not be strapped by all of this.

He had something to deal with today, anyway. There was no time to sit here and argue. Or stumble over those brats. The one, the older one, was starting to look pretty tasty. She was a teenager now. *Blossoming*. Naughty little thing, he saw how she looked at him. They weren't blood, so she wasn't off-limits. Legality rarely ever factored into Randall's mentality. He had been to jail. It wasn't so bad. Morality, maybe? Who could possibly give a damn about that? Morality was a ceiling hung too low for a tall man, and he was pretty big.

The other girl. Elsa, well. . . She was different. Smart kid, no doubt, but he didn't care for the way she looked at him. There was a quiet condescension. Almost *pity*. Too smart for her own good, unlike her sister who was dumb as a sack of hot shit.

Just like her brainless mother, Randall thought.

But she still had that ass. . . Pale as the day, little goosebumps all over, a freckle or three.

Mountain mama, wild as hell. And that kept him coming around, no matter what a bitch she could be.

He could deal with that, and she had a type that he fit like a custom mold.

No matter. He needed to shake off their morning spat like black coffee eventually overtaking a hangover. He had grabbed Elsa pretty hard this morning when she spilled that glass of milk. . . Maybe too hard. She was a tough girl, barely made a sound, but she was so small and fragile. Her little arm had felt like a dry twig as his rough hand snatched her off the bar stool. She hit the stained linoleum with a thud. Turned to face him as he yelled at her. Looked him right in the eye. He had pulled her up off the floor by the other wrist, before the mom had intervened. He had seen her do just as bad with them, but he was the *outsider* after all. The live-in boyfriend. Who just happened to pay for every goddamned thing they ate, the heat that would keep them warm on these chilly nights. They *owed* him, they really did.

Fuck 'em. I've got work to do.

Ten minutes later, just as his truck had started to warm up, he pulled into Rooster's driveway. Rooster lived high up on the hill. Way back in the woods. They had gone to grade school together, and he used to kick his ass up and down the playground when they were kids. Randall had to think hard about what his real name had been. Way back then. It hadn't been impressive, but he knew the nickname had come from the cockfights he liked to host a few Saturday nights a month.

Randall looked at his crooked little house with a smirk. He knew that every wood panel, every mildewed pane of siding, even the black mold growing under his disgusting kitchen sink existed only because of his charity. He worked for Randall. Randall owned him, and he had always known it.

But, the boy could really cook the hard stuff, and he did it pretty well. God must have peered down from his cloudy kingdom and said,

"Well Rooster, you ain't getting much, but I guess I'll give you some rudimentary understanding of chemistry. Just enough to get by. Use it how you will, you poor, inbred fuck. Best of luck to you."

Randall viewed himself as his only source of luck, and he was pretty pissed at Rooster when he pulled into the driveway. Maybe God would help him; maybe not.

A few more of his boys were gathered around an old Camero, rusted to hell, sitting with the hood open right out in the leaf pile Rooster called a yard. A half-ass oil change or something in the works. Randall got out of his car all casual and lit a cigarette. The boys postured as he walked across the yard. His boots crunched the dry leaves with each step, and he pretended not to notice their expressions go from a dumb happiness to quite serious. Most studied the ground as he announced himself. Rooster included.

"What are you boys doing out here so early? Shouldn't you have been up late cooking my shit last night?"

A ring of smoke encircled him as he exhaled. He was a head taller than all of them. Country-bred muscles moved smoothly under his work shirt. Hat brim low over his brow. He was the *man*, and everyone on this godforsaken hill knew it. Test him. You'd find out for yourself. You'd bleed for it.

"How ya doin', Randall? It's been a hot minute. Think it was. . . when? That poker game? We were up working so late last night. Just stayed on up. Right, boys?"

Rooster spoke to break the ice. His hick voice fell flat in the morning quiet. His idiot friends nodded.

"Is that a fact?"

They continued to nod.

"You know, I heard that we lost a site up here last week. Read it in the papers, actually. That old cunt sheriff was all about it. Said he was going to shut us down for good and all that. Then, the bastard had the nerve to grace my driveway and ask me about it all. Told him I didn't know what he was talking about. That my boys knew better than to cook that close to the goddamned road. We had a good laugh, oh yeah. But he wasn't kiddin'. And, I don't like strangers, or the Law, or anybody coming up my driveway. You know the cook spot he's talking about, right, Rooster?"

"Um, yeah. I think so, RJ."

"You were on that one, right? It was your place?"

"I guess. . . We have so many right now. That's why the money's been coming in so easy. We've been bustin' our asses to move that shit. Working day and night. Right? Right, boys?"

There were some nods. One of the younger guys had plain walked away. The air was terse and suddenly had a bitter taste.

"Look, RJ, there was this guy. Some fuckin' jogger or something up here that Larry saw talking to the cops. Way up the road. Near where we cooked that batch. He told on us or something. Had to, right?"

"Who?"

"A guy out jogging. A runner."

"A runner?"

"Uh-huh. Larry said he thought he was a teacher or something."

"Up here?"

"Yeah. He talked to the sheriff. For sure. Otherwise, nobody would of known it was there or said anything."

Randall laughed. A genuine laugh. It momentarily set the other guys ill at ease. They didn't typically see him so much as crack a smile.

"You're telling me that some guy was running up here, and he just happened to meet the sheriff and tell him that there was a meth cook site up the road?"

"I mean, yeah. That's what we heard."

"Who would be such a damn fool as to *go running up here*? What, is he stupid?"

The guys laughed. Nervously. Forced.

Rooster had one hand on his hip. The other, his right, rested on the hood of the old car just inside the open hood. Randall moved quickly. He knew what he was going to do, long in advance. The prop clanked against the metal frame just as he brought the hood down on Rooster's hand. The slam echoed into the trees and all the boys instinctively jumped back at the sudden clamor.

Rooster withdrew his hand from the hood and backstepped in one motion. The look on his face, blank. Shock. It hadn't even started to hurt yet. Before the nerve endings signaled *pain*. Before the drool from the Kodiak dribbled down his stubbled chin. Before he could even take a breath, Randall planted his big boot right below the smaller man's chest and he was back-peddling across the yard.

Rooster, unable to breath, ribs and hand now engulfed in white heat, panicked. Crawled like half-dead roadkill away from his attacker. He began reaching down his stained blue-jeaned leg into his oversized Justin's for something. His boot slid down his skinny leg as Randall's long stride closed the gap between them. White sock exposed. A leather band, a tattered holster. The pistol looked about as pathetic as its owner. Worn, useless. Unable to function properly. He never pulled it from its seat, as Randall grabbed his arm and took it out himself.

"Aww, hell! What do we have here, boys?"

Randall brandished the little hand-me-down pawn shop plinker around like a schoolyard bully holding up some little kid's lunch money. Rooster continued to crawl away. This time on his stomach.

"What you goin' to do with this, Roost? Shoot me?"

Randall's laughter echoed like the clamor of the hood across the yard. Just as flat. Just as cold.

He pointed the pistol at Rooster. Cocked the little hammer. Aimed right at an oil stain on his upper leg and pulled the trigger. Rooster just stopped crawling. There was no sound anymore. He eventually rolled over with his hands raised. Tears visibly streaming down his face. Dry leaves and dirt all over his hands and cheeks.

"What, Roost? Were ya going to try to take a shot at me? How'd that work out for ya? Huh? I thought you were smarter than that. Jesus, you stupid fuck."

"I'm sorry, RJ. . . Please don't kill me. Please don't shoot me again. I know what I done. I know. It'll never happen again! Please!"

Randall aimed the small pistol at his head for a minute or two. He moved in close. Rooster could see down the barrel only inches away from his tremoring face. Let him really think about it. Then, he lowered it by his side. Spit at Rooster. It hit his chest and neck with a disgusting splat. Rooster only flinched. His eyes were still fixed on the gun. His leg was on fire. A warm wetness was spreading over his filthy jeans. Barely more potent than a pellet gun, it still hurt like nothing he had ever felt before.

Randall, still puffing on his cigarette, finally opened the cylinder of the pistol. Emptied the remaining five .22s out onto the ground and threw the piece into the woods.

"Rooster?"

Rooster nodded, hands still raised high for no apparent reason.

"Two things. Cook your shit deeper in the woods. You know better than that. That's *my money,* you understand? Last thing I need is that cop coming up here snooping around, you hear me?"

Rooster nodded vigorously.

"And, two. You ever try to pull a gun on me again, and I'll fucking kill you so fast it'll make *their* heads spin. Yeah?"

Randall motioned back to the other guys. Most were now tucked behind the Camaro. Peering on like frightened rabbits.

Rooster nodded. The color was slowly leaving his face. He looked dead, but his heaving breaths beguiled that assumption.

Randall walked back towards the car, passing the boys. No one made eye contact. He could have yelled "Boo!" at them and they would have pissed their pants.

"Why don't you boys give him a hand? He's still my best goddamned cook. I don't want him to bleed out over there in his own shit."

They scurried to Rooster's aid. The leaves crunched deftly as Randall strode back towards to his truck. The door opened and closed with deep, metallic clatter. The engine purred to life, Myrle Haggard crooned over the radio. Randall backed out the way he had come in, navigating the rough driveway with ease as he looked over his shoulder. Arm sat relaxed over the backrest like a Sunday morning drive. Like he hadn't just put a man in the hospital. He glanced back at the lesser men still struggling to get Rooster off the ground in the derelict yard. Mainly, he was making sure none of them had gotten cute and pulled a shotgun while he was looking the other way.

They hadn't. Damn straight. It felt good to be the *man*. To watch cowards piss their legs at his feet. He was a bully, sure. . . Always had been. It was like a calling card. And it was his forté. Skilled as any big wig CEO or cheese-dick politician. No need to finesse. He had his nest egg, he didn't have to make the whistle call on the lumber yard like his daddy, or fight in a war like his granddaddy. Come back the brittle shell of a man with a bum leg. He just had to stay mean. Stay smart. Stay out of jail, and he'd be more than fine.

He opened the leather glove compartment as he caressed the steering wheel on the rough mountain road. Old leather flask. Familiar as a best friend. Jack Daniels corroding the cheap metal within its frame. Went down smooth, every blessed sip. And he sang along to the radio as leaves fell all around. Mumbling every third word as he hummed the tune. Tapped the wheel in time.

Death was everywhere, burning in golds and reds, and man– it was a fucking gorgeous day.

Rylan

She came in with the rest of my first period, as she always did. Perfect attendance record. Bright blue eyes always scanning the room, a little nervous, a little too small for her age. She had been the only student to ace my last unit exam. She aced everything, and that was the question mark.

The poor thing had about three or four outfits that she wore each week. They were always clean, and I had the feeling she might be doing her own laundry. I assumed she had enough to eat, four walls, the necessities. . . But, I knew, there wasn't much to fall back on at home. I had read her file. I had sat through the counselor's off-hand and clumsy recitation of all the 504four and free-lunch kids' family details. Elsa was no exception to these melodramas, In fact, she was worse off than many at home. There seemed to be two factors at play: a useless mother and a low-life step-dad figure who lived with them.

And, as I passed out study guides for our new unit on American Romanticism, the step-dad was firmly on my mind.

I hadn't said anything as I passed her seat. She offered a quiet but very polite, "Thank you, Mr. Wilder," when I had set the study guide down on her desk. Every other kid had either said nothing or groaned as I waxed on about *my favorite period in American literature*. The more I hyped the content, the more they knew to complain. They understood my slight sarcasm, as that was the preferred language of pre-teens. You had to speak the language of the tribe, even as a teacher.

Her "thank you" was met equally with "You're very welcome, Elsa. Doubt you need this." And I tapped her desk with my knuckles as I moved to the next seat. But right where her Mellow Yellow T-shirt sleeve ended, just above her elbow, something caught my eye. A pretty significant bruise. Fresh purple. Black and blue. Not a common place for a childhood scrape. It looked like it hurt pretty badly, but again, I only saw it in passing.

At lunch, I emailed the counselor. That was protocol. That bruise had weighed on my mind all morning. The way it disappeared under her yellow T-shirt. How much further up her arm did it go? How had it gotten there? Again, the step-whatever and the mom weighed heavy in my thoughts. Maybe she bumped into a door. Or fell down some steps. I doubted it, but short of sliding her sleeve up right there in the middle of class, I couldn't be sure.

The counselor, Kathy McDonough, emailed me back as I ate my sandwich and chips. I only had lunch duty three days a week, and I was enjoying a little low music in my quiet classroom in the absence of forty watchful eyes. I could hear her annoyingly sing-song voice in her message. It was palpably bad. I wasn't surprised by the quick reply, either. She had that phone glued to her face at every turn, as it were.

"Hi, Mr. Wilder! Happy Monday!

Thank you for emailing me about this. Our Elsa is such a sweetheart, isn't she? Anyhoo, I'm not too worried about a little bruise. Probably just a scrape. Maybe she bumped into a door frame or something? Happy to discuss further if you feel that is necessary! We just have to be careful not to rock certain boats, and not to jump to any conclusions, ya know? We do quarterly check-up calls with our most at-risk students living in difficult households, so I will be sure to plan one with them soon.

Best,

K."

I rolled my eyes and almost closed my laptop after reading this condescending waste of an email. I wanted to respond, but ultimately didn't.

Wouldn't want to rock the boat or jump to any conclusions, ya know?

Later that afternoon, I saw Elsa in the hallway. Right before the first bell rang. She was getting her red pillow out of her lockers, and I was off-handedly reprimanding two boys for running in the hall. The snap of my fingers at them got Elsa's attention.

She looked right at me, smiled a big smile, and then looked right back down at the floor, self-consciously. I motioned for her to come over to me, and immediately regretted it. I wanted to ask about that bruise, but had no script planned or strategy prepared. That Kathy was right about one thing: this was a sensitive topic, for sure.

She bounced over to me in a few elfin skips, her eyes aglow and blonde curls bouncing.

"Yes, Mr. Wilder?"

"Do you have just a second, before your bus comes?"

"Yes, sir. I'm on third bell."

"Cool. Mind if we talk really quick?"

She nodded. I propped my door half-way open with the stopper and motioned her inside. Rule number one: never talk to a student, alone, in a closed room. Rules weren't my thing, but this one was the exception. Self-preservation was very important to me. Maybe my strongest instinct, in fact.

"I'm not in trouble, am I, Mr. Wilder?"

She sounded genuinely worried. There was an extreme innocence to this little creature in front of me. Something lost along the way, for sure.

"Oh, yeah. The worst trouble. . ."

I smiled when I said it. Her face furrowed at first, then she beamed, too.

"I'm kidding, of course. No, I just wanted to check in with you for a minute. I know you don't have long before your bus, but we haven't had a chance to talk much."

"Uh-huh."

"So, what do you like, Elsa? Any sports? Any fun activities at home? You're certainly doing great in school."

"I don't think that I'm too good at sports. . . I like to read. I like to write stories. That's why your class is my favorite, Mr. Wilder."

"Oh, yeah? What do you like to read? I'm glad that you like my class. If only the teacher was better, right?"

She giggled. Instinctively brought her pillow up to her face out of shyness.

"No! You're a great teacher! My favorite. Well, I like Mrs. Townes, too, but you're also my favorite! Anyway, I like to read a lot of older books. I think they are called the Classics. I just finished one called *Great Expectations*. It was very good. I like Charles Dickens. And Jules Verne. And Hawthorne. And–"

"You just finished *Great Expectations*? Like, the whole thing?"

"Well, yes! I couldn't just read half of a book! How would I know what happened to the characters?"

"That's cool, Elsa. That's not an easy read. Did you like it?"

"Oh, yeah."

"What kind of stories do you like to write?"

"I used to write stories with my grand-mom. We would talk about them. Make up characters. Make up plots. We especially liked ghost stories."

"Do you still live with your grand-mom?"

She looked down. Instantly sad. A sore subject. A reflex, almost.

"Um, no. She passed away. I miss her a lot, though."

Shit. I had forgotten that from her file.

"Oh, I'm sorry, Elsa. That's too bad."

"Yep."

"Well, you're going to really like one of our assignments coming up pretty soon. You're going to get to write your own ghost story for class."

"Really?"

"Yep."

"Oh, cool! I'm excited. I want to be a writer when I grow up, actually. I would love to move to Europe. Maybe Paris, like they did in the 1920s. Write in cafes. Use an old typewriter. Have a little *flat*. That's like an apartment over there. That would be nice. I dream about that a lot. I have a poster of the Eiffel tower in my room at home, actually. My grand-mom got it for me."

"That's awesome, Elsa. I think you can do whatever you like. I really look forward to reading your books someday."

"You would read them?"

"You bet."

The third bell was ringing as we talked. She instinctively looked up towards the ceiling as if she didn't know where the sound was coming from above her. I, too, looked up before catching her gaze again. My wheels were turning. How to approach the real reason I called her in here?

"Hey, Elsa. Really quick. I know you have to go. Um, I couldn't help but notice that bruise on your arm in class today. I just wanted to make sure you didn't need to see the nurse or get a note for PE. . . Is that thing okay? It looks pretty bad."

Her face turned red, as I knew it would. She brought her opposite hand across her body to pull at the sleeve on the bruised arm. I also surmised that this child in front of me would be utterly incapable of lying, and I hoped that I was correct.

"Uh, my arm? Oh, yeah. This bruise. . . It's nothing, Mr. Wilder. Just a bad bump. It barely hurts. I should probably get to my bus, if that's okay? I don't want to miss it. My mom would be very mad."

"Sure thing. Go ahead."

I opened the door fully for her to leave. Then stopped her, right as she was walking out into the hall.

"Elsa?"

"Yes, sir?"

"Take care of that arm, okay? There are a lot of people at this school who really care about you, okay? We don't like seeing you all bruised up like that."

She nodded, looked down, and then looked back up at me with a smile. Her Hello Kitty backpack and little pillow both dangling almost to her knees.

"Thank you, Mr. Wilder."

"You bet. Now scram before you miss your bus."

She nodded rapidly and then bolted down the hall. Quick little thing. Could sign her up for track. Her Converse made little sound as they cleared the long hallway in no time flat. Her footfalls were not silent, but very quiet. Present, but in the background. Resonant, just like the girl who wore them.

"Jesus, son. Take it easy. Frustrating day at school?"

I had finished a pretty hard run a few minutes prior, and now Uncle Ray and I were slamming some weights in his garage. Sweat burned my eyes, and I was perspiring too much to put my T-shirt back on. I had just made an audible grunt as I completed a super set on the bench press, and Uncle Ray was doing some bicep curls in the corner. His skin, taut but beginning to wrinkle, screamed 'fit old guy' to the rafters. I was proud of him.

"What's that? Sorry, Uncle Ray. I was in my own little world."

"I can see that. I asked if you had a frustrating day at work? You've been grunting and growling around the garage ever since you got back from your run."

"I mean, I'm working with a hundred pre-teens with hormones and smart mouths who hate school but for some reason like me, so. . . Frustrated? I mean, maybe. That probably describes my general demeanor of late."

And the thought of a little girl coming to school with bruises on her arm, but I didn't want to hash that out at the moment.

"No, you're fine. You just seem to have an extra dash of man juice today is all."

"I feel like it."

"You *look* like it. Those are some scary veins running up those arms and legs, Ry. You doing any races? What was your run today?"

"Ha, I haven't planned to, Uncle Ray. Maybe, though. I'm feeling fit. Today. . . (I consulted my watch) I did five this morning, really easy, before work, and another eight this afternoon in 47:21. I got moving along pretty well, I guess."

"Wow. You should *definitely* get in a race. There's a big one up here in the fall. You remember? That mountain race? The one with the Scottish shit and bagpipes. I think there's some prize money, too."

"Yeah. I'll consider it. Could be fun. Good for my *man juice.*"

We both laughed at that.

"How's the girl thing going? Your aunt saw you texting up a storm on the porch the other night?"

"Yeah? I actually met someone pretty cool – at work, of all places. We've been hanging out a little. You'd like her. She's smart, attractive. Sexy librarian deal going on."

I stood from the bench and jumped up to knock out a set of pull-ups.

"Oh, that's my type."

"Right?"

I could feel no burn in my arms. No strain. I just kept pulling my 140lb frame up and up and up. How could you not love this feeling?

"Good, Ry. I'm glad things are looking up for you, son. What about that apartment you were talking about? Are you going to up and leave us so soon?"

"Well, I sold the ring. Don't know if I told you. It wasn't much, but it was enough for a deposit on a cool spot close to downtown and the first two months' rent. I hate to leave, I do. You guys have been so great. But I feel like I'm free-loading and want to get my own place. . . You understand."

"Completely. Your aunt will be sad, and so will I, but I know you like her cooking and you like to run these dirt roads up here. You'll visit with frequency, yes?"

"You know it. Nightly, basically."

"When can we meet the young lassy who has stolen our Rylan's heart?"

"Never if you talk like that. . . Otherwise, probably soon. How's next week sound for dinner? We can go out. My treat. I get paid Friday."

"Your treat, eh? We'll see if we can work it into our busy schedules."

We laughed. Uncle Ray resumed his familiar series of seasoned gym-rat exercises. I continued to push my body onward. It would let me know when it had enough. Until then, I continued to grunt and growl. An animal nature, a fire that, at times, burned too brightly. All fires eventually die, but I was young and strong and virile. I would worry about death another day.

For now, to feel so potent was a beautiful thing.

I sat in the parking lot of the Glenn Stowe apartment complex waiting on the realty guy. A Bruce Spencer from Mountain Realty, to be exact. I remember seeing their commercials when I was in school up here. They were good for local adverts, but still had that *hometown* flavor with some 90's soft jazz and a baritone voiceover in the background, as the brothers Spencer pretended to work with prospective homebuyers and vacation renters. After the climatic handshake was complete on some million-dollar property up on the mountainside, the younger brother Daniel would look straight at the camera, the music would get an octave lower, and there it was.

"Hey there, ya'll. I'm Daniel Spencer and this is my brother, Bruce. Come see us for your next slice of heaven at Mountain Realty. We're one big family here, and we welcome you to join us in the High Country. Life's a little better in the mountains, after all."

Classic. Simple. And the 90's music resumed as the camera panned back over some ancient ridge and drifted high above the trees, making even the mountains look small below.

And here I sat. Relaxing after another hectic day at school. Had the music on and my seat back a few notches in mild repose. The early-fall sunlight felt warm on my face as the Earth tilted away from its source and the cooler months approached. Like two lovers after a quarrel. All the pain and cold of winter's separation from the Light rapidly approaching, awaiting Spring's reunion and the return of Warmth. I let my mind drift momentarily back to Teresa. Our time together. And just a few weeks ago I had longed for the cease of our Winter. The return of our Spring. But now, the thought of her was hard to conjure As far away as the distant sun. And like the sun, just an idea, really.

I was finally sleeping better. My head was clearing. I could focus again, and the hole in my middle that she had created was starting to heal. All that was good. I was a diver emerging from the dark sea just in time, not a second too soon. It was a hard for a man to live underwater, after all.

A sharp little sports car pulled into a space a few over from where I was parked. The Mountain Realty folks. Bruce, and. . . A lady in the passenger seat. Must be my direct leasing agent or something. I sat my seat back to its normal position and got out of my car to see this apartment. That little bit of money I got from the ring and a few very modest teaching paychecks were apparently burning a hole in my pocket. But, with a fresh space came freedom, and a chance to try to start afresh.

"Rylan?"

"Yes?"

We were standing in the middle of the apartment's living room-to-be, nodding at light fixtures and commenting on the fireplace and whatever else people do when viewing a prospective home. I had drifted off in thought, as I am liable to do.

This woman, the one with Bruce... Something was off with her. She had a wild look. Not just in her eyes, like you might expect, but everything about her. She was disheveled, sure, but that was kind of sexy. What struck me, and I had noticed the same expression on my face the last few months, was a profoundly tortured look overwhelming her aura. A deep weariness. Something haunting the halls behind that furrowed brow. Her eyes were too sharp. Like shattered glass, sparkling. She had this scar, too, and it didn't look very old. She tried to hide it with a few stray bangs, and it almost worked.

I suddenly felt sorry for her and I didn't know why. My instincts were always pretty good about people. This ol' girl had *been through it*, and I wondered what that *it* had been to leave her so vacant. She never spoke during the showing, just nodded when appropriate, as if a mechanical hand was moving her limbs and suspending her body from a puppet string.

"Oh, I asked if you liked the space? Ha... taking it all in, are we?"

"Sorry, Bruce. I was just admiring the view out the window here. Oh, yeah. I love the space. Let's talk rent, deposits, etc. I'm sold."

"Great! Eliza? Didn't you have a folder put together for Rylan?"

Eliza... Maybe she *could* speak? She stood still for a moment as if registering the request. Then, she swiftly withdrew a Manilla folder with the necessary documents from inside her handbag. She extended it out to me. Her nails were long and unmanicured. Her hand shook lightly as it clutched the envelope.

"There you are, Mr. Wilder. I'm very glad that you like the apartment. This one of our most popular properties. I am available to answer any questions you may have."

There was a strange elegance to her voice. Like someone who had learned to speak properly through intense practice, rather than any formal schooling or upbringing. It bordered on a Hepburn Transatlanticism. I instinctively wanted to ask her opinion of *Breakfast at Tiffany's*, but I refrained. There was also an incredible coldness. Not an aloof, devil-may-care attitude, but rather a total absence of feeling. An empty well, like Murakami's, but lost to a plentiful snowfall and vanished in the wind.

Vacant, like this empty apartment.

And we continued our nodding and appreciating the fixtures. So, this would be the place I attempted to start over. I would fill this empty space as best as I could. The afternoon sunlight streaming through the uncurtained windows behind us would dim, and I would spend plenty of time alone with my tormentors in these four walls. But maybe I would eventually get some better sleep. Get cozy with my particular demons, pour them a drink. And, eventually, fill this space with the trappings of a new home for a renewed version of myself.

"Great. Let's do it. Where do I sign, as they say?"

"Will you hand me that knife over there – the butcher?"

We were in my new kitchen, a few weeks later. Everything was clean and sterile, just cleansed from previous tenants. There had been this strange herb smell, when I had moved in, that was quite odd, and it had finally vacated the space. It might have been sage or something, but I was glad to be rid of it.

She limberly leaned up on her tiptoes to reach the block and pulled the blade underhanded from its crevice. Her long legs accentuated with the movement and her fashionably cut joggers. She wore one of my college hoodies, and her curly blonde hair sat equally relaxed at her shoulders. She looked especially cozy.

I took the knife by the handle when she turned and set about excavating the large orange gourd in front of me on the opposite counter. The knife hesitated as I pressed the blade into the thick flesh. I tapped it twice with the palm of my hand and continued to push. The resistance gave way to hollowness. Now the carving could begin.

I felt thin arms wrap around my middle as I navigated the tight angles with my knife.

"Hey, you. Thanks for coming over tonight to help me carve these."

"Am I helping? I don't feel like I'm doing much."

"Well, you are here in a supervisory capacity to make sure that I do, in fact, carve these for tomorrow. There would be some fifty-odd pre-teens with very disappointed expressions on their faces if I neglected this tonight. Plus, in no reality am I going to remove the seeds and shit out of this thing. That's all you."

Lacy pinched me and let go. I fake-kicked back at her. She laughed, and it was a warm sound. I hadn't heard that in a while – a genuine laugh. We had some candles going, they flickered against my relatively sparse walls. I had just gotten a few lamps and a trite painting or two from a local 'boutique second-hand store' to give the space some character. Most of the furniture was from Uncle Ray and Aunt Linda, but I could make it look homey enough with a few more paychecks under my belt.

It had a fireplace, and within its stone belly I had lit a Duraflame and threw on a few small logs. More for atmosphere than warmth tonight. Outside, the evening descended into full night. Twilight, we say. The elder brother of Dawn. The autumn crickets had just ceased their last song of the day. Even the insects sought a mate ahead of winter's arrival.

Lacy hopped up on the counter beside where I was carving and set down some empty grocery bags to extract the pulpy innards. She was armed with a pasta spoon in one hand and her glass of wine in the other. She studied her swinging feet, and occasionally looked up to watch me fret over some errant cut in the pumpkin.

"This is good wine. The food smells delicious in the oven, too. You said we were having a roast and veggies tonight?"

"Yeah, it should be ready in about thirty minutes. I've got some rolls that we need to put on soon, too."

"You're going to spoil a girl. I can't cook to save my life. Neither can my mom. I got it honest."

"I'm just glad to have someone to cook for. Hard to cook for one, most of the time."

"You can feed me any time. I'll be your culinary critic. Like the bad guy on Ratatouille."

I laughed.

"Did you just reference 'Ratatouille'? We've been hanging around kids too long. . ."

"Oh, come on. You know you love it. It's like Academy Award-worthy."

"Uh-huh. It's great. Goes, 'Citizen Kane', 'The Godfather', 'Ratatouille', and then, I don't know, 'Gone with the Wind' or something."

"Stop it! Those are all my favorite movies."

We had dinner with three finished jack-o-lanterns watching with childish menace as we ate. Some low music played through a tiny Bluetooth speaker, and we joked and talked on a level that we hadn't yet reached before. The conversation about families and their inherent nuances came first, and then happenings at work, and then a cursory circle of our romantic pasts all rose to the surface as the wine allowed.

I didn't go into too much detail about any one thing in particular, and largely just let her talk.

"And, so, that didn't work out. . . But, the good thing is, I was two-months' single when you asked me out a few weeks ago."

She cupped her mouth with her hand as if to share a secret.

"In the teachers' lounge, I might add!"

"Hey, I didn't have your number and there was no one else around. I did my best. And you didn't seem to exactly play hard to get, either."

"How could I resist the mysterious young English teacher with just the slightest hint of brooding surliness? Me being a librarian, I thought we could wax on forever about the Bronte sisters and the wonders of Shakespeare deep into the evening!"

She said *the wonders of Shakespeare* in an English accent with a dramatic swooning effect as if she were fainting.

"Exactly."

"Speaking of English, the kids told me that our Mr. Wilder had them writing horror novellas for Halloween to be presented in class over the next few days. Is that what these jack-o-lanterns are for, to set the right mood?"

"Yeah, I've diluted the content for each grade, but they've been studying some Gothic horror, Poe, Irving, and whatnot in class. They had to choose a local piece of folklore or a ghost story they knew and expand it out into a full story. You know, an 'include three metaphors, five similes, be able to identify the setting, motif, etc. kind of project. That's what they were researching in the library last week."

"Ah, lovely. I'll drop by your room to hear a reading or two. Maybe we can invite the best ones to read them in the library on parent night. I think that's on Thursday night, which is the 30th, so perfect timing."

"You should, and that's a good idea."

"There was one little dear who was especially excited about her project. Oh, what's her name? The really small kid who carries around the pillow sometimes. . . She's actually a really smart cookie."

I decided to be coy on the subject.

"Elsa Privette. She's a sweetheart. Definitely a wallflower, but makes killer grades. What did she say?"

"Yeah! That's her. And the prettiest blue eyes. God, I just want to take her home and feed her and read to her or something. I've heard she's had it pretty rough at home. Or, really rough, actually. She told me that she had written over twenty pages and may need to come in early to type it in the library because she doesn't have a computer at home."

"Twenty pages? I only asked for five. . . Wow. Good for her. A young Flannery O'Connor on our hands. I heard from the counselor about some of her problems at home. Real dad is dead or ran off; she and her sister lived with the grandmother for a while until she died; absent mother. Not a great situation."

"And you know about the step-dad, right?"

"Just a little from the counselor. Is it Kathy? Cary? I'm not too sure about her... What about the step-dad?"

Again, I played coy.

"It's Kathy. Don't say anything, but she's fucking useless. Having a degree in 'Child Psychology' and acting like an airhead does not make you an effective school counselor. A lot of our kids just aren't getting what they need. Resources, I mean. Anyway... But, yeah, the step-dad or whatever has been in and out of jail. Lots of drugs, disorderly conduct a battery charge against their mom, and he supposedly killed someone when he was like sixteen or seventeen. They charged him as a minor, I guess."

Made sense from what I had seen.

"Jesus. No, I didn't know all that. Probably explains a lot. That poor thing looks utterly terrified half the time. We're not supposed to let her just drag that pillow around, but I don't have the heart to take it from her. She usually keeps it in her backpack or locker during class, though."

"I remember her sister, too. She's in high school now. She was the same way, but I've heard she's gotten pretty wild lately. Like most of these *'country girls from the holler'*, as they say. Lucky you, coming from a shiny Atlanta private school to join us here in the sticks."

She mock-slapped my arm from across the table, and then asked, "Why was that, anyway? I've been wondering."

"Long story... Some other time, I'll share. The short-version, though, is that I secretly love it up here. Always have. I feel at home. The mountains, the cold, the isolation. It's healing to me."

She looked up from under tousled bangs, took a deep draw of wine, slowly returned her glass to the table, and rose from the table. I slid my chair back just a few inches so she could sit on my thigh. She leaned in to whisper in my ear. My goosebumps emerged to meet her gentle weight on my lap.

"Do you need healing, Rylan?"

I swallowed before speaking. My mouth was dry. I tried to be smooth.

"Only if you are the medicine."

She moved an errant strand of hair back from my ear and twirled it in her fingers.

"I can be. If that's what you need."

We kissed in the flickering shadows of candles and fire. Low music, a reverberating blood-buzz from the wine, and a warm high engulfed me. At once, the pin-pricking roar in the back of my head began to subside just enough to enjoy the moment. Brief as flame, likely, but still a moment's respite, no less.

The same jack-o-lanterns that had witnessed a lovely romance unfold in my apartment were now adorning the front of my classroom. I had the lights out, save for my desk lamp, and a cold autumn rain fell gently outside. I moved my teacher chair near the blackboard for my students to read their novellas in between the pumpkins, like a fireside ghost story or something.

Tony, Lacy, and I sat at the back, in a row of little chairs, nodding at each other playfully as a particularly 'country' young man regaled us with a story about a demon dog that haunted his property.

"The damon dawg chased the boyy across the yerd like a hound chases a ruck'oon."

So he read, pausing to look up from his paper. . .

"Ugh, Mister Wilder? That's one of muh sy'milees, like you asked fer."

"That's great, Jake. Thank you for letting me know. Go ahead, keep reading."

Tony texted me while we sat, instead of whispering.

"Nice work, teaching those sy'milees."

"Can't wait for his metaphor." I responded.

A few more not-quite-Falkner stories were read, and then I smiled at Lacy to get her attention. As the last sentences were unraveling of a story that eerily resembled an abbreviated plot of the classic Universal 'The Wolfman' film, I motioned to my gradebook. She looked over, and I showed her who was next: Elsa Privette.

"Your young novelist." I whispered.

She gave me a thumbs-up and nodded excitedly.

The semi-Gothic girl who recited 'The Wolfman' plot sat down to a few forced claps. I gave her some encouraging words, as I had with everyone, and she beamed when I compared her story to the classic film from which it was obviously derived. Kudos for the retro material, regardless of the potential plagiarism. Lon Cheney was long dead, anyway.

"Elsa? You're next."

The girl turned with her eyes wide and a bright smile on her face. She had been sitting with her pillow in her lap rubbing the edges with her fingers. A nervous habit, I had noticed, but she looked excited to take the big chair and read her story. She left her pillow beside her desk and scurried quickly to the front of the room. The cushioned chair nearly swallowed her when she sat, and her oversized pumpkin sweater made her look like an elf atop a giant throne. There's a simile, by the way.

"Whenever you're ready." I offered.

She took a deep breath, cleared her throat, and her voice was light but strong when she spoke. After a few minutes of her reading, she found a rhythm and a confidence that I hadn't seen in her before. She was in her element.

"Okay, my story is called 'The Mirror for Ghosts'. It's about a local legend, and I. . . I am going to read it now."

'The Mirror for Ghosts'

Do you believe in ghosts? I was always told that they didn't exist, but I'm not sure that I believe that. Let me tell you why...

Under Banner Lake, there's a hidden town buried below the dark surface of the water. The mountains protect the water and all of its secrets, like Roman centurions. My grandmom used to tell me stories about the old town of Banner, while we sat on her porch overlooking the quiet lake. I would imagine that I could see the street cars and the sidewalks and the famous theater under the water, as she would tell me about what it was like even before she could remember.

In the 1930s, during the Great Depression, the TVA flooded the whole town to build Carter Dam. Everyone was evacuated from the area and had to go live in Johnson City or Knoxville, while they rebuilt the town we know today as Banner. Everyone except for one family, that is.

They were called the Hagans. Sarah Hagan and her daughter Isabelle lived alone on the outskirts of town, and never bothered with being friendly to anyone. Most people just left them alone in their tiny cabin to do as they pleased. They had no newspaper or radio, and they never heard the news in town about the area being flooded that summer. There weren't many phones then, and all of Sarah's acquaintances were afraid of her. Many even thought that she was a witch...

You see, her husband Robert had died in WW1 fighting the Germans in France. It was said that Sarah had baby Isabelle the day that her husband fell on the battlefield. This would be quite ironic, don't you think? Sarah mourned for her husband deeply each day, as they were very young and were just starting their life together. She wore all black in town and was known to have terrible fits from time to time. Sarah began hosting seances to communicate with Robert and would invite many people to come see. They say that Sarah was very good at this, and people would leave her parlor crying and frightened after she had recalled a loved one from the Great Beyond. When people refused to pay or disrespected her ceremony, it was said that she would put a curse on them and their family so that they would know her grief. She wanted everyone to be as lonely and sad as her.

She was told to stop by the townspeople, as the seances were considered satanic. She was shunned from the town after that and moved to the woods to live by herself with Isabelle.

No one from town every ventured up to see her, and many hoped that she had simply disappeared. So, when the town was flooded, Sarah and Isabelle had no warning...

The water was said to have destroyed the tiny cabin almost instantly, taking Sarah and Isabelle's life along with it. Sarah's body was found almost a mile away on the bank of the new lake, but Isabelle was never seen again. Many people think that the sheriff and his deputies purposely didn't tell the family, so that they would be drowned and an end would be put to all the bad rumors surrounding them. Maybe that was true, after all.

Now, the legend goes that on the right summer night, if you are in tune with such things, you may hear Sarah calling for her lost daughter through the trees around the lake. Her voice would crack in the twilight, and her crazed cackle would echo off the dark water nearby. Some people even claim to have seen her searching for Isabelle in the dark. I never believed this at all, until I saw her for myself.

A few years ago, before my grand-mom passed away, we were out on a summer evening in the meadow near her house trying to catch fireflies. They would glow and fade like stars in the sky, tiny Christmases floating in the air. I had just released one from my jar because I didn't want to scare it too much, when my grand-mom stopped in her tracks ahead of me. She wore a loose white gown that flickered gently in the warm breeze, and her face had turned the same color as its fabric. I had never seen my grand-mom afraid, but she was frozen like a pillar of stone.

I followed her gaze to the tree line. The flowers of the meadow seemed to dance as my eyes sought what she had seen. Then, I froze, too. There in the growing darkness stood a lady dressed all in black. We couldn't see her face because of a dark veil, but she was there, nonetheless. She didn't speak or move. We had not heard anyone approach through the trees. Immediately the legend of Sarah Hagan came back to me. I ran to my grand-mom and wrapped my arms around her waist. As much as I wanted to hide my face in her gown, I kept my eyes fixed on the woman in black.

My grand-mom's voice was tense and dry when she finally spoke.

"Hello?" she asked.

This was a question and not a greeting. The woman offered no reply. The crickets that had been chirping all around were suddenly silent. The trees behind the woman, usually a friendly audience, now all seemed to become evil spirits in the growing darkness.

I had never felt truly afraid until that moment. All of my happiness was gone. It was replaced by a deep and lasting fear as we stood in the silent mountain meadow. I finally closed my eyes and squeezed my grand-mom tighter. When I got enough courage to open them again, the woman in black was gone. Everything gradually returned to normal. I had never been so glad to hear crickets chirp and to feel the warm breeze of a summer night. . .

My grand-mom and I only whisper amongst ourselves about seeing the woman in black. We don't call her Sarah, but we both know who we saw that evening in the meadow. I have not seen or heard her since, but she finds me often when I sleep. Her black dress and mourning veil wrap around me like the limbs of evil trees, and I jolt awake as she is dragging me down into the dark waters of Banner Lake.

I will forever be haunted by Sarah Hagan in my dreams, and that still makes me afraid...

So, do you believe in ghosts? I think that I do. I think that I always will.

The End

The classroom was utterly silent as Elsa stood up from the big chair. Even the boy who always slept in class sat unblinking, wide awake. Tony had been scrolling through college football stats on his phone during the previous stories, but he sat bewitched at the edge of his seat. Lacy hit me repeatedly on my arm and was the first to start clapping. The whole class followed, and Elly's face turned beet red as she returned to her seat. She managed a meek "Thank you" that perhaps only I heard. She had returned to her normal bashful self almost as quickly as she had become a master raconteur.

I stood and sat my notebook down on the chair behind me, raising my hand to get the class to calm down. The applause was very loud, and one of the country boys was whistling like he was making a proverbial cat-call. Finally, everyone was mostly quiet and I could speak.

"Elsa, wow. That was amazing. Is that a true story?"

"Yes, sir."

"And the town below the lake? I didn't know any of that."

"Yep. That's true, too."

Lacy was nodding at me from the back of the room as if to confirm her story.

"Elsa, would you want to read that at parent night this week? I think it's perfect for Hallowe'en. A true folk-horror story. Great use of local folklore, too."

She looked down at her desk for a moment. I thought she might cry, her face was so red. The manuscript in her hands gave away a pair of trembling hands.

"Yes, sir. I think I can."

"Okay, great. I'll pick two more people to read their stories, as well. Let's see, who's next? Someone has big shoes to fill."

I had helped Lacy decorate the library for parent night during my planning period that day. The voyeuristic jack-o-lanterns that I had carved for my classroom were added to a collection of similar orange orbs all over the room. We had brought in a ton of folding chairs and moved the usual tables out of the way in preparation for the swarm of parents we expected to attend. Faux autumn leaves hung from the ceiling in little arches, papier maché and wrinkled.

It was a fact that our American sense of seasonality was a direct derivative from school gatherings such as this one. As a kid, I fondly recalled the palpability of concepts like "Fall", "Christmas", "St Patrick's Day", and every other minor or major holiday coming alive at school in the form of bulletin boards, posters, classroom decorum changes, and little parties where parents signed up to bring napkins, plates, cupcakes, and the obligatory Lay's potato chips. It was how we clocked the yearly march around the calendar, and now I felt immersed in such a cycle again. All this as I stapled a giant witch's hat to said bulletin board.

"You think her parents will bring her tonight to read?"

I was a thousand miles away when Lacy spoke, sneaking up behind me as I mused about orange and black sprinkles on stale confections.

"Who? Elsa?"

"No, Margaret Thatcher. Yes, Elsa."

"Sorry, I was lost in thought. I don't know. Her mom might. I doubt we'd let the step-dad through the door. I'm sure he's on some no-entry list."

"Is that a thing? A 'no-entry' list?"

"I may have just made it up, but Tony keeps an eye on who comes in and out of the school pretty well. What with his record and all. That you had mentioned."

"Good point. Guess we'll see."

A few hours later, we saw. . .

Tony, all six-foot-six of him, was greeting kids and their parents at the double doors at the entrance to the little school. The counselor Kathy was there and the secretary, smiling and waving and handing out programs.

I stood off to myself in the hallway. I hated events like this. I was a friendly guy, but faking all the school shit with parents was beyond my comfort zone. Right there with loud parties, big crowds, and airports. My inner wallflower was bound to come out sooner or later. I adjusted my blazer and loosened my tie. I shifted between crossed arms (too stand-offish) and putting my hands in my pocket (too apathetic) and eventually settled on something of a parade rest as parents began to come over and introduce themselves. Most were very nice, a few were very annoying, and the majority were quite backwoods in dress and manner. This was a big deal and it quickly began to have the feel of a Sunday fellowship luncheon. I was the outsider.

As everyone caroused and began to file into the library for the assembly, I remembered that I had left my gradebook in my classroom. I was certain that I would be accosted by someone, before the night was over, about an 'undeserved' bad grade for some missing homework, or an errant paper, or a 37 on a unit exam. Plus, I needed a breath. My collar had suddenly become too tight amid all the smiling and waving and being introduced in the foyer.

My dress boots clacked lightly on the tile floor as I made my brief escape. I passed the big trophy case, and the gym's double doors. Took a right at the intersection towards the middle-school wing. It was a small school, easy to navigate. The art room was coming up on my left, easy to spot with sixty-three unique works on display, each taped to the stoic concrete walls lining both sides of the door. The bright fluorescent lights of the entranceway began to fade to only the back-up lights as I neared our hallway. By the time I reached my room, it was quite dark. The kids would definitely refer to the dimly lit halls at this time of evening as "creepy", and I couldn't disagree with them.

I opened the door and stepped inside my now-familiar space. I took pause before turning on the lights. My eyes hadn't adjusted to the darkness yet. Inside, I smelled the distinct burn of cigarette smoke and a bad aftershave. There was someone in there, waiting in the quarter-light. I could make-out a shape, bringing my mind reeling back from the quiet lounge of my thoughts. I started, a flash of adrenaline startling my senses.

He stood at the blackboard, somehow studying our lesson's notes from the day, despite the gloom. I quickly turned on the light to reveal some big bastard in a red flannel dress shirt, John Deere hat, and dirt-stained Carhart khakis, standing not ten feet in front of me.

"Shit. Jesus Christ. You scared the hell out of me."

All of this had happened in matter of seconds.

"Pretty strong language for a school teacher."

"Huh? Sorry, who are you? You really shouldn't be down here after school hours."

"I think you know who I am. And now I know *exactly* who you are."

I did know exactly who he was. It was Elsa's step-dad. Fuck. . .

"Oh, yeah. We know some of the same folks. You spoke with that old cop about a few of my – um, production sites recently, yeah? Had 'em shut down. Cost some people I know a bit of money. That wasn't very nice of you, I didn't think. Running up on that hill in your little shorts. Not used to people being up there, you know? It's our property and all. We can do what we want."

His voice rattled thick with a back-mountain accent. Muddled, and deep. Like distant limbs cracking and falling in the woods at dusk. I narrowed my eyes at him and did my best to give nothing away with a stray expression.

"Look, I don't know you, and I need to get back to this assembly. Tell you what, let's pretend this didn't happen, that you weren't standing in the dark in my classroom, and I won't have to get our resource officer to have you escorted out."

There was no resource officer.

He stepped towards me slowly as he drew an invisible line along the board.

"I don't think so, teacher. *Mr. Wilder*, is it? Says it right above your door, in fact. My girl Elsa likes you a lot. Talks about your class and shit at home. That's fine, that's fine. She's a smart girl and all that, but you need to understand that we do things different up here. Probably much different from wherever the hell you're from. I'm going to say this once. Now – you need to mind your business. That's it. Just mind your business. You understand? Stop snooping around up on that mountain, quit your running or whatever up there. And I better not get another call from some uppity bitch wanting a welfare meeting about a little bruise or another on the little sister. Yeah? You hearing me?"

I swallowed a bit. He was close enough that I could clearly see the stubbled five-o'clock shadow spreading across his face and neck like a passing cloud. I could see the fine wrinkles on his face and forehead. Working outside. Dead blue eyes. Almost clear. Buzz-cut under the hat. Not quite forty, but not thirty, either. Something inherently wicked in the scowl, a bully's intimidation that had worked his whole life.

It was working now, if I am honest.

"Yeah. I get it. Your business is your business."

"Good."

He extended a hand to me. I hesitantly shook it.

He pulled me closer abruptly. Whispered in my ear.

"I mean it. Teach. Don't fuck with me. If I found you here, I can find out a hell of a lot more."

I didn't respond, but as he pushed past me to open the door, I reached my heel back to block it from swinging open. He shot a look back at me.

"Hey. Randall, right? I only shook your hand agreeing to stay out of *your* business. The girl? Well, that's *my* business, too. Let's keep our hands off her. *I mean it.*"

He smiled. Country-yellow teeth stained deeper from pack after pack of chewing tobacco. Not your real *meth teeth*, but pretty bad. He had hit the pipe a time or two.

"All right, teach. You're the big man. Now move your fucking foot. I never liked being in no school house."

I did as he wished, and he slammed the door behind me as he walked out into the hall. My diploma tilted on the wall behind my desk. My hands were shaking. Mostly out of anger, I hoped.

I steadied myself in the quiet room for a minute, waited to hear the side door open and close as Randall made his clandestine exit. I took a few deep breaths, turned out the light, and almost forgot my gradebook as I ventured back out into my little world.

I made it back to the library just in time for the assembly to start. Lacy had saved me a seat in the row of uncomfortable aluminum chairs with all the other teachers. We got a quick smile or two from a few old hens. Well, maybe side-wise glance was the better word. Two young teachers of the opposite sex seeming very fond of each other lately.

"You okay?" Lacy whispered, as Tony began his opening presentation.

"I guess. Just had a weird – um, encounter. . . In my room. I'll tell you later."

"Okay. Yeah?"

I nodded, and her eyes said enough. She patted me gently with her program on the leg to show her understanding. I really liked her. No drama, no bullshit. Just understanding, and that was all you really needed.

And about an hour later, Elsa read her story in front of practically the whole school. Pillow in hand, but it was such an extension of her fragile personage that no one really noticed her clutching it tightly.

It took her a few minutes to relax, stop her face from blushing and her voice from shaking, but in the end it was great. Really *great*. She beamed when she finished.

Everyone applauded. Even her mom clapped her nicotine-stained hands together and had tears in her eyes.

In the corners and the shadows, all the ghosts of Halloween bowed and postured as she navigated her way back to join the crowd. I was sure of it, even though no one saw them. Not even me. But, that didn't mean that they weren't there. I felt them all the time, just out of reach.

The Saturday morning after Halloween, at some ungodly hour, I sat sipping a cup of black coffee and grading papers on a barstool in my new kitchen. A mostly eaten buttered bagel sat sadly on a little saucer. A bottle of some salty-sweet sports drink rested half-finished to the side.

I paused for a moment in the morning silence. Took a deep breath to ease some nerves. Scanned the room.

This place was starting to feel like home, and I already had positive associations within these walls. Lacy and I had finally had dinner at Uncle Ray's, the night before, at his continued request. They loved her, of course. She was an instant hit. Like family in a flash. We talked for hours, ate a delicious meal, played Trivial Pursuit, watched a horror movie, and snuggled on the couch, like kids, as my aunt continued to tease us with popcorn and Hallowe'en candy. She kept waiting for Trick or Treaters who never came – they lived too far out for that sort of thing. So we felt obliged to humor her until much later than planned.

Uncle Ray eventually saved us from further gluttony and seasonal enthusiasm.

"Hey, Rylan. Don't you need to be getting to bed? I told all of my friends that you were going to win that race in the morning. You better not let me down. It's almost eleven o'clock. A star athlete needs his sleep."

Also upon Uncle Ray's suggestion, and at the coercion of some co-teachers at school, I had, in fact, registered for that mountain race everyone up here went nuts over for whatever reason. That would take place in just a few short hours, and I was beginning to feel some butterflies. I hadn't run a race in forever. I had no idea what kind of shape I was in at the moment, compared to my most competitive days, but I figured *What the hell...* People look at you less strangely when you tell them you run ten miles or more a day if there is some arbitrary 'race' attached to the end of the sentence.

This was my get-out-of-jail-free card for a vague, borderline OCD and lots of pent-up aggression. It kept me on the level, but no one really understood what that meant.

And, more frightening, I had an intuitive suspicion that I did, in fact, have a chance of outright winning the thing.

That particular pressure is something unique that only a certain personality type can understand. A potential win was far more threatening than the comfortable certainty of loss. I figured that boxers and jockeys and presidential candidates all knew that feeling, as well. To win at anything meaningful was to set an ever-mounting precedent of *expectation*, and that was the worst pressure of all.

I heard Lacy stirring in the bedroom. The ruffle of sheets at this quiet hour was enough to garner my attention, and then she called my name. Half asleep, the two syllables that comprised my existence drifted out of the cozy room like soft jazz playing down a candlelit hallway somewhere in a lofty country estate. Beckoning and haunting, I was thrilled beyond measure to have this woman in my life. Even if it was temporary, as all things ultimately are, I wanted to cherish this particular gift. She had inadvertently pulled me back from a very bad headspace, and I tried not to view our current relationship under the umbrella of doom, with which I often shaded my worldview.

I liked the shade, for sure and more than most, but sometimes I could darken the light a bit too much. With her, I was willing to put my sunglasses away and let the light shine into my vacant little room.

"Yeah, babe? I'm in here. You want some coffee?"

Her voice came drifting back to me.

"In a minute. Come see me."

I got up from my bar stool and sauntered into the bedroom. She looked like a lioness furrowing within my sheets. Queen of the Satin. A Destroyer of Worlds.

"How are you feeling?"

"Pretty good. I'm getting oddly nervous, actually. I haven't raced in a while."

"Oh, yeah? Well, can I do anything to help you relax? Distract you, maybe?"

She gave me a look. Her eyes burned with blue fire in the morning dim and distant lamp light. She rolled over dramatically in bed. Arched her back and lifted up with only the top sheet covering her lower half. It struggled to maintain its duty, and then drifted off seductively, leaving her intoxicatingly exposed. She looked back at me, tossing an errant curl out of her face and motioning to me with an enticing gesture.

"Do we have time?" she asked in her sexiest voice.

"Probably not, but who cares?" I casually replied, with a shrug, and then crawled into bed with predatory fervor.

The morning light seemed a bit brighter, perhaps more offensive, at this altitude. The air was cold, but I didn't notice. My breath came out in crystalline puffs as I leaned into the incline. These switchbacks were just impossible. They seemed to never cease. We were a little more than half-way up the five-mile route. Moving through time and space as we climbed from a starting elevation of 3000ft and ended 5800ft above the sea. I was securely in second place at the moment, having left two guys out of sight once the steepest climbing had begun.

This guy in the lead looked strong. Bright yellow jersey. He was part of a semi-professional group in the area. He literally got paid to lace up and win footraces. What a concept.

But, alas. There it was. I caught him glancing back over his shoulder before he disappeared out of sight just ahead amid the rocky, craggy turns that careened up the mountain.

This wasn't over yet: we were both hurting just as bad as the other, and this guy was running scared.

We had passed all the Highland Game activities being arranged in a big clearing near the famous mountain's visitor center and entrance gate, a mile earlier. There was still a decent pack of runners at that point, before things drastically separated. Men wearing kilts and tartan moved about. Tents were being erected to later sell cheap trinkets, fried foods, and flat beer. A crowd of early risers cheered from either side of a twine fence as we breached the woods, crossed the highway, and came into sight before attacking the access road which led to the summit. That's where the real racing had started, and that is where the real pain had met us with a waiting grin.

The grade reached fifteen percent or some ungodly slope at that point. Even if you slowed to a jog, even if you *walked*, this course was still going to take you to a special place of self-imposed despair. I could not believe Uncle Ray had convinced me to do this. Even Tony, from school, had pushed for me to run after studying the collegiate All-American plaque, hanging dustily in my classroom, one day after school.

I wondered who had originally concocted this hair-brained race for just a moment. It had to be someone with no intention of ever running it themselves.

Something like, "Oh, Hell, Charlie! What do ya say about a footrace up that there mountain? Be pretty up there, won't it? People would come from miles around to run this one! We can get a big car dealership to pay out some cash to the winners, and they all can stay to watch the caber toss and eat a turkey leg, after it's over!"

Yeah, something just like that, I bet.

I couldn't tell.

Was he hurting? Was he hurting worse than me?

My legs were struggling to maintain their cadence up the hill. Lactate within my cells was rising like a tide, my stomach occasionally tightened into a knot, and even my neck muscles were straining, focused on that yellow singlet appearing and then vanishing ahead in the blinding sun and into the shadows.

I remembered the first time I had ever visited this mountain when I was in college. My dad had never taken us when I was a kid. Wasn't his thing. He liked boats and water, and this was far from any such riparian distractions. All they had up here was a three-state view and a makeshift zoo housing several local rarities. Teresa and I had taken advantage of our student discounts to visit the so-called park, and it had been a similarly fine fall day. It had been a bit earlier in the year, though. It wasn't cold yet, and they close the mountain after this weekend every year. The annual Highland Games was the send-off into the waiting onyx of winter for such altitudes. Snow would come, and everything presently around us would be blanketed in an inhospitable whiteness. It would happen soon. Maybe this week, the forecast had said.

We had a great time that day. I remember clearly having a group of strangers take our picture on the footbridge that connected two small ravines at the summit. She had on a blue Patagonia half-zip and her hair blew about wildly in the wind. We looked happy. And so young.

That picture had stayed with us all the way to the end. I remember idly staring at it one afternoon during the worst of it all. A physical discomfort shooting through my body, a vague nausea ever present. As my mind returned to the task at the hand, to the yellow line on the pavement beneath my feet, a fragment of that feeling came reeling back at me like hot shrapnel. It was strange, that I could just call it on like that. Summon its reappearance.

I needed to live in that place right at this moment. An empty room decorated only with Hate and Insecurity. My masculinity had been thrown deeply into question by it all, and this was enough to make any young man *very angry*. Perhaps I had enjoyed wallowing in my bespoke despair a bit too much. It made everything more potent. Food tasted better, music aroused more feeling, drinks and sex had been more satisfying. Perhaps I could revel in this empty room, host and guest all to myself.

And then my mind drifted to that little girl for some odd reason. Her bright eyes. Her inherent kindness and all the things that she wanted to become. Those bruises on her arm... The sonofabitch who put them there. God, nothing had made me madder. I hated a bully, and again, I hadn't spoken my true mind when he was in my presence, just two nights prior.

Maybe though, all said, I simply *hated* myself. Hated my inadequacies, my perceived shortcomings. I felt no conscious masochism, but I could never be sure. All I knew is that it drove me onward. Fueled me forward. Gave me distinct purpose and made me want to be better. To do more and not waste a day. To fight harder, and to win, if only for myself, but that is all we truly have. The mirror, our reflection.

He had fifty meters on me. Maybe less. Kept looking back over his shoulder like a coward. That was a chicken shit thing to do. Either take the lead and hold it confidently, or don't take it at all. I didn't know his name, didn't really care, but I'm sure he had an athletic resumé a mile long. NCAA berths and national championships. A modest stipend from some big shoe company to go along with his trust fund and absence of worldly debt.

I had some talent, had shown that talent on many occasions, but I had no such dalliances in regard to making a living off running a few races and otherwise playing video games all day.

As he looked back one last time, I channeled my deepest hate in his direction. A quiet rage that burned like wildfire, somewhere deep within me. He didn't deserve it. He was not to blame for anything. He looked innocent and startled as I pulled even with him in the last set of switchbacks. He looked intimidated and afraid, unaccustomed to losing anything short of an Olympic-caliber race. We couldn't have been running much under seven-minutes per mile at this point in the race as the relentless climb reached its maximum tilt, but we were both going *all-out* with every muscle fiber in our bodies working at full capacity.

I caught a momentary glance of his blond hair and reddened face from the effort, as I passed him unceremoniously. He didn't fight with me. He surrendered the moment I pulled ahead. All that awaited was one final ascent to the finish at the top of the summit. I drove my knees and pumped my arms with an impossible forward lean. I could feel the little muscles in my lower legs beginning to cramp from the acute stress of the occasion. My lower back ached as it worked to stabilize my lean body.

As I heard the bagpiper begin to play upon my approach, the hairs on my arms stood at attention and all the pain momentarily vanished. Goosebumps riddled every inch of my skin, and a deep elation outrivaled the anger I had conjured to make that last push up this godforsaken pile of rock.

I had family and friends and kids who looked up to me waiting at the top. I had Uncle Ray and Aunt Linda. I had Lacy. I had practically the whole obsessed town screaming my name as I broke the tape.

Feeling the tape give way on my heaving chest, I didn't celebrate with any dramatic gestures. I just stood trying to catch my breath. Tasting Hemingway's copper pennies. Feeling the blissful chill of accomplishment, a relief akin to bloodletting or exorcism.

I felt Lacy's arms wrap around me at some point. I smelled her perfume and shampoo as she hugged me tightly. A little girl handed me a medal. A big guy in a neon vest slapped me on the back as I cleared the finish chute. A reporter wanted to chat much too soon upon the run's cessation. The world spun and the air burned. Invisible flames scorched the earth.

Everything was wonderfully ablaze, but nothing was destroyed.

And I never once looked back.

I struggled with a glass ketchup bottle at a dive bar a few hours later. I was surrounded by all my favorite people,

"Hit the Heinz logo."

Lacy whispered in my ear. She hadn't required ketchup for her Caesar salad, so easy for her to advise from afar.

It worked, though, and a glob of red plopped onto my plate to accompany my burger and fries. I took a long sip of my beer, dipped a fry, sat back in my chair, and put my arm around Leslie. Uncle Ray raised his Old Fashioned to toast my race, and we all clinked our glasses satisfyingly all around. I felt like the king of a small Mediterranean country. Or an untouchable war lord. Or a Prohibition-era gangster. Other runners and their families had also made haste to get to the *Axe & Shield* for lunch after the race, and many had come over to say congratulations as we ate.

It had been a red-letter day so far, and I was in high spirits. Even the ridiculously sticky tabletop couldn't abate my elation. In fact, it enhanced it. Lunch was on me, because I was a thousand dollars richer after killing myself to climb a steep fucking hill.

But, still.

I had this lingering sense of dread somewhere in the shadowed corners of my mind. The places I went during a race were never pretty, but I had kept seeing that girl's arm. I had kept seeing Randall's stubbled face so close to mine. I had felt my fangs pierce the skin there for a minute. They had gotten pretty sharp, and the urge to bite was impossibly strong.

I felt equally tethered to both Elsa and Randall for some reason, yet in the moment so detached. My happiness slept toe-to-toe with her lack thereof. It slept beside his inherent meanness, as natural as Death. Born into him like a cancer.

And maybe that's what bothered me the most. I, too, had a bit of that in me. I, too, could get nasty. I just tempered it better and was raised to keep it in check. I had the deepest feeling that I would see him again, and I feared that it would be a little like looking into a reflective pool. What I could have been if not privileged by circumstance. My broader, flannel shirt-wearing doppelganger.

It bothered me, and suddenly the room and all the celebration fell on my deaf ears. Lacy and Ray were toasting. I was still smiling and nodding, but I suddenly felt exhausted by it all.

I was ready to go home. I needed to rest. My thoughts had gotten too loud again.

Part II:

A Long Winter, All Too Brief

Eliza Stone

The stick-it notes on her desk hung like little yellow flags off a galley on the stillest day of the year. The MLS wasn't updating, and she couldn't focus. Daniel was running around, ever busy, and seemed to be purposefully avoiding eye contact with her. Like he had for almost a year. Ever since the accident.

The first flurries of the year fell outside. Very early for the South, but not so early for Appalachia. The whiteness of the flakes was impure to her. White had become a painful color, and she could practically feel the flakes, falling outside, chilling her fragile bones through the dingy window.

The brothers had decorated the office with a forced sense of cabinesque décor. There was the obligatory stacked-stone fireplace, the elk head mounted on the wall (there hadn't been elk in the area for several centuries), the copious cedar, the leather couches. . . Mountain Realty to them was an idea, an obsessive pursuit, but the money they made was quite material. Much more palpable than the overdone decorum, the glass eyes of the long-dead elk, or the pseudo-snow falling outside.

Daniel had a call come in on his cell phone and stepped into his side office, out of view. His light voice flittered off into a temporary distance. Eliza's nervous movements and flittering eyes suddenly became more apparent with no one else in her presence. In her desk drawer, buried beneath a thick layer of file folders, there were two prescription bottles. Both contained very strong narcotics. Both were from two different prescribing doctors and had been filled at two separate pharmacies.

She wasn't supposed to take any more pills until much later that evening, but today was not a good day. Earlier, she had popped a few little blue pills and one of the white ones that got stuck in her throat on her way to work. She was beginning to feel too much, so she had given herself a pass lately. An OD was unlikely and would be welcomed at this point, she reasoned.

The snow falling outside was bringing something to the surface of the dark lake that her psyche rested upon. If she let this unbearable *something* breach the surface, she knew a maelstrom would follow. Being at work, being the talented actress she had become, mimicking normalcy as best as she could, this would be unacceptable. She didn't know exactly what was stalking under the false placidity of her façade. She was unafraid of that darkness, welcomed it even, but her life as Eliza Stone would no longer exist if this Blackness were to ever reach the Light.

She knew that whatever it was would ultimately bring pain and chaos. It desperately wanted out of its layer, like a demon seeking leave from beneath the iron gates of a midnight Hell. So she quickly took a handful of her pills and swallowed them down without water. When alone, she chewed them so they went to work faster. She always twitched and her cheek would tilt up to one side at the acrid taste, but within minutes the wonderful emptiness would return. It felt like drowning when the drugs took effect. Just like the *hard* drugs used to when she was young. It was like lying with a familiar lover when they hit her bloodstream. The sensations, the building climax, the after-effects were always the same. Yet, you kept coming back for more of that familiarity. Without this human draw to sameness, there could be no lasting connection.

Her file drawer opened and closed with a benign clatter that would draw no attention. Daniel knew she was in pain and was always kind. The brother Bruce was indifferent, but still kept her on despite an obvious decline in work performance. But neither knew the extent to which she lingered on the ledge of some eternal precipice. This job and a feeble attempt to make Lilly proud were all that kept her glued together.

And just then, from out of the gently falling frozen flakes, came a ray of light like she had never seen before.

The bell above the door sounded the arrival of two new entrants to the pretentiously cozy space. A young mother, quite attractive and wearing a nice coat, and her daughter. Eliza's eyes fell on the latter like a reptile narrowing-in on some unsuspecting rodent. She felt at once a wave of nausea and something akin to bliss. Then, the little girl turned and Eliza got a full glimpse of her face.

Lilly?

Blonde hair and an angelic passivity washed over the child's face like warm water in a bath. Innocence, personified. Just like her daughter, but not lost to the void and mystery of a questionable afterlife.

"Brittany, be sure to stamp your feet on the mat. We don't want to track this slush all over their nice office."

The young mom's voice was gentle, like any good mother's, and the child obeyed immediately. She stood there stamping her feet for too long as the mom scanned the room and got her bearings. She smiled at Eliza, whose mouth may have been slightly agape from the recent dose of meds and the fact that she was staring at a slightly older version of her own daughter in front of her. Back from the Dead. A reflection and a glimmer of her own blood manifesting in the form of this child. So close she could grab her, yet she did not belong to her in the least.

How lucky this woman was, Eliza thought. She had no idea. What was it like to lie down on the couch beside her daughter for a nap? Every bath, every episode of fitful crying, every diaper change, every kiss on the forehead. She still had that right beside her.

And to Eliza, it was only a haunting memory that was pulling her down into an inescapable fog.

"Hello. My name is Katrina Reynolds. I had an appointment with Daniel Spencer to go over some listings, I believe."

Eliza blinked slowly. She immediately hated this woman. She had money, obviously. A college education.

Glancing out into the snow, a new BMW. Maybe some domestic disturbance had brought her in without a man, but that might have been the only hardship she had ever endured. It was written across her face like a bad tattoo.

"Ma'am?"

It had been several long seconds. Eliza finally came back to the moment. Blinked rapidly, and managed to speak. She had focused so intently on the girl that each square on her pearl-colored down jacket had become intensely fascinating.

"Oh, I'm sorry. I must have been lost in thought. Mr. Spencer is on the phone and should be out of his office in just a moment. You're welcome to sit by the fire. We have coffee, if you like."

Her eyes never left the daughter. This imposter named *Brittany* and her bitch mother.

As the two sat on the leather sofa by the gas fireplace, browsing the magazine collection for something reasonably kid-friendly, practically on each other's laps, Eliza could only fantasize about running her hands through the girl's light hair. Caressing her neck. Reading the words on some page of *Highlights* to her and watching for a reaction.

There really was a striking resemblance between this kid and her late daughter. It was a bit eerie. Even an outsider would have potentially remarked. The girl was a few years older than her daughter. This was even more haunting to Eliza. It was like seeing a ghost in future tense.

A shade of things yet to pass. And they would never come to pass, because her sweet girl was gone.

Eliza couldn't help herself anymore. She wanted to be near the girl. To touch her. To get her scent. To live out a fantasy that had inhabited her waking and dreaming mind for almost a year.

"Ms. Reynolds? Would your daughter like a cookie? We have fresh chocolate chips?"

"Oh, that's so nice! Brittany, would you like a cookie?"

"Yes, ma'am."

Eliza had already uncovered the Tupperware on the coffee table and placed two homemade cookies on a plate. She had baked them herself. They were Pillsbury, but still. They were baked by her.

She walked slowly over to the couch. Brittany's eyes beguiled no anticipation of her coming treat. They were bright blue, just like Lilly's.

"Here you go, sweetie. I hope you like them."

"Brittany, what do you say to the nice lady?"

"Thank you."

Her voice was like a coo, a precious sound that only children can produce. Innocent and unpretentious. Hopeful. Her sky was yet unclouded. She had known no loss or pain. In the time capsule that is our mortal bodies, this stage is the oldest artifact to be found.

Childhood, fleeting and impossibly beautiful.

Eliza smiled at the girl as she ate her first cookie with a small, little-bird bite. The girl smiled back. Fully trusting, all-believing.

Eliza shifted one glance to the mother. It was cold. It hid a vicious nature. Dark thoughts were passing through Eliza's shattered mind as she studied the woman's perfect make-up and pretty face. She hated her. An ultimate hate that was hard to conceal.

And why should she be so lucky?
And why should I feel so empty?

Eliza's thoughts were wild. Untamed monsters under every bed, all the skeletons in all the closets, all the demons in Hell moving just below the surface. She felt an evil rise in her that was without name. But, looking into that sweet girl's eyes as she ate her commercially processed homemade cookie, Eliza Stone felt something that she had not felt in a long time.

Purpose.

Randall Lightner

Damn girl was a fucking mess... *Too much of her mama in her. Jesus Christ. I don't have time for this today, and of course she's out of town... Visiting that useless sister of hers in Charlotte. The breeder with, like, five kids or something. Married well, sure, so she had brains. Am I even on Jenn's parent list or whatever? Fuck...*

Randall pulled into the high-school parking lot, his truck neglecting the two speed bumps lining the drive like they weren't even there. He had gotten a call a few hours earlier from some annoying secretary trying to explain that Jenny had gotten into a fight, and she was being suspended for two days, and a parent or guardian needed to come get her as soon as possible, and she was waiting outside the principal's office, and they had tried calling the mother to no response, and his number was also on file... And so it went.

He had been up playing pool at a buddy's on the far side of the mountain when his phone buzzed. He was two beers into an easy afternoon, had just scored some coin off a deal, and was ready to burn a few and kick back. He ignored the first ring, seeing that it was from the school, but then it buzzed again not three minutes later. He answered grumpily, struggled not to hang up on the secretary, and said he'd be there when he could.

He had played two more games to win his money back, shared a joint with Ronny, and took a beer for the road. It had been consumed and dispersed somewhere out the window before he reached the city limits. The sound of glass breaking as the wind whipped through his window was very satisfying, the cold air careening across his face and bare arms. It had to be damn near freezing for Randall to consider a jacket. And even then, he burned hot.

Did I need to go inside? *No way. I'm going to call.*

Randall called the school, spoke briefly to the secretary (Carla? It's Lightner. I'm outside to pick up Jenny. No, now. I don't have time to sign any forms. I'm in a hurry. Send her out for me.)

Carla sent her out as she was told.

Jenny came out the doors with the sullen temperament of any teenager, but with a special shade of irritability that only she could muster. Her dark hair, so different from Mama and Elsa, blew in the breeze and the holes crafted into her skinny jeans revealed little glimpses of olive skin beneath.

Her daddy must have been damn-near Indian, Randall thought, as he stared her down at the school's roundabout. Patches of snow lay around in the dead grass from the early dusting they had a while ago, but the girl wore no jacket, either. She, too, burned hot.

She opened the heavy door, had to take a huge step up to get into the cab, and slammed the door behind her. She put on her seatbelt instinctively, crossed her arms, little bracelets and charms jingling, hoop earrings dangling, and looked out the window with a pissed-off expression. She smelled like Dollar General perfume and bubble gum. Her lipstick was a deep red, her make-up too heavy, her eye shadow made her look like a gypsy who had dressed in the dark. She was still riding with her training wheels, but she was the type that would skip the bike altogether and move on to the *motorcycle.*

Randall hit the accelerator, and off they went without a word. He smiled and laughed to himself as the school vanished in the rearview.

Nearing the Dairy Queen up their way, Randall broke the silence. It was a little after one o'clock, and he was getting hungry.

"Hey, little sis. Want some lunch?"

"Yeah. I guess."

He pulled into the parking lot and was alone at the drive-through. A few minutes later, they were sitting with cheeseburgers, fries, and a chocolate shake for the elder Privette girl, a few miles up the road. Quiet pull-off near the river. Randall didn't have a sweet tooth, but he could put three burgers down with ease. Especially coming off a little high and a few beers.

Everything had an easy haze and rocked like a boat on a reasonably calm day. Coming back to shore, nearing a full stop. He would have to go back out soon, or else his tide would change for the worse. And that was never good.

"So – a fight, huh?"

Jenny shook her head emphatically. Cracked her knuckles. Sipped her shake.

"Bitch. I don't even wanna talk about it."

"Talk about it. It's just us. Your mama ain't here to yell at you."

"I been talking to this boy. At school, right? He's cute, and this chick Dana knows we're sweet on each other. She went and started texting him, and now. . ."

Randall wasn't listening at all. His mind was a thousand miles away, and at once prowling over her slender body. Every curve was both mysterious and familiar. He had paid for everything that made her who she was, this young hellion sitting next to him in his big truck. He wasn't into kids or anything sick like that, but this Jenny. . . She wasn't a kid anymore. She was curvy, or she stuffed her bra. Maybe both. He liked a bad girl, and she was heading down Bad Street like a steam train with no breaks. He was a man with enhanced appetites, after all, and she had become more than an hors d'oeuvre over the last few months.

"That's too bad, baby. Sorry about your boyfriend. Did you get a good shot or two in, though?"

"Yeah, I bloodied-up her damn pig nose. She barely touched me."

"Good. I bet you did. You hurt your hand?"

"A little, but it's fine."

"Let me see it."

She lifted up her bony hand in front of his face. Randall took it in his big rough mitt and kissed it better. He rubbed his scruffy beard over her smooth knuckles.

"Quit, now! That tickles!"

She giggled as she protested. Randall kissed her hand again, and she did not pull away. Her pupils dilated as he slowly began to suck on a finger or three, the purple polish of the last week fading and cracking. She blushed, and he could see goosebumps pop over her skin like grass growing through the lens of a hyper-speed camera.

She sighed, her breathing accelerating, and he finally stopped. Looked her right in the eyes. She looked away. Ashamed and suddenly embarrassed. He rubbed her neck as she looked out the window, her face red as a summer sunset.

"You ain't got to be shy, girl. I'll leave you be."

She was almost panting. He could see the rise and fall in her chest and stomach with each breath. She seemed to be unable to speak.

"Randy?"

"Yeah, babe."

"Do you think I'm pretty?"

"You know I do, little sis."

"Would you kiss me?"

"I would, but I'm not going to."

"Why not?"

He pushed her gently with the palm of his hand. Shook her by the arm in jest.

"Cause you know why, stupid! It ain't right."

She paused. He saw her swallow. Her throat tense and tight in the tension of the moment.

"Would you if I was older?"

He smiled at her. Malice cutting through the air like a knife. He didn't reply, but stole one of her fries and dipped it in her milkshake.

Oh, sis. I'd do more than kiss you, he thought in some untame recess of his mind.

He turned the radio up, lit a cigarette, and studied the river below as it flowed briskly to nowhere. Virgin snow lay around and ice shimmered in patches as the dying sun faded overhead.

Eliza Stone

Eliza waited in the vacant lake house for what seemed like an eternity. The late autumn sun waned over the shimmer of the water, and the leaves had long died. Their corpses lay all around, littering the ground with the remains of a year. Time passed at odd intervals – for her, anyway – but she checked her watch, paced around the small kitchen, and sat back down on the couch. It was cold in the room, and she shivered once that thought entered her mind.

Where the hell is he? He's very late.

She checked her phone. No texts or calls. She spun the keys to the cabin around a bone-thin finger. She tapped her foot. She scratched her arm and had to make herself stop. She pulled at her hair and straightened the back for no good reason. The only sound in the room was the tick of an old grandfather clock. It had distracted her from the moment she stepped inside the dusty rental. The incessant bastard had gotten inside her head. Like Time itself, it simply wouldn't quit announcing every miserable second. The Spencer brothers spared no expense in their decorating, and she was pretty sure that thing was authentic.

She couldn't care less. She just needed something to take the edge off, and her man was very fucking late.

Before she left work earlier that day to show a house, she had looked up the combination to a door lock out here on the lake. She had driven out the highway, turned off onto a side road, and then took another, which was unpaved. And then down a long gravel driveway, there it was: 3223 Lakeview Court. Out of the way, and vacant, with no one around. This was a perfect meeting spot. She had always chosen perfect meeting spots.

She studied the room as she waited. A dead mallard posed, frozen in space, on one wall, an antique shotgun hung above the stack-stone fireplace. A wood-carved mama bear and her cub greeted guests near the door. The sight of this depressed her further. A cruel reminder of the loss she tried daily, hourly, to avoid.

It was a futile pursuit. A foregone conclusion.

She was just wondering if that rusted shotgun might still shoot when she heard the distinct sound of tires crunching over gravel outside. Headlights filled the room as the twilight reached a peak. She stood, turned on a lamp for some additional light, and met the man at the door as he strode up the porch steps.

She opened the door before he could knock. He looked up with no measure of being startled and let himself into the room without permission. She closed the door behind him, and instinctively turned the bolt. When he passed, he smelled like pot and beer. Again, she couldn't care less.

"How ya doin' there, Liza? Goddamn. Did you find the hardest fucking place on the map for us to meet? Most folks I do business with just come by the house, for Christsakes. You and this cloak-and-dagger bullshit. . ."

Eliza stood before him, unblinking. Her face was hollow and her futile attempt at makeup did nothing to conceal a pallor so deep that even prison held no candle. Her look alone prevented him from finishing his sentence.

"You're late, Randall."

"Am I? Sorry. Must have lost track of the time. Had to drop my little Jenny off at the house and make sure she was. . . um, settled, with her sister. You know. Mama's outta town and all."

"Uh-huh. Do you have my stuff?"

"That I do, missy."

"May I see it?"

Randall wore a small, military-style backpack over one shoulder. He removed it, unzipped it, and started to remove its contents onto the kitchen table.

One by one, he laid out two syringes with needle attached, a bag of something dark, a bag of something crystalline, three prescription bottles, and a Ziploc bag of red pills. Eliza's eyes glistened darkly as she saw the contents appear like mirages on the wooden grain of the table. A tickle ran down her spine, and an excitement ran through her like she hadn't felt in years.

She probably hated the man in front of her. His veiny hands motioned to each item with a brief explanation, which she drowned out, and he was dressed in his typical uniform of flannel work shirt and carpenter pants. His thick stubble ran too far down his neck. His Adam's apple moved too prominently when he spoke. Every word and every syllable crackled out in a rolling-river hick accent, which she had grown to despise.

However, he was an entirely necessary evil in her life. She relied on him. Really, honestly, more than anyone else. It was an easy association, because she had no one else.

"What do I owe you?"

Her voice came out strained and terse. He wasn't finished talking about how some 'queer in jogging shorts' had disrupted his supply chain of whatever was in the bag of crystal. Again, she couldn't care less. The devil was in the details, as they say, but he was also deeply inside of Eliza Stone.

"Yeah, so. How does a cool grand sound for the whole set?"

"Yeah. Sure."

He looked up at her from examining one of the prescription labels. His eyes were chilling blue lightning bolts in the low lamp light.

He lay the prescription bottle back down and stood between the woman and the drugs. Her gaze shifted slowly from her prize strewn out neatly on the table. He had the look of a man waiting for the cards to play out in a high-stakes poker game. He looked her over.

She wasn't unattractive. Not really. Her bangs hung over one eye, partially concealing the deep scar on her pale face. She probably had a good figure some time ago, but now she was withered into something rather skeletal, streamlined. Like a painting of Venus made of driftwood, raw and brittle. An ancient goddess emerging from the first Water.

Something in her eyes just wasn't right, though. There was something primal, reaching back in time. The echo of an alternate beginning, perhaps. Lilith seducing Adam; Eve serving only as an idea.

Pandora, and her box of wicked tidings.

Randall moved the long strands of dark hair out of her face. She never blinked, never moved.

"You know, Liz, I don't need your money. You could always pay me some other way."

Her stare intensified. She didn't respond.

His rough hands caressed her cheek. Her skin was cold, like opening a freezer door.

"In fact. . . Why don't we just say to hell with the thousand bucks. It can be on the house this time. And the next, if you like."

"My purse is on the couch. Please move."

She brushed away from him and walked to the sofa. She reached inside, removed a sizeable amount of freshly dispensed cash, and was counting it when she felt his presence closer behind her. A floorboard creaked. His shadow appeared on the wall in front of her, cast and shattered in the lamp glow. He wrapped her tightly but was surprisingly gentle. He kissed her neck, kissed her shoulder. Slid her bra strap away and nibbled her collar bone. She didn't resist, but just let out a deep sigh. His hand slid across her chest, and he pressed against her backside. All she could smell was alcohol and bad aftershave.

"Randall?"

"Yeah, babe."

"If you do this, I won't stop you."

"Uh-huh."

"But let me tell you something first."

"Yeah?"

He was petting her in places she hadn't been touched in years.

"It better be worth it for you."

"I'm sure it will, Liz."

She craned her neck around to whisper in his ear. Her voice had achieved a subdued sensuality like he had never heard before. It was the ideal female voice, not her usual hushed murmur. It gave him goosebumps, at first.

"Because I will find out where you live. It's my job, you know? I know your full name, and that's more than enough. When you least expect it, I will be there. In your house one night. I will make no sound, and I will drain you like a slaughtered goat. It will be my pleasure, like this will be all yours."

The man swallowed. His mouth was suddenly dry. A latent fight or flight reflex overtook him.

Her voice cracked once more from somewhere even deeper in her seemingly fragile frame. She reached back to massage his crotch with her fingers.

She whispered again.

"And, Randall? I keep my knives very, very sharp."

She arched her back slightly against him as a final temptation, but he had fully relaxed. No longer capable. She felt his hands leave her body. Felt him step away.

Randall Lightner had been threatened before. More times than he could count, even. It had never amounted to jack shit, though. So why had this one hit him right in the gut? He felt physically assaulted by her gaze. He had believed her every word. He felt like his throat was already cut and all the blood in his body was spilling out onto the rustic cabin floor.

She slowly turned to face him. Finished counting the money in her hands. Stepped towards him and placed the ten one-hundred dollar bills in the front pocket of his pants. He followed her every movement, and when she stepped away he took his first breath for what seemed like an era. He felt small in her presence. Embarrassed at his lack of rebuttal. He felt dazed and just wanted to get out that cabin and back into his truck. He wanted away from this haunted woman with her haunted eyes.

What the hell is she doing to me?

His stomach made a grumbled sound as she stared at him. A wave of nausea came and went. He took off his hat, scratched his head. Looked around the room one last time before he could speak.

"You're not right, woman. Fuck, you need help."

Eliza didn't speak. She moved past him again and placed the arrangements from the kitchen table into her purse. One by one. When she was finished, she smiled at Randall. In the lamp light, she looked ghastly without effort. Her chin tilted down, her visible eye narrowed, her cheeks hollow caverns where no light could dwell.

Randall put his hat back on and started walking towards the door. He kept looking over his shoulder at Eliza, half expecting her to transfix into a wolf or vanish into the Ether. Or float across the room and make good on her threat. Nothing would have surprised him in that moment.

Through the screen door and back outside, he tripped down the stairs and almost fell face first into the hood of his truck. He climbed into the driver's seat, slammed his door, locked it, and was overjoyed to see his headlights fire and shine some light into the gloom. As he rolled up the passenger window with an ill-disguised form of panic, a chill ran down his spine.

Back inside the rental, Eliza Stone began to laugh in spite of herself. It rose through her very pores and escaped into the forest outside. Drifted up to the patient moon. She felt powerful beyond measure. Invincible, and protected by the darkness stretching all around the cabin, the woods, the lake, and the whole miserable world.

Randall Lightner would never share this story with anyone. He would try to forget it in the whiskey and the weed. His own ugliness simply could not compare to whatever was eating that woman alive. Or *keeping* her alive, on the flip side.

He was certain of that much, at least.

Rylan

Over a month had passed. Thanksgiving came and went. Of course, Aunt Linda had put on a show for Lacy and me: all the works and more. We spent that government-ordained but lovely holiday up at their place for a night, and then went over to Lacy's the following day for a redux with her family. She let me do the cooking and entertaining, as we all got to know each other. They were great people, and the conversation was easy. My dinner came out perfectly as planned. Her dad and I seemed to really hit it off over a few pours of whisky. Her mom made Lacy blush more than once by mentioning how often she talked about me. What a great guy I was. And how she was positively smitten.

I beamed in the candlelight and whispered to her when no one else was looking that I felt the same way. She nudged me with her forehead and squeezed my leg tightly under the table.

There was much to be thankful for, lest I often forget in my comfortable little life.

Now, sitting in my classroom in the early morning quiet, I took a deep breath and felt relieved to slow down for a while over the next few weeks. Enjoy my break. Clear my head. The kids could feel the holidays approach like a magnet drawing flecks of iron, and they probably needed a break from me, as well. We had just finished a hard unit and end-of-quarter exam. They were drained, and I was having difficulty faking my enthusiasm even more than usual.

I was very happy to put on *The Nightmare Before Christmas* today and see them all off after lunch for an early release. Then, all that remained for the year was a bus duty, some deep cleaning of this messy room, and submitting my grades. Leslie, Tony and I were planning to go out for celebratory drinks as soon as the clock struck three, and it couldn't come too soon.

Then, a slight knock at the door. I almost didn't hear it.

"Come in!"

I recognized her immediately. The little red pillow was the first thing I noticed. She wore an equally red sweater with The Grinch emblazoned on its front, and green corduroy pants to complete the festive ensemble. In her other hand, there was a small gift bag. I pretended not to notice until the time was right.

"Well, looks who's all dressed up this morning."

"Good morning, Mr. Wilder."

"Hey, Elsa. What's up?"

"Not too much. I'm so excited for Christmas! Aren't you?"

"Oh, yeah. I need a break. Your classmates have worn me out this fall."

"I bet. I hope I wasn't any trouble, Mr. Wilder. Um, I brought you a present. I hope that's okay. I couldn't get gifts for my other teachers, so can this be our secret? I don't want to hurt anyone's feelings. But, you're my favorite and I just had to get you something to say thank you for teaching us so much this year."

"Oh, you didn't have to do that, Elsa! Thank you so much. You know you're no trouble at all. You're one of my favorites, too."

She beamed as I took the bag out of her tiny hand. It read "Happy Birthday" and looked like it had seen better days.

"Would you like me to open it now?"

"Yes, please! It isn't much, but I thought you would like it."

She gently clapped her hands with anticipation as I reached into the tissue paper. I pretended to search vigorously in the small bag to add suspense. She giggled. I withdrew what was obviously a book from the bag and flipped it over to read the title. It was a hard-cover, all red, with a gold emblazoned title that read 'Paradise Lost, John Milton.'

"Oh, cool. Look at this! Thanks, Elsa. Wow. Where'd you get this? It looks old."

"It was my grandmom's. She had a ton of old books that I got to keep. I know you always look at that big painting in the library, and it has a John Milton quote on it, so I thought this was. . . What's the word, Mr. Wilder?... *Apropos*?"

She pronounced it phonetically, but damn. . .

"Yes, very apropos. This is awesome. Are you sure you want me to have it?"

"Absolutely! It's a Christmas present!"

"Well, this made my day. Thank you again."

"You're welcome."

She kept standing in front of me. Suddenly a bit more reserved, but still smiling.

"Mr. Wilder?"

"Yes?"

"Do you ever have dreams that you think might come true?"

"Um, I mean, maybe? Like déjà vu? Do you know what that means?"

"Yes, I know what that means. But a little different. Like dreams of things that might happen later, in real life?"

"No, I can't say that I am gifted in that way, young lady."

"Well, I think that I sometimes do. I don't know. Last night I had this weird dream, though."

"Yeah? What was that?"

"Oh, it was probably nothing. But I wanted to tell someone just in case. I dreamed that one of the first grade teachers on the other side of the school left a candle burning in her classroom. It was near her bulletin board, and there were little drawings of Christmas trees on construction paper above the flame, and, well. . . Oh, I'm sure it was just a dream."

"Huh? Have you ever had a dream like that come true, Elsa?"

"Occasionally, but it's usually about bad stuff."

"Like what?"

"Um, let's see. I dreamed that Gerald's grandmom was going to pass away a few months ago."

"Did you tell him?"

"No. I didn't want to scare him, but somehow I just knew. And she did die a few days later. It's usually about bad stuff like that. Or the school burning, like in my dream last night. I don't really want to talk about that, Mr. Wilder, but I did want to tell you about my dream."

This was more direct than I was used to hearing her. She stated this plainly, and without hesitation. Something in her tone changed, and I didn't press that matter. Weird kid, for sure.

She continued. "Will you go check later today?"

"On what?"

"The candle, silly! I don't know which room it was, but I know it was in the first grade hall. They have a sign up that says "Merry Christmas, First Graders!" that was in my dream, too. There are only four classrooms on that hall, so it shouldn't be too hard to find. I'm sure it's nothing, but I would feel better if someone checked."

"Sure, Elsa. I'll check before I leave today."

"Thank you, Mr. Wilder."

I wasn't sure if I had any intention of walking all the way down there after school, but something in her voice was remarkably convincing.

"Cheers!"

Tony clinked beers with Lacy and me. We were at the local brewery. It was crowded with the Friday regulars. It smelled like old beer and cedar. Eclectic artwork decorated the rustic walls, the tables were all decommissioned whisky barrels, and a band was about to strike up with some folksy tunes. Nothing negative could be said about our special little hang-out. In the moment, at this time, it was always perfect.

"Well, my friends, another fall has come to a close. How are we feeling? Rylan, you haven't said two words since we left the school."

We had all taken my car. Tony had big plans to get blasted and his wife would come pick him up later. Lacy had driven with me to work, which was no longer causing myriad oohs and aahs to emit from our co-workers in the staff parking lot.

"Cheers. I'm good! Sorry, I didn't realize I had been so quiet."

"As the grave! What's on your mind? Perk up! We have drinking to do, and I'm getting hungry. You're buying us dinner from the food truck for being a sour puss."

Lacy rubbed my back as she spoke. Teetering dangerously on her barstool. Her Belgian Triple was already almost finished. I had barely touched my IPA. My mind was crossing the county line and drifting into another zip code, but I figured what the hell – I'd let them in on the events of my afternoon.

"So, you guys know Elsa Privette, right?"

"Um, yeah."

Lacy sarcastically said, and Tony nodded as he studded the foam on his lager.

"She came by my room this morning and brought me a Christmas present."

"Uh-oh, Tony. Little Elsa has a crush on our Mr. Wilder here. He with his Johnny Depp surliness and–"

"No, nothing like that. She brought me a book, and we talked for a bit. And she told me that she had this dream last night about a fire at the school. Said that there was a candle burning on the first-grade hall in her dream, and it might catch some papers on fire, and that she was worried it might burn the school down with everyone gone for the holiday."

They both were quiet now.

"Dramatic, right? Well, she asked me if I would go check after school. To make sure there wasn't a lit candle down there. I didn't really think anything of it, you know? Kids being kids and all. But, she was very earnest and for whatever reason, I believed her."

Lacy narrowed her eyes. Tony continued to nod as he took a big gulp of beer. The band was beginning their first song in the background, but I had their full attention for a moment.

"So, I debated going down there after the kids left for the day. Why not, I figured? Worst case, I got a few extra steps in today. Or, on the other hand, what if she was right? I know this sounds crazy. . . But, I did walk down there after the bell rang. And I saw this very specific 'Merry Christmas' sign she mentioned from her dream. And I looked in two classroom windows, and there wasn't a candle that I could see. But, then in the third. . . And I'm telling you guys, I got goosebumps when I looked through the little window in the door, but there it was – a candle flickering with papers right above it. Just like she said. And I watched her walk right out the door after we talked, no way she could have snuck way down the hall before or after to see that candle."

"Shit."

Tony finally spoke. Lacy's long lashes blinked slowly and her perfect eyebrows raised.

"I had to go find the janitor to open the door since it was locked. And I went inside and blew it out, obviously. And yeah, I guess it might have freaked me out a little bit."

"I have told them a thousand times, no candles! They just don't listen. . ."

Tony was animated when he spoke. His mind lingered on the physicality of my story, not the nuance of the girl's pseudo premonition. Lacy, however, rocked back on her stool. Her eyebrow still raised. She didn't speak. She patted my thigh under the table. She believed me. What I was trying to say.

"So, yeah. Elsa was right. She literally dreamed about a candle burning specifically on that hall, and damn if she wasn't one hundred percent correct. What do you do with that? She's such an odd bird, but I mean. . . Holy shit, right? And, what's weirder. . . she alluded to dreaming about that Gerald kid's grandmother dying back at the beginning of the year."

Lacy wrinkled her brow. Tony was still on about the stupid no-candle rule. And I still felt on edge.

Lacy finally broke the moment's feigned tension.

"You really believe she dreamed that, don't you?"

I didn't answer. Didn't need to, really. Tony spoke before I could concoct some philosophical treatise that neither of them probably cared to hear. They were just out to have fun, and I knew that I was dragging down the mood.

"Yeah. Super weird. And I'll definitely send an email out reminding those airheads to blow out their candles or, better yet, keep them at home."

"Oh yeah, you do that Tony! Get 'em! Send that email!" Lacy replied, jokingly.

We all laughed. Mine was loosely sincere. The band began to play "Cat's in the Cradle"; I took my own big swig of bitter beer. But yet, my mind remained on that strange little person who apparently was gifted beyond the fragile bonds of our known world. Second sight and dreams. Premonitions and ghost stories.

And with Christmas right around the corner, with its ethereal lights illuminating ancient beliefs, it somehow all made sense.

Eliza Stone

She pulled into her assigned space outside the snow-stained and water-weathered apartment building that she called home. Her tires squealed to a halt and the old car visibly jerked as she slammed it into park.

Eliza stepped out in a haste, a run in her pantyhose and skirt starting to look threadbare around the seams. Her hair was in her face. She wore no makeup, no lipstick. She couldn't find a reason, so she stopped looking for one.

She slammed the car door, remembered her purse and her bag, opened the door, grabbed them, then slammed it even harder the second time. The recoil almost caused her to twist her ankle on her too-tall heels. She took them off, realized that she had on two different heights, and cussed under her breath as she stormed up the steps to her place.

Fucker. . . I hate you.

She continued to swear audibly as she struggled with her key. Struggled through the door. Caught a neighbor's wandering eye from down the way, gave him a look that spelled M-U-R-D-E-R, and he raised his hands in a gesture of peace as she vanished into her small apartment.

God damn it! Fuck!

Screaming now, she threw her purse and heels and leather bag against opposite walls. She half-fell and half-lay down on her dingy carpet floor in a heap. Sobbing. Pulling at her hair and clothes. Misery incarnate in a dark and tiny cage.

Bruce had called her into his office that afternoon, before she left. Reprimanded her for a series of infractions. Being late. Being distant. Being rude to prospective clients. Not doing her job the way he wanted her to do it.

Acting odd. Very strange. What's up with you? Why are you behaving like this? You used to be so on top of things, and now. . .

His accusatory questions and implications rang between her ears like a gong. He had ultimately threatened her job in their pained ten minutes together. The one thing she had. Her only distraction, apart from the drugs and the booze; her only reason for getting up in the morning.

Dan had looked at her with a quick glance of pity bordering on empathy as she made her way out of the office. He couldn't do too much to help her. He had to agree with Bruce to a large extent. Hell, she knew she was fried and fucked-up beyond belief. She didn't need Bruce to point that out to her. It was practically written across her forehead, and she could no longer contain the clawing demon scraping behind her eyes.

It would eventually either escape or devour what remained of her scattered brains in a hearty holiday feast inside her pale skull.

She liked to picture this fellow, this demon, with his icepick constantly poking her insides. Every time he poked, the pain came back. The pain's name was *Lily*. The pain was a physical thing, and it draggedher daily into the world's deepest, loneliest well.

Her psychiatrist had insisted that we all had our demons. Some people kept them buried; some people took up a new hobby to combat them; some people succumbed to them and let them win. Her job, this good doctor had proclaimed, was to rise above this demon. Get her life together. Find little ways to *start forgetting her child* and eventually move from the tragedy of last winter.

You could take up art. Maybe painting? Or music? Do you have any interest in music, Eliza? Can you play an instrument?

Eliza always just sat, stunned, in these appointments. She rarely spoke. She couldn't believe what she was hearing from this fat cow absorbed into her fat-cunt chair in a cold office with too-bright lights. Her attendance to these therapy sessions was short-lived. Otherwise, she might have killed that woman and spent the rest of her miserable life in jail.

It would have been worth it.

Eliza's sobs eventually turned to laughter. Maniacal? Probably. Cathartic? No, that was just bullshit.

The only catharsis is death.

Eliza mused as she reached for her cigarettes out of the scattered remnants of her spilled purse. She crawled for her lighter. Was already puffing the white stick to life as she stood inelegantly and drifted like a specter into her kitchen. Dirty dishes in the sink. Old food scattered all around. It probably smelled disgusting in there. She didn't care. The smoke she inhaled masked any smell like a bad perfume in her nostrils.

She reached for a semi-clean glass off the counter. Reached in the freezer for one of her bottles. Poured the icy deliciousness into the waiting container. Two fingers of Russia's cheapest filled her mouth with cold anesthesia. It no longer burned going down. She didn't feel a thing.

Two more fingers in the glass. Hesitated imperceptibly. Added another quick pour. Her throat pulsed visibly as she tossed it back. She let-out something between a growl and a roar from deep inside her belly.

Two fingers more, scurried to find some pills in her bag, downed them like candy, and chased them hastily with more vodka.

The alcohol haze was starting to sway her body and ease her mind. The drug cocktail was beginning to pull her molecules and neurons asunder. This was her favorite part. The finite in-between. The moments before she was completely zapped yet still teetering in her present state. She would light a few candles. Turn out the lights if any were glowing. If she could, before she teetered too far, she may even make it to her pawn shop CD player for some music. Sirens would start wailing in her ears soon, but nothing a bit of Mazzy Star or Stevie Nicks couldn't help soothe.

Now, she could begin to unwind and think on this demon fellow living behind her eyes. She had gotten to know him very well, but each greeting was always the first time.

Handsome bastard, aren't you? Charming, too. Let's skip the small talk. Wanna fuck?

He agreed, an eyebrow raised, and Eliza Stone made love to nothing on the dingy floor of her dirty apartment. Her skirt up high, tossing on the floor. In flairs and moans, rolling with the demon suiter, her mind crackling like live wires, fading embers, and then a blissful nothingness.

She pictured black Satan sitting in her patched-up armchair. Satan the voyeurist. Always watching them. Always entertained and always happy to join in when summoned.

And believe it. He had been summoned.

Eliza Stone hosted such threesomes on the nightly. Her company was always the same. She reveled in what few friends she had, after all.

Time would pass slowly in the afterglow of whatever fantastic sex she had concocted. Whatever fantastic chemicals she had found to penetrate her ice-cold blood stream. Her thoughts were varied. She mused on Death, Hell, heaven – the whole thing.

Her Lilly had been her heaven. She didn't believe in angels or harps or whatever else Michelangelo had painted in that Italian chapel, but she had believed in her baby girl. Eliza's heaven had lasted only a few years. Painfully brief. It had been enough, but she would burn the world to spend just five more minutes with her daughter. Hate and anger consumed her.

This was the result: a broken woman lying on the floor of a cold, dirty cell with enough booze and buzz in her system to float a frat party for days.

She felt a new emotion now, too. It was *jealousy*. Every kid she saw. In the grocery store, on the street, at work. She wanted them. It was a strange sensation. To deeply need that warmth again. To be willing to take it from someone else and not think twice about it.

Especially that little Reynolds girl. And her spoiled-bitch mother with her Lululemon ass and Pepsodent smile.

Woman, I could make you bleed. I could cripple you. Your daughter could belong to me and I could make her mine. She would grow to love me. I could show you...

Eliza pulled and tossed her hair. She tried to stand, fell back onto the floor. Finally managed to climb the wall to get on her feet. Caught a glimpse of Christmas lights glowing outside on the railing. Their reds and greens and whites hurt her eyes. They looked like headlights to her.

As she began to slide slowly back down the wall, nauseated and exhausted, she caught a final glimpse of her Satan. He was no longer in the armchair. He was standing somewhere in the dark. The candle flicker could not illuminate his form. She could only discern his silver eyes gazing back at her amid the gathering night outside.

As she blacked out for the night, in that tiny moment between oblivion and numbness, he spoke to her. His voice was kind; almost gentle.

He told her two things that night.

He told Eliza that she had lived through Hell. That it didn't get any worse than that. There was no fire, no eternal torture.

He told Eliza that she should take what she wanted. She would be under his embrace. He would keep her safe for a time.

I want you to be happy, even if it's only for a fleeting moment.

Eliza Stone slept soundly that night.

When she awoke, she had to start making plans.

She had to *nest* again.

———

And plan, she did.

The next time she decided to go into the office, her mind was not on Bruce's condescension and scrutiny. He could die in a dark well for all she cared. She worked with fervor. Answered her pointless emails and deleted anything that resembled the clawing hands of the outside world.

TJ Maxx had an offer for her.

She no longer needed new clothes.

A local landscaper wanted to survey her lawn.

She had no yard to tend.

Her old hairdresser wanted to see when she might come back in for a styling. Appointment slots were going fast!

She no longer gave a hot goddamn about how she looked. Bruce had only reinforced that fact in his practiced and cruel speech.

She caught a glimpse of him in his two thousand-dollar suit, sitting pompously, like a sad emperor clown, in his posh office across the way.

A pity to bleed-out all over that expensive fabric, you arrogant prick.

Anyway, back to her real work for the day.

She had to find the perfect new home. A special place for her and the child. She had a good idea of where to take her. It would serve as the perfect cocoon for Brittany Reynolds to blossom. To become Lily Stone again. To morph like a beautiful butterfly. To be hers and hers alone.

It was high on a mountain. Away from everyone. She would have only to pick the time. It needed to be later. After the tourists left. After they vacated these hills, like migratory birds, back to their miserable lives in miserable little cities and towns. Passing their idle hours spinning madly on this depressing rock. *Waiting for Godot* in an absurd one-act play that failed to fully entertain.

She had seen her just the other day. Walking out of her perfect little elementary school. So young and so pretty and so untouched by the world. She followed her with her eyes fixed. Captivated like a night owl on its unsuspecting prey. She wanted to grab her. Smell her hair. Breathe life back into the memory of her daughter, like an animated little doll. And she knew she would. She waited patiently out of sight as her mother appeared in her shiny car. Always dressed to the nines, only to stay at home.

Did she really dress like that just to come to the pick-up line and maybe see a teacher or two?

She always got out of her car to help her daughter inside. Eliza knew she would do the same if in her shoes. Had she been given the chance, she would open the door for Lily. Take her bookbag. Dress her in the best clothes she could afford. Help her get her seatbelt fastened. Drive the speed limit and ask her about her day.

As *the plan* began to unfold in her mind like a brood of spiders spilling from their mother, Eliza grew wild with confidence. She met Bruce's stern stares with indiscretion. She walked a little taller around the office and in town. That is, whenever she decided to briefly emerge from her solitary life. Even hermits at heart had needs. They needed to occasionally break their own spell.

Eliza haunted grocery-store aisles like a benign wraith in her simple blacks and grays. Something strong was almost always coursing through her veins. Riding her capillaries like broom-bound witches in the night. Elderly women gave her strange looks; homely little families moved aside to let her pass. The food she bought was rarely for her. Little frozen meals and peanut butters and jellies. Little Debbies sat like doll-eyed twins in her buggy. Chef Boyardee rode shotgun beside them. She stockpiled anything that wouldn't rot or mold or otherwise disintegrate. She stored the special goods in baskets to take up to her secret little heaven when the time presented itself.

The time was almost right. Just a few more short months. It was almost midnight in the mind of Eliza Stone. There would be no going back, and no reason to retreat.

And in that veil of darkness, when the world was sleeping their happy dreams, she would reap her harvest with fine-tuned strikes from a visceral scythe. She would consume and devour. The sleeping world was her oyster, and she would suckle every last drop of the saline poison she craved.

Lilly, reanimate.

Lilly, be mine again.

Rylan

I had bought a real Christmas tree. I had somewhat decorated my apartment. I thought it all looked pretty good, especially with the lights low and a wood fire crackling as the centerpiece. Teresa always hated the holidays. Thought they were tacky and "commercial" and all the other predictable yuppy bullshit. Lacy, however, enjoyed the season. She had grown-up in church, same as me, and seemed to revel in the old observations.

I was indifferent. I liked holiday lights. I liked Norse darkness and yule logs. I liked spiced cider. I liked the idea of a Victorian Christmas. On the TV, in concurrence, George C. Scott portrayed a miserly banker dealing with depression and shouting anti-social pseudo-swears at all-comers.

I could relate. The Ghost of Christmas Yet to Come be damned. He was probably just a bit of undigested cheese or something, as Dickens was quick to illustrate, after all. My own misanthropy had not been born from some parental slights in my youth or a deep greed for money. I had a good childhood and I made a whopping thirty-six thousand dollars a year in a resort town, so those two things were irrelevant.

Mine seemed innate. I had never liked people much. I had always chosen the outskirts of social life and preferred to proudly wear the loner's badge. I was the observer. A writer at heart. I don't know why I'm this way. Blame Conrad or a sociopathic great-great-great grandfather. Regardless, I hid it well. I cared for those who couldn't defend themselves. I hated bullies and the political cartoon characters on the news. I distrusted the government and the façade of social media. I liked Clint Eastwood and old leather. I liked silence and candlelit rooms. I should have been born in another time.

But, as I lay on my couch massaging Lacy's scalp and feeling her warmth against my body, my mind drifted – as it had for weeks – once again to that girl in my class.

What did her Christmas look like? Did she get gifts at home? Did that asshole stepdad get drunk on Christmas day and ruin the whole thing for her?

I didn't know. Why did I care? It wasn't like me to harp on such things. Some weird connection there. Takes one to know one, or something. Perhaps we were indeed kindred spirits having crossed paths in some older life. Like I said, I should have been born in a different time. Did she too feel that way?

Certainly, she must.

And as the Ghost of Christmas Present exposed his two secret stowaways on screen, Ignorance and Want, I wondered if she was perhaps the latter? A child, hidden beneath a cloak of the Present, exposed in the cold for wanting to be better. For wanting something more than her mother could give. For wanting the strength to get the hell out of here, someday.

I thought, that night, warm and cozy on my couch with a beautiful woman at my side, that if I could give anyone a Christmas present this year, it would be Elsa Privette. And it would be something really nice.

She really deserved it, after all.

Elsa

It was two nights before Christmas, and all through Elsa's house. . . Not a thing was really different than any other night. She had helped her mom put up a little fake Christmas tree in the living room, but that was about all. There was no mulled cider or basted goose or even a single strand of garland to be found. No carolers came to call. No church bells rang off in the distance to the tune of some ancient hymn.

Dickens had done her a disservice in that regard, but she was in good spirits, nonetheless.

Randy was only a little drunk, her mom was in a decent mood, and Jenny was actually sitting in the living room with them watching TV. She was absorbed with her phone screen, but she was at least present on the dingy couch. This was about as good as it got. Elsa did not take such moments for granted. They were all too brief in her little world.

Then, Randall spoke.

"I need some smokes and some more beer. Jenny, you wanna come with me to the store?"

Jenny looked up from her phone. Blew a big pink bubble with her gum and quickly twisted its remnants back into her mouth.

"Sure. I'll go."

Randall patted the arms of his big chair and lifted his weight up with a grunt. He pulled at Jenny's ponytail playfully as he passed the sofa. He never did stuff like that to Elsa. They didn't have that kind of relationship, she guessed.

"Take Elsa with ya, Randy. And get me some Slims while you're there. I'm almost out, too, and I ain't smoking your menthol crap."

April was pitched up on the opposing chair with cigarette smoke enveloping her like a wreath. Elsa gave her a look that begged 'no', but Randy didn't protest her going as he usually did.

"Whatever. Get your shoes, E. And you could say 'please' every now and then, woman."

He mockingly mouthed 'Go get my Slims' a few times while donning his jacket.

"*Please* get me some Slims. I'll make it up to ya later, Randy. You know that."

A few minutes later, the three were riding down the mountain at a speed that Elsa thought was too fast, but no one else seemed to be bothered by the jarring turns on the loose-gravel road. She sat in the back where there was no seat belt and had to steady herself on the big seat with every switchback. Randy and Jenny sat up front talking and ignoring her presence, which was honestly preferred.

They did this a lot, Elsa had noticed. Go off together on rides and to run errands. Elsa thought it was weird that Randy could nearly knock Jenny's teeth out one minute and then they were best friends the next. They play-hit each other and laughed and fought over the radio station in the front seat as Elsa studied the darkness outside the window. Lost in her thoughts, finally getting a good grip on the door to keep her small frame from bouncing into the floorboard with each twist and bump in the road. An empty beer can hit the seat beside her as Randy had tossed back his last cold one and dramatically crushed the can as he drove.

They always went to the same gas station. An old Shell that had a little butcher counter in the back, where they served biscuits in the morning and cuts of meat during the day. It wasn't the closest one off the mountain, but it was only a few extra miles down the road. Randy knew the owner and he always took a few freebies, while he was inside, without anyone saying anything. The closer station was owned by an older black gentleman, whom Randy didn't like for some reason. Elsa thought he was nice the few times she had been inside. His grandson went to school with her, and she thought he was a nice boy, too. He always looked a little lonely to her when she saw him at lunch or at recess. She could always relate to similar feelings of isolation when everyone else was laughing and playing with their friends. They were silently kindred spirits without having the chance to fully get to know each other.

The Shell station glowed around the next bend in the road, like a sudden sun appearing in deep space. It was always busy, even at this time of night. They didn't have much, out on this end of town – mundane destinations such as the two convenient stores, the bait and tackle shop, the little restaurant with the too-low ceiling – but they were the social hotspots. There was also an old bar and pool hall, but Elsa had never been inside there before. That was Randy's favorite place, so she didn't think she would like it very much, anyway.

Randy parked at a weird angle that wasn't quite in an official space. It was obviously blocking someone in, but he didn't seem to care. He and Jenny hopped out of the truck mid-sentence and it was understood that Elsa would stay behind. They disappeared into the store behind the ATM machine and Elsa felt relieved at her moment of peace. She took a deep breath. Browsed the parking lot. Recognized a familiar shape at the closest gas pump. It took a moment for her young mind to identify the form so out of context. And then, another shape she recognized opened the convenience store door and stepped out into the cold air.

Mr. Wilder and Ms. Elridge!

She almost squealed with excitement. Her little hands struggled to roll down the window. Each hurried turn of the crank brought her closer to two people she so adored.

They had no idea how much. Not a clue.

She called out into the dark and the cold and the too-bright fluorescents.

"Ms. Eldridge? Mr. Wilder?"

Lacy turned mid-stride and Rylan looked up from the gas pump. They were dressed differently than she usually saw. Ms. Eldridge had on more make-up, a really nice necklace, and a purposefully loose-fitting holiday sweater over some tight blue jeans. Mr. Wilder had on a black sports coat and a deep green mock turtleneck. To Elsa, they looked like they had been having fun.

Maybe they had gone to a party? Why are they together, in the same car? Out late.

Elsa's mind spun at the thought.

Oh... They must like each other. Like, really like each other.

Her teachers waved at her, confirming who they were. Rylan finished at the pump, Lacy put a bag in his car, and they walked over, hand-in-hand, to Elsa's open window.

"Elsa Privette! Isn't it past your bedtime?" Mr. Wilder joked. Elsa laughed genuinely.

Lacy added, "What are you doing out so late, young lady? You're going to scare Santa away!"

Elsa giggled again. "Hey, Mr. Wilder! Hey, Ms. Elridge! I'm out with my sister and Randy. They're inside the store. What are you two doing tonight?"

"We went to a little teachers' party out this way. We're headed to stay at Rylan's uncle and aunt's house for the night, so we don't have to drive back into town. We're going to spend Christmas with them this week, anyway."

"Oh. That will be lots of fun. I didn't know you two were such good friends," Elsa chirped from the backseat, unassumingly.

The two adults looked each other, smiled, and then laughed a little.

"Yeah, we are great friends, Elsa. The best."

Elsa smiled back at Mr. Wilder.

The convenience store door opened, just as Rylan was asking about Elsa's holiday plans. Randall and Jenny appeared on the sidewalk. They both were holding big paper sacks. Jenny turned around and punched Randall on the shoulder as they chatted and joked. He pushed her gently and pinched her butt. She screamed in her pajama pants and flip-flops. Yelled "Ass!" at him, for all the world to hear.

Rylan's eyebrow went up momentarily. He looked once at Elsa, and then to Lacy. Lacy's expression changed from a big smile to a big frown.

"That's my sister, Jenny. And that's. . ."

Elsa's words were drowned out in the moment. Rylan, especially, bristled as they approached them, all blowing smoke in the cold night air.

Randall looked up at the two standing beside his truck. Vaguely recognized the man, and the woman was a special kind of attractive.

It dawned on him, despite the hour and the drink as he neared his vehicle and the two strangers talking to Elsa.

"Teach! What's up?" Randall yelled.

Rylan nodded apprehensively and gave a slight wave as the bigger man staggered toward him in a weird kind of strut.

"And who do we have here? She's a bit out of your league, don't you think, Teach?"

Jenny had already excused herself from any interaction and was already back in the cabin of the truck. Elsa's little face and bright eyes looked on from the window like a dainty puppet. Rylan put his arm gently around Lacy to indicate *'It's time to go'*.

"Evening, Mr. Lightner. We were just saying hello to Elsa over here."

"Is that right? Checkin' in on little sis again, right? Makin' sure the big bad wolf ain't gobbled her up?"

"No. Nothing like that. We were just wishing her a merry Christmas."

"Oh, yeah? Elsa, is that right?"

She nodded in the seat. Unsure of what to say or if she should speak at all. The sarcastic way Randy was talking had an edge to it that Elsa had learned to interpret. It made her nervous.

Rylan took advantage of the pause. Patted Lacy definitively on the arm. She was staring a little too disgustedly at Randy as he cracked open a Tall Boy right in front of them in the parking lot, the piss smell of cheap beer emanating into the night air.

"Well, then. I guess we'll be on our way. Good night, Elsa. Mr. Lightner, I hope you all have a safe night."

"Uh-huh."

They walked quickly across the lot. Lacy whispering all sorts of insults about the other man to Rylan as they approached his car. She glanced back twice to see Randall talking to Elsa in the backseat, roughly handed her his bag from the store. Rylan was counting the seconds until. . .

"Hey, Teach. Hold up."

Damn it. . .

"Here. Take the keys. Get in the car, Lace."

Lacy protested, but then acquiesced for a moment under the bright pump lights. Randall was walking towards them, and his stride wasn't playful this time.

"Yes?"

Lacy got in the car, cranked it from across the seat, and let the window down so she could hear them. Rylan kept inching closer to the car himself.

"Cute chick you got there."

"Thanks."

"Now, look. I been hearing that you're still damn insisting on going for your runs or whatever up on my road. Several folks I know seen you up there, and they tell me everything. So, I figure, after our last little talk that you're either *stupid*, or you plain ain't takin' me seriously."

He touched Rylan's jacket. Looked him right in the eye.

"And you don't look stupid to me, Teach."

Elsa had been straining her ears to hear, but then she thought it was best to roll her window up in the truck. She didn't think it was polite to eavesdrop.

Rylan looked down, perturbed. Glanced back at Lacy in his SUV.

"Randall, yeah. I go for runs up on a dirt road near my uncle's house. That's it. I like it up there. I'm not snooping around or whatever you think I'm doing. That one time you or whoever saw me talking to the sheriff, he *stopped me* up there. I wasn't intending on ratting out your still or your cook site or whatever you have going on up there. Again, not my business."

"Uh-huh. I guess I believe that. But, that ain't what we agreed. I asked you not to come up there. It makes my people uneasy. They start bugging me to go do our thing elsewhere. Hell, some of 'em even think you're a cop, yourself. They get antsy, you know? But, you know what I think? I think you're snoopin' up there to check on our girl, Elsa. Make sure your little girlfriend ain't livin' in squalor or whatnot."

He laughed at his own comment. Rylan did not.

"Ultimately though, Teach, all I'm sayin' is that we had an agreement. A gentleman's handshake. You stay off my hill, stop getting the school all riled-up every five minutes about this little bruise or another, and I play nice. Leave you and the girl and her sister alone. Now, it seems to me that you ain't holding your end of the bargain. So, why should I hold mine?"

He gave Rylan a light push to drive his point home. Rylan folded his arms defensively. Staggered his stance a bit for balance. Randall took another big swig of his beer. Swallowed deeply, like his throat was sore.

"And, Teach – like you said. Your uncle and aunt live just down the road. Let's see? I bet I know which one. The nice one right on the river? The one with the separate little guesthouse? I'm guessing so. Maybe I'll pay them a visit, too. See if I can get you to take me seriously next time."

Rylan's mind was humming like livewire. If the man in front of him was just a little more drunk, Rylan might have been tempted to take a swing at him. They were standing face to face. Both men unblinking under the light. The tension was palpable.

Instead, he lowered his voice to almost a whisper.

"I'm going to leave now, Randall. But, just remember one thing. You don't *know* me. I don't *know* you. Whatever reputation you think you have up here, I don't really give a damn. This is the second time you've singled me out for some schoolyard push and shove, and I'm personally getting tired of it. So, please back out of my face and try not to kill that little girl in the backseat of your truck driving back up the mountain. She's worth fifty of you."

Randall's eyes widened. He pursed his lips sarcastically and gave Rylan a light smirk, snickering to himself.

"Nice speech, Teach. You practice that in the mirror?"

Rylan waved his hand up at Randall dismissively as he turned to walk away. He was finished with their conversation. He glanced back twice in the three yards between where they were standing and the driver's side door of his car. He half-expected that beer can to come flying at his head. Lacy had rolled up the window and her eyes were still fixed on the piece of redneck trash standing just feet from her window.

Randall blew her a kiss, and Lacy finally looked away. He had one last thing to say as the young teacher opened his car door.

"Hey. *Rylan*, is it? I hope you don't have to find out who I really am, boy. You wouldn't want to *get to know me*, as you said. I *am* the big bad wolf, you hear? And I know who you are, too. You ain't shit. Fucking pussy."

Rylan closed his door as Randall was still speaking. Locked them. He and Lacy both stared out the window at the man until he finally walked back to his truck.

Elsa saw this all from the rear window. Her bright eyes taking it all in, every gesture and movement. Every word exchanged she imagined through the thin glass. She was so angry at Randall she could scream. She wanted to *hurt* him for embarrassing her in front of two of her heroes. Literally, they were heroes to her in the fragile little world she inhabited. She cracked her knuckles nervously in the back seat, as Randall got back inside. She expected the worse to be directed at her, but he just started talking to Jenny like nothing had happened.

She felt sick to her stomach the whole ride back home. She didn't say a single word.

The big trees in Gerald's backyard yawned downward towards his grandmother's headstone, and nothing made a sound as the world turned blank white. Snow fell in gentle waves, like slow-sifted flour. It was Christmas Day, and Elsa was happy to be with her friend.

The two kids sat together by a little fire Gerald's mom had built on their loosely-covered back porch. Smoke blew this way and that, but they didn't seem to care in the least. Elsa's teeth chattered in the cold, but she felt warm inside. They even had spiced cider. It was hot and sweet, and Elsa let out a little 'umm' with each sip.

"Oh, guess who I saw the other night?"

Gerald lifted his hand out of politeness as he finished chewing a piece of candy cane.

"Who?"

"Mr. Wilder and Ms. Elridge. At the gas station. They were together. Like, *together-together*!"

"What? Really? I can see that. Good on Mr. W."

They both giggled conspiratorially.

"They looked happy together. We talked for a few minutes, but then. . . Well, it doesn't matter. What was your favorite gift this morning?"

Gerald rummaged through his stocking. Offered Elsa a chocolate Santa, which she gladly accepted. Moved on to a block of divinity himself that Santa Claus had somehow procured from the local gourmet general store. They both unwrapped their treat in noisy synchronicity. Gerald's face, with its retained baby fat, moved in harmony with his chewing as he spoke.

"Um, I don't know. My mom got me a bunch of clothes, but my dad got me a pellet gun. It's really nice. Has a scope and everything. That's probably my favorite thing. Oh, and I got a new skateboard. My other one was losing its tread."

"Neat! I saw the BB gun in the living room when my mom dropped me off. It looked brand new."

"Pellet gun! You have to pump this one like three times to shoot it. What did you get, E?"

"Oh, not much. I love the books and hat your mom got me. They were great. Definitely my favorite things."

She pointed skyward at her new beanie with a cool Hurley logo on it. She had hugged Gerald's mom twice for the nice gifts. She had even teared up when she gave her two wrapped gifts. It was more than she was used to at home, and she was grateful to her core for the surprises.

Elsa looked out over the yard and the snow. It was so peaceful to her. So clean. Mrs. Yonah's headstone peered vaguely out of the whitewash. Only the bottom portion remained visible. Her name and birthdate and death date were all covered by winter's tears. It erased her to the naked eye, but Elsa could feel her all around. Freed from the ceiling of time and the boundaries of a human form. She could also feel her own grandmother in the snow. It was her favorite season, winter.

Maybe they were together in some world just beyond our own? Friends, kindred spirits. Untethered to anything or anyone. Truly free.

The wind broke the silence and moved both snow and wood smoke around in a spectral dance. Gerald studied his divinity closely. Removed an errant piece of pecan and put the rest in his mouth with a look of deep satisfaction. His frame filled the entire camp chair, his feet firmly on the ground. Elsa sat like a diminutive marionette on hers. Her head rested just below the Coleman insignia and her Conversed feet swung underneath.

They appeared opposite in every way, yet were somehow so close. Two orbs circling the same axis. Bound to meet at some point along their arc. Any circumstance or incarnation bringing them together on a special day.

Then, something told Elsa to look down. Closer to the house and the moment. In the snow, a black spider crept towards them and the modest fire. Braving the ice and the cold. A state of diapause slowing its activity but enhancing its meaning. Bringing it to its strongest form. It reminded Elsa of a dream she had been having lately. It was almost a nightmare, but it was the certain kind of dream she had learned to heed. Such dreams, in her brief but profound experience, were often prone to come true.

"Gerr?"

"Yeah."

"Look at that spider."

He looked down from perusing his stocking.

"Whoa. It's big. Don't they die in the winter?"

"I don't think so. I think they just aren't as common. Or, we don't really notice them as much. They are cold-blooded and pretty tough."

"Oh. Cool."

"I think they're cool, too. That one reminds me of this dream I've been having lately. You know the dreams I have, how they sometimes come true?"

"Yep. Weirdo."

They both laughed. The spider paused as if to eavesdrop on their conversation. To figuratively warm itself by the fire. It froze in place to form a perfect triangle between the two humans. The fire a common bond between them, the snow a familiar backdrop to such earthly coalescence.

"I've had this dream lately about a woman. She's very sad. She makes me feel a little bit afraid. I see her wandering in the snow. She's looking for something, dressed in black. That's why this spider reminded me of her. I don't know why. They have the same. . . aura, I guess."

"What's that mean?"

"It's hard to explain. It's like a feeling that a person gives off. Something you can't put your finger on, exactly."

"Oh."

"Yeah, but like I said, she's wandering in the snow and she's very sad. I know that much for sure. But then it always ends up in a very dark place. Like in a house, but different. It's always nighttime. And I start to feel panicked in my dream. Like something awful is happening that I can't control. I can hear her laughing, but there's someone else there. A kid. Younger than us. I don't know. It's not a good dream, Gerr. I didn't mean to bring it up."

Gerald looked up from his stocking. Studied Elsa like he had the candy. He didn't know what to say. He knew that the girl in front of him was the smartest person he knew. He knew that they would always be friends, but sometimes she scared him a little. The way she talked. The way she was so certain of her dreams. Her eyes. . . The way they danced and sparkled. She wasn't like anyone else he knew, but that was his favorite part about Elsa Privette.

"It's okay, E. You can talk to me."

"Thanks, Gerald. I like talking to you."

The old screen door opened behind them and Gerald's mother appeared. She looked pretty in a dark gray Christmas sweater, her jet black hair pulled straight back into a ponytail. She had a kind face. Sad, too, but kind.

"You kids ready for dinner? I think everything's almost done."

Both of them nodded enthusiastically. Elsa was starving, and she couldn't wait to enjoy the big meal the younger Mrs. Yonah had prepared. They both popped up from their seats in a way only youth can provide. Light and free. Unburdened, even though their lives were far from perfect.

Without notice, the dark spider had disappeared just as suddenly as it had arrived. It had listened intently to Elsa, had warmed itself by the welcoming fire, and had moved on to explore the expanding whiteness encircling the world. It would build for months to come. Everything would be silent but for the wind. The cold was cleansing, and time would pass gently towards the violence and deep blooming of the impossible spring.

Eliza Stone

Later...

Something potent coursed through Eliza's veins as she strolled through the wooded lot. She knew these woods well. They brought back a flood of emotions, and she could feel every molecule shifting within each cell of her being as she danced among the trees in the gathering gloom. Off in the distance, hiding between the rows of trees, the dark lake cast an inky backdrop to the scene. The moon would be out, soon enough. Its pale reflection would provide the only light, and some things thrive best in the dark.

That much is certain, and we know those things as *fear*.

Every few steps, Eliza would lift up onto her toes with a surreal levity. Feet bare in the cool air, over the leaves and sticks but feeling no pain. She would spin about, twirl, shimmy. She hummed a tune. Perhaps a song she had recently heard, perhaps a hymn or a nursery rhyme. Its character changed from note to note, and she lost herself in a purity of inspiration. Her hope was at a crimson peak as she flirted with the high of reunion.

This would be the night that she would find her daughter again. Her *new* daughter. Take her somewhere safe from the world. A place where they could be alone, and they could be together again.

Just ahead, not a quarter mile away, the backyard of a house appeared. A soft light shown through the windows. A mother was inside. Maybe preparing dinner. The father was probably on his way home from work. And in the backyard, playing on her new swing set, was a lovely young thing who had just finished her homework. Her mother had given her a brief leave to go outside before nightfall, and she swung high above the growing grass. With each dip and rise, she would smile. It felt good to soar above the ground, and she wished that moment of flight would last forever.

Eliza's black hair and black dress shifted in waves as the gentle breeze seemed to carry her along. As she spun through the trees on a flight of her own, silence enveloped her in an unnatural camouflage. She could not be seen, yet there she was. She could not be heard, yet she sang in the gloom.

She smiled a wicked sneer as she saw little Brittany Reynolds playing alone in the yard. The scar on her face and the mess of black bangs only added to the aspect of menace. To her, there was no Brittany. There was only the ghostly reflection of Lilly, and Lilly belonged to her. She was simply reclaiming what was hers from this imposter family.

When Eliza walked silently across the smooth, cool grass of the Reynolds' family yard, she walked unseen. Brittany's light frame moved from front to back only yards away. With one silent step, and then another, a darkly dressed woman with pain-stricken eyes inched ever closer to the girl. She could almost smell the sweet scent of the child. Her shampoo. The detergent on her clothes. Senses reeled, she could almost hear her heart beating right there before her.

And when she grabbed her, the girl lifted seamlessly from her seat. It was as if Nature held her breath and no noise could escape from the void. Even the air was still, and nothing dared make a sound.

The mother was reading from a cookbook in the kitchen and had just stolen a peek out the window to check on her daughter. She had been there, giggling on the swing with each push forward. This had made her equally happy. She loved seeing her smile, as any parent does.

Not five minutes later, Katrina Reynolds stepped out onto the back deck of their newly purchased house. Her daughter was no longer at the swing set. She was no longer in the yard. Something primal seized her at once. She looked left and right. Her throat tightened. She called out in vain, hoping to hear her daughter's voice echo back just out of sight. Perhaps exploring the woods, testing her limits.

But, no. There would be no reply. Only the gathering darkness stared back at her. It made light of her terror. The worst feeling she had ever felt overtook her. A gnawing pit consumed her insides. An Abyss, and a Nothingness that could only live in the dark places. In the shade and the blackness. In these dense woods, and in the basement of our thoughts we lock without a key.

Brittany Reynolds had simply vanished. She was gone without a trace.

Sheriff Scott

There were already two patrol cars in the Reynolds' driveway, when he arrived. It was dark, and he could feel the tension in the air before he even got out of his truck.

His wife had answered the phone when it rang less than an hour before. Its clamor had interrupted the meatloaf dinner and cold Budweiser he had just sat down to enjoy. He could still taste the perfectly browned edge of basted Ketchup and thought vaguely of retirement on his drive out to the lake.

To just sit and exist. Drink his beer and watch a ballgame. Maybe go fishing when the weather was nice. Wait for Death in a rocking chair out on the front porch. He would kindly stop by in his tinted black car, and it would be on to the next life.

Dream on, the aging sheriff had thought at that fleeting fantasy. He was a realist, after all.

Reality was always just a bad phone call away, and tonight it had called right at dinner.

He stepped stiffly out of the truck and a young deputy jogged across the yard towards him before he could announce himself.

"Hey, Sheriff. Sorry you had to come all the way out here. You heard the report?"

"Yeah. Missing kid. What's the scoop?"

"Yep. Looks like it. We combed the woods for her the last hour or so, but she ain't back there. No sign of her."

"Where's K9?"

"Um. . ."

"Call 'em. Get a dog or two out here. These woods go for miles. Any potential suspects? A jilted ex? A relative?"

"No, sir. Family says they don't have any enemies or anything like that."

"I'll go talk to them."

"They're inside, Sheriff. In the living room."

"All right. Get those dogs up here."

The baby-faced deputy nodded. He looked worried, genuinely worried about this supposedly missing girl. He was a good kid, but this job was going to wear him out like a shop rag.

The sheriff nodded to the other deputy circling the house with his flashlight. He nodded back. He was older and harder-looking than the kid presently calling for K9 in the yard behind them. There was no need for the two men to speak. They had seen this and much worse a hundred times before. Sometimes it worked out for the best; sometimes it didn't. They both knew that "policing" was more about luck and appearances than the crime shows would have you believe. Most days, you were simply a mediator drifting between the various shades of gray in the murky pool of human behavior. Ever unpredictable, yet certain repetitions could at times give you a second sight. Like reciting the lines of a familiar movie, or a boxer knowing the precise moment to juke and jab.

And the Maglite beam searched desperately in the dark for any sign of tonight's missing girl. It penetrated the blackness with its tiny scope, and its light could only illuminate just so far into the night woods beyond.

The sheriff knocked twice on the freshly painted front door before letting himself in to the house. This place was big, very nice. Someone had some dough to buy this spread out on the lake. Property was getting very expensive out this way, as it was no longer just vacation homes and cabins from the seventies lining these backroads near the water. He knew from the station that this was a young couple, just moved to the area from somewhere up North. Dad worked for the massive charity conglomerate in town, which paid very well and drew the right employees from far and wide. Mom stayed at home, and the girl in question was six-years old.

She had disappeared that evening around dinner time. Right before dark. Had been playing on the swing set out back, the mom had just seen her from the kitchen window, and then she was gone. Nowhere to be found. Seemingly spirited away in a span of five minutes.

That's all he knew. He had some swirling thoughts and ill-formed opinions on the matter, but he would keep them to himself for the time being. That was usually best.

The husband and wife sat together on a stark white couch in the den. Mark and Katrina Reynolds. The former had an expression of disbelief on his clean-shaven face, delicately balancing the emotions of the moment as best as he could. The latter, surprisingly, smiled when she saw the sheriff and stood to greet him before he could announce himself.

She was very attractive. Very elegant and graceful, despite the situation. She was made-up pretty as a picture, despite only wearing a green Dartmouth half-zip and fashionably distressed jeans. Her dark hair was pulled neatly in a bun with a few errant bangs caressing her smooth brow. The sheriff removed his hat and offered his hand to shake hers, already outstretched.

"Sheriff? Oh, thank you so much for coming all the way out here. We really appreciate it. What a night, right? Here, come sit down if you like. We're both nervous wrecks, but I'd be happy to get you some coffee or something."

"Thank you, Mrs. Reynolds. It's no problem at all, and I'll pass on the coffee to save you the trouble. I can only imagine what you folks might be thinking, but we see this sort of thing all the time. Your daughter will probably turn up in an hour, under a bed upstairs or playing hide and seek with one of our deputies."

Katrina forced a short laugh. Mark feigned a tight smile. The sheriff wasn't joking. Less than a month ago, a little boy had indeed hidden for four hours under a bed while his whole neighborhood looked for him outside. But, this already felt different to him, somehow. An intuition, perhaps. There was some sense of peril in the air that he would almost deem palpable. Couldn't quite put his finger on it, but he reckoned that tight-lipped father on the sofa was feeling it, too.

This young mother, however, was an *optimist*. Apparently, she was one of the rare and delicate sprites that nothing bad had happened to in life, up to this point. The naïve bliss of white elitism was stitched into her very being, like the fine fibers of the carpet under his dingy boots. She couldn't help but have the utmost faith that this, too, would pass, and the sheriff felt like he was only fueling that cold fire.

"So, we are expanding a search perimeter at present. Down to the lake, through the woods, and back up to the highway. We're getting more men up here, and a K9 unit as soon as possible. My gut tells me that she probably wandered a little too far from home, right at dusk, and got lost in the woods coming back. These woods are very thick, as I am sure you've noticed, so she might not be able to hear the boys calling her name out there right away. Do you have any neighbors nearby that she might have gone to in a pinch? Any hiding places out there that you know of?"

Katrina spoke after a pause.

"I mean, we've only met one set of neighbors. An older couple that lives down a little closer to the lake. Honey, what was their name? They were so nice. They brought us a loaf of banana bread when we first moved in, a few months ago."

"The Carlisle family, if I remember correctly. There are only a few houses on this side-road, so she wouldn't have many options if she did end up in someone's yard." Mark had swallowed deeply before he spoke. Wet his dry mouth. It looked painful for him to produce words.

"Okay, great. Have you called them? We'll send somebody down to their place right now, and then we will go door-to-door out here if we need to keep looking."

"Yes, and I left them a voicemail."

"Very good. And, I have to ask – do you happen to have any enemies? Anyone who might want to hurt you or your girl?"

"No. None."

Mark answered flatly. Katrina shook her head emphatically, her eyes begging a "but we've never done anything wrong" sentiment.

"Have you had any prowlers out this way? Anything like that? Nothing creepy?"

"Sherriff, no. We haven't. We would have told you already."

"Understood. I just have to ask. Trying to get a clear picture."

"Do you think she's been, what? *Kidnapped?*"

Katrina's voice pitched higher on the last word.

"No. Not at all, Mrs. Reynolds. I'm just doing my diligence. Like I said before, I'm sure she will turn up before daylight. We'll get her home, safe and sound."

The couple didn't have much to say after that, and the old sheriff was starting to feel a bit awkward sitting on their couch with little consolation to offer. So, he excused himself after a few more moments and showed himself the door.

Outside, the patrol car closest to the house rested like a dark sentinel just outside of the porchlight. Sherriff Scott pulled a can of Grizzly from his back pocket, tapped it a few times out of long-born habit, and took a big pinch. It had just started to work on stimulating his neurons and transmitters when headlights appeared through the trees in the distance.

K9 had arrived, and it was about to be a long night.

Before dawn, two things were fairly certain.

Brittany Reynolds was indeed missing, and she was lost in a forest far deeper than the patch of hardwoods circling a lake, which concealed a forgotten town beneath its placid waters.

Randall Lightner

The wife was asleep, and he stood in the kitchen with the younger girl. Neither he nor Elsa spoke as she poured a bowl of cereal and he drank a cup of jet-black Folgers. His head was throbbing from finishing off a bottle of Jack the night before, and he was in no mood to hear the Saturday morning cartoons careening cheerfully from the TV in the room beyond.

Elsa smiled at him as she added milk to her dollar-store Fruit Loops. He nodded in return, then turned his attention out the window.

That girl was one of a small handful of people on God's green earth who he could not hold eye contact with for more than a few seconds. She made him uncomfortable on some deep level that he could not explain. Like she could see right through him. See his most base nature exposed in the daylight, like a holiday parade. Her smile, a Mona Lisa glance. Put simply, she was not afraid of him. He could hit her, throw her against the wall, scream until his echo was deaf, but she was still largely unafraid of him.

It was odd. His father, who was long dead and buried, and his older brother, who was in prison for murder, had him equally under their thumb in the quiet children's corner in which he sometimes hid his true self. And, then, there was this little girl. Weird as hell, too perceptive for her age, with piercing crystals for eyes and a demeanor that was almost lethal in its placidity.

Out the window, the first blossoms of spring sprang like fireworks off the trees. And beyond, just then, an old truck pulled into the driveway with a Tanawah County Sherriff's emblem on the side panel,

Randall took a long, last sip of his coffee. Turned to Elsa who had retired to the living room to watch Scooby-Doo and felt a sinking in his stomach at the sight of the cop car in his driveway. He knew that someday his yard would be filled with cop cars. Probably not today, given that it was only one policeman in that old truck, but he knew. Soon, they would all come for him. The whole damn world would demand his blood for crime upon crime, and he would share his brother's fate. Eventually, we would all share his father's, so what did it really matter?

The sheriff got out of his truck too casually to be arresting anyone this morning. That was some mild relief, Randall supposed. He momentarily pondered how that would go down. Right there in the front yard. He was younger and faster and meaner than the old policeman. He could get into the dresser drawer and have his pick of Glock or Colt in less than a minute. Go out the back door. Come around the house. Get the drop on the gray bastard.

And. . .

Pop, pop. Goodbye.

Where's the shovel?

But, all was easier said and imagined than done. He had never killed a cop. And something about Carl Scott had always bothered him somehow. He was a measured man, intelligent. No stories floated around in the ether about him ever being on the receiving end of an ass-kicking or in the direct path of a shrieking bullet.

Randall, on the other hand, was wily, like a mad fox or a famished coyote. He could *get away and stay gone* if the odds were in his favor. That said, he had never been in a straight firefight. He had always obliged the upper hand somehow. And he knew that if the man now standing in his yard really wanted, then Randall Lightner, in all his façade of menace, might end up catching one between the running lights.

Luck had its limitations, after all. Fear of reprisal ultimately keeps every man in check to one degree or another.

The old man spotted him through the dingy kitchen window and gave him a slight wave from the yard, imploring him to come outside. Randall poured his remaining coffee on top of a pile of dirty dishes in the sink, told Elsa to stay inside, and walked out into the annoyingly bright sunlight.

"Morning, Randall. Sorry for the early call."

"Did you *call*, Carl?"

Randall stood with the screen door propped against his foot, not fully willing to commit to interaction with the sheriff.

"Um, no. Just an expression. I meant my coming to visit you so early. Never mind. Come on out here. I got a few questions for you."

Randall stepped with a few swaggering strides out into the yard. He leaned against the hood of the truck, stretched out his shoulders informally on its frame, lowering his strong, dense body down to the bumper and back up to full height. The sheriff was unamused and cut right to the chase.

"You look like shit, Randall."

"I feel worse."

"Well, that's all your business. I didn't drive all the way up here for a wellness check. Look, I'm sure you heard about this missing girl. The Reynolds' kid. It's starting to look like some kind of kidnapping, or worse, and I just wanted to ask you a few questions."

Randall looked up from the truck with a tired expression on his face. A deep fatigue. The drugs and the booze only formed an outline to the hangover of daily life. He looked generally miserable, like some proud ape trapped in a zoo. Resigned. He could get depressive, and today was one of those days.

"Sheriff. . . Jesus Christ. I ain't done nothing to some little girl. Now, damn it. You know that. I got two of my own I can hardly stand. I don't need some other brat. . ."

"I wouldn't have just strolled up in your yard if I thought you did, Randy. I'm getting older, but I'm damn sure not getting dumber. Anyway, listen, I know that you *know* people. Especially up here. I'm going door-to-door to find out anything I can. See if anyone has heard anything. I have a few rap sheets right here that I want you to look at for me. Sex offenders, mostly, that have either skipped town or we've lost track of out here. I'm thinking somebody we might know has a taste for little girls, and you hang out with a colorful crowd."

The sheriff reached into his jacket pocket and pulled out a few folded pieces of paper. They each had names and mug shots and other petty details about a few perverts that certainly looked capable of snatching up some poor girl and taking them god knows where.

"Know any of these guys? Know where to find 'em?"

Randall reluctantly glanced at the pages. He held one closer to his face. Scrunched his brow. Sat the page down on the hood of the truck.

"I know this one. Grew up with him. He's a real son of a bitch, but I ain't seen him in years. I ain't never seen the other two."

"Robert Brown?"

"Yeah."

"Think he might've taken that girl?"

Randall looked the sheriff right in the eye. Studied his furrowed brow and unblinking eyes that were beginning to droop on the edges. Admired his flannel shirt, neatly tucked into a pair of Levi's with a Winchester belt buckle right on the gig line. In another life, these two men could have swapped roles. One the good guy, one the bad, but the Universe had made that distinction long ago.

"No."

"What do you mean 'no', Randall? He's a registered sex offender, has a history of violence, and we can't get a hold of him."

"I mean, *no*. I don't think he's got that kid. She's too young. He liked big tits, teenage girls, at least. Used to practically have a brothel of high-school drop-outs he'd pay for sex out in that shack he inherited from his mama. He's got this old shed with dirty pictures all over the wall. Used to do a ton of hard shit, too. Some nasty business happens up there, but again – he likes them *almost* of age. I don't think he's your man."

"Do you know where we might find him?"

"Not really. At his *house*, maybe? You been up there yet? I don't know. You should ask my boy Rooster or Tom Redford. They know him way better than I do."

"I may do that. And this 'Rooster'. . . What's his real name? Um, Charles. . . Charles. . . Anyway, how's his leg? I heard he had been walking with a limp and ended up in the ER a while back. Some 'accident' involving a small caliber pistol. Know anything about that?"

"Ha. Sheriff, you going to book me for shooting some goat-fucker in the leg? Or are you thinking I'll spill my guts if you bring that up? I've been to jail. A few times, actually. It ain't so bad. And I don't know anything else about that girl of yours. All I know is some yuppy family moves up here to the sticks, they forget where they moved to from some suburban Stepford, and somebody snatches their precious little girl. They should have kept their eyes on her, is all I'm saying."

The sheriff removed his hat. Scratched his head. Put it back on and considered what Randall had said. He wasn't stupid. Sly like a fox. He had a wicked gleam in his eye. Water about to boil beneath the blue glass. Randall didn't break eye contact, held his gaze. The rising sun was obviously painful to him in his present state, but he was handling his hangover woes pretty well.

"You're not wrong, Randall."

"Nah, Carl. At least can we agree on that."

"So, can you think of anything else before I leave? You *know* people, as I said. And you know people who *know* people. You've lived here your whole damn life. You got anything that might help us out? I promise, I'll return the favor if you do. God knows you could use a favor, cause if I was younger you'd be. . . Well, I just need something to go on, all right?"

Randall spit into the grass behind him. Stood from leaning against the truck. Wiped his hands on a dingy Dixie Outfitters T-shirt, and turned his head to belch quietly into his arm.

"I got one thought, is all, Sheriff."

"Yeah? What's that?"

"You're looking for a man, right?"

"Yes. Obviously."

"Well, what if you're wrong?"

"What do you mean?"

"Why ain't you considered a woman? And I ain't talking about any weird sex shit. There's more than one reason someone might kidnap a little girl."

"Who are you talking. . ."

"The realtor, sheriff. The fucking wack-job realtor who lost her kid. The Stone woman. Look, I've had some dealings with her. Under the table, she's on some hard shit, if you care to know. And, well. . . I'll admit it. She scares the hell out of me. Something ain't right upstairs, and she's always out near the lake." He tapped the side of his head for emphasis.

"Stone. . . First name?"

"Eliza. Elizabeth, I guess. The one whose kid died last year in that car accident. In the snow. Slid into the truck or something."

"And you think that she would kidnap somebody's child to – what? Replace her daughter or whatever?"

"Maybe. People have fucked-up motives."

"Any real reason I should pursue this, Randall?"

"Call it a gut instinct, Sheriff. I don't know. You asked my opinion. I gave it. What more do you want?"

"I'll look into it. Seen this woman lately?"

"No. Not in a while."

"Like, how long? Where did you meet her last?"

"No, Sheriff. This is where I go back inside."

"Hey, listen. If this comes to anything, I'll let you know. And one more thing: in the meantime, keep your hands off that little one. And her big sister. If I hear one more report from the school, I'm going to have to take you in. Understand?"

Randall Lightner was already walking back in the house. He nodded slightly, waved his hand over his head, and opened the screen door without a proper goodbye. He had drawn the line, and Carlton Scott understood that boundary well enough.

When kids play cops and robbers on the school yard, they aren't expected to get along. The whole point is to shoot at each other, after all, and sometimes you don't get to choose your side.

Fate and circumstance determine which ones wear the badge and which ones always have to run.

Eliza

Eliza had planned all this for weeks. Carefully, it had consumed her. Her mad mind spinning the details from a broken loom, their threads connecting with odd precision. She somehow knew that she would get away with this. She would take her, and no one would stop her. Reclaim the daughter she lost, if not in body, but in essence and presence.

That would have to do.

She had drugged the girl heavily. She rested in the trunk of the old car in dreamless sleep. The headlights were low as Eliza navigated the dark roads that led from the lake to the ski resorts. She passed a few commercial trucks, riding the breaks down the steep climbs as she ascended. On her right, an austere slope of craggy rock and cold moss reached straight up towards the night sky. To the left, far below, a river flowed over equally ancient rocks like a vein of dark blood rushing through some arcane giant. And that giant, forever in slumber, the true natives had called *Appalachia*.

Eliza, at her core, was even older than those Natives. Equally exiled, but by a God she had scorned. Soon to be hunted in a Wild of her creation. Wild as any serpent in any garden. Just as Original, and just as Lost.

Eliza focused on her destination. She had the address memorized. She had the key code for the door memorized. She knew it would be unoccupied for quite some time because she had removed the listing from the Mountain Realty site. The brothers were awful with anything computer-related, so they wouldn't immediately wonder why the big condo at the Winter Ridge Ski Resort hadn't booked. Ski season was already fading backwards into family Polaroid albums, after all. She would largely be alone at the top of that cold mountain.

Well, perhaps not alone at all. She would have her surrogate daughter, and that was all the company she cared to keep.

Two days earlier, she had taken all of Lilly's clothes and toys and trinkets up to the lonely condo. The sky was flat gray outside as she prepared a bedroom for the Reynold's girl. She hummed nursery rhymes to the vacant air as she worked. She sang to herself and smiled. The condo was fully furnished, so her new Lilly would have a nice bed and a nice place to play.

There were only a few other cars in the complex's parking lot, and she had made sure no one saw her comings and goings. She had already stockpiled her groceries. Enough to last a long time if needs be. She had bought all of Lilly's favorite things: Frosted Flakes, peanut butter, those little meals with the Penguin on them, frozen fish sticks to dip into tartar sauce, Chef Boyardees.

She painted this fantasy as she drove. A fantasy that she hoped would end in her being called 'Mommy' again. A fantasy of reading books, getting ready for school, playing hide and seek, going to the park. She might get to do all of that. Maybe not here and maybe not now, she knew. She wasn't that naïve or wrecked by her potions just yet, but maybe she would in another place and time. Somewhere on a higher plane, perhaps.

She would be good to this girl. Take the best care of her. And then, through the drugged haze and dim headlight glow, reflecting off the black road yawning ahead of her, a flash of reality.

She had kidnapped someone's child, she was causing pain, and she would be hunted. Quickly, Eliza repressed those thoughts. She asked the Darkness for them to pass, and so they did. She was master of the night, and she could have whatever she wanted.

If only for a brief while, she would. Life is too brief, she reasoned, reaching for her purse. Skillfully opening a small Ziploc. Skillfully swallowing two or three or four pills without any water. Without changing her expression. She caught sight of her gaunt face in the rear-view mirror. The shadows in the dark car gave her a skeletal, strained, and demonic aspect.

She knew herself to be all of those things, but she was also a mother. She had opted to adopt this time around, and with the Devil himself riding comfortably in her passenger seat, she would have her chance to parent again.

Sheriff Scott

"Warrant's in, Sheriff. All good."

The young deputy stood at Carl's desk, warrant in hand. He looked almost giddy, in spite of himself. He had been on the job only a few months. This whole kidnapping deal was the most exciting thing he had ever experienced in his twenty-four years. Carl had known his dad for years and years. DOT foreman one county over, looked just the reflection now standing before him with a sappy grin on his face. His ruddy cheeks and curly blond hair made him look like a ten-year-old boy dressed as a cop for Hallowe'en. Or a cherub in khaki uniform.

Carl squinted over his bifocals at Deputy Dawson. He had been trying to copy and paste some text from an email on his old Mac but had failed to master the dexterity needed to guide the mouse. No text had been copied or pasted before he was interrupted.

"Robert Brown?"

"Yes, sir. We have the warrant."

"You said that. Let me see it."

Dawson handed the warrant note across the desk. It was partially sealed in a very ordinary looking envelope.

"Did you see the address on here? Almost across the state line. We've got a little drive ahead of us."

"I didn't open it, Sheriff." Carl gave him a look. "But, I did search his name in our database and found the address."

Carl let the moment hang in the balance while he perused the notice. The only sound in the Sheriff's office was the ticking of a Ducks Unlimited clock hanging on the wood-panel wall. His desk was not necessarily *neat*, but it was organized to the Sheriff's specific liking. His secretary and the cleaning lady knew not to so much as move a pen on its surface. He had no nameplate. No family photos. Besides a few trinkets of his own, like the Ducks clock, a coat rack partially made of elk antler, and a large calendar on the side wall, sponsored by various local restaurants, it was perhaps the world's most boring office. Even the filing cabinets looked bored as all hell sitting in their lonely corner.

"Good. As you should have. Wanna go out there with me to serve it?"

"Me? Um, yeah! Yes, sir. I'd love to go."

"Before you get too excited, let me just say. I have it on decent authority that he isn't our man. I don't need you packing the Tac gear or anything. We're just gonna play it cool. Go have a look around. Understand?"

"Got it. I understand."

"Good. You drive. I need gas in my truck."

Carl had already served two such warrants the day before, to no avail. He had asked for a net of fifty square miles around the town for any known sex offenders or pederasts. It had turned up a nauseating number of possible suspects – twenty-four grossly depraved, disgusting hicks who he would prefer to be rotting away in a cell somewhere.

Most *were* in jail, either for the aforementioned offense or some other petty crime, but ten were still very much at large and seven were not presently wearing ankle monitors. Today's house call would hopefully mark three stand-up citizens off his list.

It would, otherwise, be a very eventful day if they did turn up anything related to the disappearance of sweet Brittany Reynolds.

The sky overhead was corpse-gray as the deputy drove them through town. Snow was always a possibility at this altitude until at least May Day. Sheriff Scott looked skyward, nodded to nothing in particular. It could definitely snow, the wolf clouds overhead proclaimed, and it was cold as a witch's tit outside.

The university kids littered the sidewalks off Main Street in varying degrees of hurry. Off to class, off to an early lunch, off to smoke a joint in the dorms with a few friends. Despite the generation gap and all evidence to the contrary, Scott had never belittled the college students who cohabitated his ol' town, like many men his age. He knew the university brought civilization to an area that could use it. He liked the music, and the restaurants, and the football. He took pride in seeing the teenie-boppers grow into young adults somewhere beautiful and supposedly safe.

A few years back, there had been a few murders on campus. It was all over the news. The paper had a field day, as that sort of thing was largely unknown in the city. Two girls, walking alone on separate nights, found themselves dead as doornails before daybreak. It happened over four or five days, but it had felt like an eon to the sheriff and his deputies. Parents were irate, a curfew was put in place, and they had worked around the clock to chase down any possible leads. Sheriff Scott clearly remembered walking through the main campus one evening. The sun died slowly overhead, late spring twilight burning like a bonfire. He studied every passing face. Every young movement and energetic gait. Every frown. There had been no definitive suspects, and then – he saw it.

An ATM right beside a bus stop. ATMs always had cameras. The first girl had been found face-down in the muddy drainage creek not 100ft from the kiosk. Big Wells-Fargo lettering, bright and red and right in front of his eyes.

It took hours, but eventually they gathered the footage. They poured over the tape. Every moment on the night of the murder was pivotal. They had three possible suspects within an hour's time-frame of the murder. Two had been duds, but one. . .

Sheriff Scott had made the arrest himself. He had not been gentle. He could still feel the violent kicking and struggling under his knee as he fought to handcuff his man. The feel of his oily hair as he forced him against the tile floor. The definitive click of the metal cuffs as he finally snapped them together.

There was an absolutism to the moment. It was why he had become a police officer in the first place. He reveled in the chase, but he was also a true believer in corporeal justice.

He hoped that this most recent disappearance would yield a happy outcome. He hoped that very much, but his mind was starting to lean towards the realm of *justice* rather than salvation for the girl. Time was cruel in these matters, and they were going on *three days*.

And then, the young deputy broke the silence of his thoughts.

"Do you know this road? Cane Gap?"

"I've been out there before. It turns to dirt pretty quickly off the highway. About a mile from the skate rink way out there near the Tennessee line."

"Okay. Let me know when we get close."

"It's a ways yet. Just relax. The boogie man can wait. And slow down. You're going ten over the speed limit."

The house was ramshackle. They had each expected as much, but this was pretty noteworthy. Even for this part of the county. Lawnmowers in disrepair, rusted bed springs, garbage strewn everywhere. . . You name it. A mangy dog barked and growled at their approach. He guarded with intent ferocity what remained of a dilapidated front porch. There would be no element of surprise, but that was fine with the sheriff. He liked to announce his presence. Found it was safer that way.

The two men strode cautiously up to the porch. The elder peered through a dingy window on the side of the small house; the younger tried to get a look through the front window without getting bitten by the drooling Chow centurion. He had his hand firmly placed on his pistol, and the sheriff rolled his eyes when he saw this semi-procedural gesture.

"Dawson."

"Sir?"

"Please remove that dog from the porch."

The boy looked at the dog. His barking was growing louder. He could basically smell him only a few feet away. He was dug-in like an Alabama tick. He snarled and growled. His black tongue held the young deputy's attention like a charmed snake.

"How would you like me to do that?"

"By calling out to its owner."

"Hmm? Oh. Right."

The sheriff stepped back a few paces. He had his eye on an old shed at the back of the house. Thought he had heard something back there when they pulled up. There was a rotten fence which circled what remained of the derelict backyard. Something Lightner had said about that shed. . .

Dawson's voice cracked a bit when he first called out. It lacked confidence. The sheriff knew it would come with time. It takes years to develop the presence required.

"Robert Brown? Sheriff's Department. Why don't you come on out and get this dog, so we can talk? Come on, now. We've been out here long enough."

He turned to the sheriff for approval, but he wasn't where he was formerly standing. He had moved with impressive stealth to the side of the house. Even the dog had momentarily stopped barking and shifted to the far end of the porch to keep a closer eye on the old man.

The sheriff motioned to his deputy to go around the other side of the house. "The shed. I think he's in there. I heard something. Go around the other side of the house," he whispered.

"Yes, sir."

Dawson jogged to the other side of the house and carefully hurdled over a plastic chair and what looked like a rusted-out washing machine to get around to the back. The whole place needed a tetanus shot. And a bulldozer.

Sherriff Scott heard a voice in the shed. Then another. Then some rattling around in there. A latent feeling started to stir in his belly. Like an old friend come to visit. Adrenaline and the thrill. He almost smiled. Almost chuckled aloud.

It felt too good. He could see his breath in the cold air. The sky remained a crackling gray overhead. He got goosebumps as he put his hand on the big Colt at his side. Its rubber grip greeted him like a warm handshake.

"Robert Brown! Come on out of that tool shed. I have a warrant to search your property."

The sheriff's voice lacked no confidence. Wayne and Eastwood and whoever was in Gunsmoke nodded in approval.

Within ten seconds, the shed door burst open and Brown (apparently) appeared in a stained A-tee and dirty underwear. His pants hung around his knees as he struggled to get them up and make a run for it. He darted clumsily to the fence, finally getting his pants mostly on as he limped like a three-legged dog through the overgrown yard. He kept looking back at the sheriff. Obviously guilty of something.

The sheriff never moved. He just watched like a hunting dog.

Dawson appeared at a full run from the other side of the yard. He slid like a MLB pro right under the pervert's legs. The sheriff was impressed. Brown flew through the air like a rag doll. He landed in a heap on the ground. The air left him in a huff like a deflated balloon. He struggled to stand back up, tripped over his jeans. Fell again. And that was that. Dawson had him. Handcuffs and cussing and spit. The boy easily overpowered him.

The sheriff finally broke his statuesque pose. There was someone else in that shed. She was cussing a blue streak in some awful, high-pitched, East Jesus Dolly Parton twang. The chow was still barking up a storm, but never left the porch. The sheriff kept checking, just to be safe.

A girl appeared as Scott neared the door. Same dirty tank top like Brown had been wearing and a cheap red thong. Hair a mess. Pale as the day and bone skinny. A few ill-drawn tattoos here and there.

She was calling both officers every insult she could muster. Hands waving. Double birds flying.

The sheriff blocked the door so she couldn't try to run, too. He raised a hand.

"Hey. Shut that up. Stop it. I said *stop*, damn it. What's your name?"

"Don't fucking matter what my name is. Who the *hell* are you? Where's that *warrant*, asshole?"

The girl obviously wasn't Brittany Reynolds. That much was certain. She looked about seventeen. Maybe a little older. In the shed, there was drug shit scattered all over the place. Empty liquor bottles and beer cans. Dirty clothes laying around. Filthy homemade Polaroids on the walls. An equally filthy mattress on the floor. An electric heater burned dimly with electric coils bright orange. The heat and the smell were almost nauseating.

Why are they out here and not in the house? the sheriff thought.

"Lady, I need your name and I need to know what you are doing up here."

"Fuck you."

There was a mean, ugly disdain in her voice. The world had been cruel to her, and her instinct was to bark like that disgusting dog on the porch.

"How old are you?"

"I's twenty."

"Bullshit."

"I's eighteen."

"Maybe. Are these yours?"

Sheriff Scott picked up a tiny bag of what looked like homemade meth from the ground. It was open, and some fell out onto the plywood floor.

"That ain't mine."

"No?"

"It's his. I'm clean."

She motioned into the yard. Dawson had Robert Brown up to his feet. Handcuffed and walking towards the sheriff. Both were covered in mud and grass from tussling around in the yard.

"You're clean? Right."

"I ain't done that shit. Ain't mine."

Her teeth and skin begged to differ. A blood test would definitely differ, as well. Regardless, she looked cold. The sheriff could see goosebumps all over her arms and legs. She wasn't wearing a bra, and that was obvious, too. He motioned to the pile of clothes beside the mattress. She started to dress in whatever was available. It wasn't much.

"Grab some for him. Come on with me. Both of you. To the porch."

He motioned to Dawson who was struggling to keep the vagabond restrained in the yard. Took the girl by the arm. She didn't protest, despite his expectations. She was probably too cold. Within a few minutes, both Brown and the delinquent were sitting on the dilapidated porch beside the drooling dog, wrapped in emergency blankets from the patrol car. It was quite the scene.

The sheriff loosely questioned them about the missing Reynolds kid. They didn't know what he was talking about. There was no earthly reason not to believe them. He uncovered the girl's name and they decided on a disputable age somewhere between sixteen and eighteen. Brown was around thirty but looked fifty. His hair was patchy and his beard was mostly gray. Damn teeth looked like something out of a horror picture. Skin was pocked with scars and drug acne.

Meanwhile, Dawson searched what remained of the old house. Apparently, the floor had collapsed in places and the walls were rotten with mold. It was mostly the dog's home now, given the piles of dried shit and the heavy smell of animal inside. No wonder they were shacked-up in the tool shed. It was sterile by comparison. The only room that seemed to be in some working order was the kitchen. They had been cooking more than food in there from the looks of it. Amateur chemists abound.

Who knew?

But, and even though these two were definitely jail-bound, there was no sign whatsoever of Brittany Reynolds. This whole episode had been a goose chase, just as Randall had told the sheriff it would be.

So far, the sheriff and his department hadn't turned-up so much as a footprint. The city PD was on board to no avail, either.

They had not found so much as an errant mitten. Nor a blood-stained piece of clothing. No body, and no hard suspects. They were all searching in the dark, and the girl's parents were blind with fear at this point.

It had been three full days and one long night. A minor eternity for anyone who cared. The local media was having a field day. Even press trucks from Johnson City and Winston had rolled into town.

As they drove back towards civilization, the sky finally relinquished and Carlton's foretold snow began to descend all around. It was almost pretty, but there was no purity in the falling whiteness and deepening cold.

Later that afternoon, after bookings and paperwork and visiting the jail, Sheriff Scott was getting ready to call it a day. His clock had just crested five p.m., and that was good enough for him. He had a cell phone if anyone needed him.

He always said the same thing, as he strode out of the office, to anyone who cared to listen.

"I'm off."

There was hesitancy in his statement. It was simply a fact. Usually, only the secretary wished him a good evening. His deputies would be either out on patrol or home with their young families. And that was fine by Carlton. He often wished the world were quiet at night. No crime, no pain, nothing that might require a badge and a gun. He was tired, and he believed in rest while the sun was sleeping.

That was rarely the case, and he had one stop to make before reconvening with his wife that evening. It would likely be a waste of time, but he knew that time for the Reynold's girl was in short supply. If, of course, time was still a concern of hers.

He hoped that it was. He really did.

In the passenger seat of his truck, there was a small, wrapped present and a sealed card beside it. He had not needed gas earlier when the deputy drove them out to East Jesus on the edge of the world, but he didn't need his greenest deputy seeing much sentiment from him, either. It was the sheriff's wedding anniversary. He had booked a reservation at a nice steakhouse for them to enjoy. Have a quiet meal and conversation. Always the best conversation.

He had written his wife a special note in the card, below the pre-fab note on its right side. She was a kindness when all was strange and everyone a stranger. He did love that woman. Had for thirty years or more. She was his rock. He liked to keep everything about her separate from his work. Separate from Death, and Grief. And Evil, if there was such a thing. He thought that there was, indeed. He had seen it. He was currently pursuing it. And that pursuit carried him through the gloom as the flurries fell and the road froze beneath the wheels of his truck.

The yellow line would disappear overnight. The edges would soften. Ice and snow would reign, and order would collapse until dawn. Such were Carlton's thoughts as he pulled into the Mountain Realty parking lot. He had called ahead. Didn't say why. Just asked when they closed for the night and politely requested that they wait a bit longer so that he could ask a few questions.

They had obliged, and both men were waiting in the ambient space when the Sheriff came through the door.

"Dan. Bruce. Thanks for waiting on me."

Dan spoke first. He was the more affable of the two brothers. Shorter than Bruce, painstakingly clean-cut, always dressed to the nines. He had a lighter voice, a bit effeminate. There had been small-town rumors and small-minded accusations about Dan's personal life. The sheriff couldn't care less. He had always been a perfect gentleman the few times they met, and everyone he knew had nothing but the best things to say about Daniel Spencer.

Bruce, on the other hand, was the behind-the-scenes business mind of the two. The numbers guy. Salt and pepper down to his beard, more severe lines on his face, reserved. He looked uncomfortable at the policeman's presence in their office, but then again, he looked uncomfortable even in his own skin.

Dan shook hands heartily with the sheriff, like they were the best of friends. They barely knew each other, but any onlooker would have never believed that. Dan was in sales, and he wore that badge as well as the older man standing before him.

"Carl! Great to see you! It's been– what, almost a year? I think we saw you at the Christmas silent auction last year, but man. . . Too long. What can we do for you tonight?"

Bruce just nodded in their general direction, forced a smile, and then fumbled with some papers on a desk as they conversed.

"Hey, Dan. Good to see you, too. I don't want to take much of your time tonight. I know it's getting late."

"No problem at all, Sheriff. Just let me know what you need. Hopefully we aren't going to jail for some unanswered misdemeanor, or. . . Did Bruce not pay his income taxes again?"

He was full of jokes. Carlton's expression remained serious. He quickly got the hint and stopped laughing at his own sense of humor.

"That's really funny, Dan, but I do have something rather serious to discuss if ya'll don't mind. You aren't in any kind of trouble, but I do have some questions about one of your employees."

"Oh? Sorry, Sheriff. I didn't mean to make light of anything. Which employee would that be?"

"Do you have an Elizabeth Stone that works here?"

Dan turned to Bruce, then back to the sheriff.

"Yes. We do indeed. As a matter of fact. . ."

"Has she been to work lately?"

"Well, that's what I was about to say. We haven't seen or heard from her in a few days. Maybe a full week. Is she okay, Sheriff? We were starting to worry, but she's had such a hard year. . . She's been known to miss a few days in a row for some personal issues, so we didn't want to pry."

"She lost a kid recently, right? A daughter?"

"Yes, sir. Last winter. Terrible accident. She still hasn't fully recovered. But then, who could recover from thing like that? It was absolutely tragic."

The sheriff reached into his jacket and pulled out a small notebook. He liked the old ways. Pen and paper. When he was a kid, he read Conan Doyle with fervor. Every story, every case. He never went the detective route in his career, but Sherlock Holmes. . . He liked his style. His *process*. His patience. The character's methods had loosely trickled into his own practice, but he was far from overly observant and lacked the sleuth's moodiness and tendencies towards addiction.

Carl was just Carl. Steady, arrow-straight. Well-defined and always direct.

"When did you last see Miss Stone?"

"Like we said. It was over a week ago."

"How was she acting when she was at work the last few weeks?"

Bruce spoke this time.

"Odd. She's an odd bird. Hard worker, very sharp. Actually a good saleswoman, but she's always been a bit weird. Last few months, she's been a ghost. Comes and goes without a word. Here, present, but not really here. Off in her head somewhere."

"Do you drug test, Bruce? Your employees, I mean."

"Huh? No, we don't do that. I doubt anyone that works for us is on any drugs, Sheriff. We're particular here, and don't have many employees either."

"Right."

"Why do you ask?"

Daniel now.

"I have it on good authority that she might be on some pretty hard stuff. And a good many prescriptions on top of that."

"Well, I have seen her take a few pills out of her purse. All prescription, of course. I mean– like I said, she's been through a lot. Probably just anti-depressants or whatnot."

"Uh-huh. You've heard about the missing girl, right? Brittany Reynolds?"

"Oh, yes. We are so sorry for that poor family. Have you had any leads yet?"

"A few. . . Can you think of any possible connection between the Reynold's girl and Miss Stone?"

Bruce furrowed his brow. Daniel looked back at his brother. Both were silent for a long moment.

"Well?"

"Um, maybe. She actually helped sell them their house out near the lake. She did the walk-through for them. The initial showing. I, technically, was the realtor of record, but I gave her the commission on the sale. . ."

Sheriff Scott stopped scribbling in his notebook. He raised an eyebrow. Looked around the room, suddenly interested in its décor. Randall Lightner's rough face appeared somewhere in the recesses of his mind. His drawl echoing in its more cavernous expanses.

If that man's lead holds any water, I'm retiring tomorrow.

"And, not to insult you, but you didn't think to call anyone about this? Missing girl, unstable woman working for you, showed said girl's parents a Mountain Realty property, and then two of the parties go missing? Nothing strange there to either of you?"

There was a series of mumbles and umms and ahs. Daniel's face turned a bit red. Bruce's thick eyebrows did a strange dance.

"Now, Sheriff, we have no reason to think Miss Stone did anything to that girl. Of course we didn't report it: There's nothing to report! Elizabeth is a gentle person. Sad, but I've never seen her so much as hurt a fly."

Bruce was a bit agitated. Rightfully so. He was just basically called an idiot and had one of his employees accused of grievous kidnapping. Or worse.

"Look, I understand your stance, Bruce. She's not my first suspect, either. But I've beaten the bushes the last few days trying to find this girl. I've looked in more *obvious* directions and haven't turned up so much as a strand of hair. What's Miss Stone's address?"

"I don't know if we have to give that out, Sheriff."

Daniel looked at his older brother. It was a condescending glance.

"Bruce, stop being ridiculous. I'll get her address off our payroll files. If anything, someone needs to check on her, anyway. I should have gone by there, myself, this week."

Bruce rolled his eyes. Shook his head. The sheriff never blinked as he squinted at the elder realtor. It was a long and awkward moment while Dan opened a computer and scribbled the address down on a Stick-It note.

"Here you go. I don't expect you'll turn anything up except for a woman in her house robe bawling her eyes out and watching old movies. But we want to help. I know the Reynolds family must be devastated. Tell Liza we miss her and to come back to work whenever she's ready."

"Thank you, Daniel. Much appreciated. I hope you are right. Alrighty, I've taken up enough of your time. Dan, Bruce – have a good night."

Bruce all but turned his back as the sheriff made his exit. Dan stood lightly wringing his hands. His face was riddled with a concern and worry that he couldn't hide.

Noted. Something's up and he knows it.

Sheriff Scott got back to his truck. Checked his phone. His wife had just sat down at the restaurant for their dinner. He pictured her sipping a big glass of chardonnay and browsing the menu. She knew exactly what she would order. Always did at every restaurant in town. She was a creature of habit. His rock. Stable as the temple's pillar.

As the old man left the realty office, he made a quick call to the station. Instructed one of his deputies to run an errand: an immediate wellness check at the address of Elizabeth Stone.

Report back ASAP.

Fucking A. Randall Lightner.

But work would have to wait for a while. Probably another wild-goose chase, anyway.

His stomach was growling and he was craving a big piece of grilled meat. His little woman was waiting on him in a cozy booth to celebrate an anniversary of the happiest day of his life.

Hold on to that. Celebrate those days. Appreciate the finite, because Infinity is only a second away.

You'll see.

Part III

The Spring, and The Fall

Eliza

Somewhere in the recesses of her fragile mind, a woman pushed a girl on a swing set. It was spring, and the birds and the flowers and everything was happening. There was no snow and no cold. There was laughter, and "Mommy", and sunshine. Kids ran around to and fro at the perfect park, in her mind. It was an image she kept safe. A perfect day she would always remember.

Eliza Stone had not had much growing up. Her father was one weekend a month; her mom barely got by doing this and that for minimum wage and a little help from the government. Her mom worked hard. She remembered that. She remembered waitress aprons and steel-toe boots and a box factory at night. She remembered being independent from a very young age. She remembered being bullied in school, but doing well. She remembered her teachers and their casual concern. She remembered going to bed almost too hungry every night.

She had wanted more for her daughter. So much more. She had a good thing going. She was rising above her station. She was sober. And then, everything had vanished in an impossible second. The walls of her stage crashed down and the set imploded. The cast scattered to the aisles.

Eliza, alone, was the star of an unsung tragedy. She sank beneath the waves like an ironic Titanic. Her machinists were faulty, as well. All hands beneath the icy Atlantic, and gone.

But, hark, here was her second chance. Watch her reanimate her Lilly. See her dance and draw and sing in a vaulted room on a mountain's top. The child is confused. She knows this a wrong, but she's too tender to know what has transpired. She's afraid, she misses her real mother, but she has not been abused. Quite the opposite. She doesn't like the shots. The lady says they help her sleep. Whenever they hear someone outside, it's always the shots. She's not allowed to go outside or call her parents. She's tired of eating the same things every day.

It's dark in here most of the time.

She doesn't like how this woman laughs. She plays differently than her mom. She gets to draw on the walls, though. They both do, but the crayons are the cheap ones. She doesn't know who Lily is or why this woman wants to be her mom. She doesn't know where she is or how long she will be here.

She is innocent, but she has been taken by a wolf.

She is a babe, but she knows this is wrong.

She misses her mom and dad and puppy.

She really, really wants to go home.

And when she cries at night, Eliza sings to her in a candle-lit room. Her soft voice echoes into the walls, and the melody shatters into a million pieces as it drifts into the sleeping hills beyond.

Sheriff Scott

The aging man rolled out of bed reluctantly. He could smell coffee wafting through his bedroom door, like a familiar incense. He liked setting that timer on the percolator and having a hot cup of black joe waiting for him in the kitchen each morning.

His wife rolled over and muttered something as he stood beside the bed. He wasn't wearing any clothes. Neither was she, for that matter. Their anniversary had gone very well. Despite their advancing years, that fire was still alive. Maybe not as bright. Maybe not as hot. But even embers smolder and burn when stirred.

Carlton checked his phone. Even though it was only five thirty a.m., there was string of texts and several missed calls. One of his men had obviously been trying to reach him. The last text read:

Hey, Sherriff. I know you're probably sleeping and were off-duty tonight. I'm sorry to bother you. Weird shit up there at that apartment you wanted me to check. I don't know what to make of it. I'll hopefully catch you in the morning at the station.

He laid it back down on the bedside table. Got back into bed with the Mrs. Kissed her on the forehead. Kissed her neck. More wrinkled, weathered like a river stone, but just as lovely to him as when they first started dating.

"Anything interesting on that phone? You had that look. . ." she asked, already knowing the answer.

"Yeah. . . I guess. I don't know what to make of it yet. Today's going to be a long day. I can already tell."

She patted him on the arm. Squeezed it gently.

"I'll make you a quick breakfast."

"Thanks, Lou."

"I love you, Carl. I had fun last night."

"I did, too."

"You be safe out there today."

"I always try to be."

"Well, try especially hard. For me."

The world was a dangerous place. They both knew that. Experience was a cruel but useful mentor. They had plenty between them.

Carl Scott, Sheriff of Nowhere, eventually rolled back out of bed. Took a quick shower, dressed in his usual, grabbed the egg sandwich and thermos of coffee his wife handed him. Kissed her goodbye.

He was at the station a half-hour early. Night shift was still on duty, and he had one deputy he needed to speak to with some urgency.

He had a feeling about this one. He had a feeling that circumstances were about to pull him in a direction that he was getting too old to navigate. He could combat age. He could combat bad men and the wicked mundane. He would now have to combat a special Darkness, and there was no light for him to grasp in the gloom he would soon delve.

He knew this somehow in his very bones. He did not know why, and he didn't believe in premonition.

"What did you find over there last night?"

The deputy in question, usually drinking too much coffee for someone bound for bed at this hour, stood uncomfortably in the Sheriff's office. He was rubbing his hands together as if he was cold. The deep khaki of his uniform matched the fluorescent light in the room like a camouflage. He was a bit older than most of the men at this station. Early-thirties. Five-o'clock shadow. Tall and brooding. Nervous energy and sharp. Carl liked him. He was reliable and alert.

"So? You went over there, right?"

"Yes, Sheriff. I did. I know you got my text. I went over there. Knocked on the door, no one answered. I happened to try the doorknob after a few tries and it was open. I wouldn't have gone inside, but you mentioned a wellness check. None of her neighbors were around, so. . . Anyway, I went inside."

"And?"

The younger man looked to the floor. His face was paler than usual. Something had disturbed him. That much was obvious.

"The place was empty, Sheriff. No sign of the Stone woman. Looked like she hadn't been there for a few days. Place was a wreck... Bed was unmade, stripped, all the linens were on the floor. Like she had been sleeping *beside* the bed? There was a bad smell, and her underwear– I mean, her clothes were all over the place like she had just dropped them on the floor every day when she came inside... She had drawn on the walls. Like a little girl's picture, and some kind of dog? There were a lot of them. I don't know. It was weird. Really weird."

The sheriff didn't speak. He just kept staring inquisitively at the man standing before him.

"Lots of pill bottles and empty dime bags... A few needles and some straps. Place was a real mess, Sheriff. That woman... I bet we find her dead in a ditch, somewhere."

Carl might have blinked. Maybe not. Travis cracked his knuckles.

"Oh. And, one more thing. She left her phone. It was on the counter in the kitchen."

The Sheriff perked up. He raised an eyebrow.

"Did you take the phone?"

The deputy reached into his pocket. He looked like a guilty kid handing back a cookie he had stolen from the cookie jar.

"I did, Sheriff. I figured... It might be important. I think I know why you wanted me to make that house call. I know I shouldn't have taken her property, but... Here. The battery is dead, but I'm sure we can find a charger."

The sheriff told him to find a charger and they'd take a quick look. Assuming there was no password to guess at for a million hours. It would be off the record, and they'd return the phone together that afternoon. This was not exactly legal. They both knew it.

"Sheriff?"

"Yeah?"

"Does this have anything to do with that missing girl? The Reynold's kid?"

"It might, Travis. It just might."

The man nodded. He raised the phone in a sort of salute and left to find a charger.

The Sheriff liked that boy. He was good at his job.

The phone screen illuminated with a little robot figure floating amid a myriad of suspended geometric shapes. A less-common telecommunications company logo appeared after the theatrics, and then. . . A password prompt appeared.

The sheriff looked up at the Travis. Raised an eyebrow.

"Four numbers. Go."

Travis shook his head. "Do we know her birthday?"

The sheriff turned to his desk. He had a file on Elizabeth Abigail Stone at the ready. It wasn't thick, but she did have a few priors. More importantly, all her essential information was neatly assembled. Carlton grabbed it and opened the manila folder. Paused briefly. It only took a second.

"Try 3-3-8-7."

Travis typed the digits with his thumb. Shook his head to the negative.

"Or 0-3-0-3?"

The same response.

"Sheriff, we don't have too many attempts, I don't think. These things usually lock for a while after a few tries."

The sheriff nodded as if to say, *I know how phones work.*

He flipped through a few more pages. Found what he was looking for quickly.

"Try 1-0-1-3."

Travis smiled. Nodded affirmatively at the sheriff.

"Well, that was easy enough. Nice work, Sheriff."

"The daughter's birthday."

"All right, what are we looking for on here?"

"Why don't you comb through her text messages, emails. I don't know, Travis. See if you can get on her social media or whatever."

"Got it. Give me a little while."

A little while had passed. During that brief spell, Carl had posted a patrol car at Eliza's apartment complex. Just to be sure they were there to greet her in case she came home. He had called the Reynold's family to give them his promised daily update. They were utterly beside themselves and bordering on resigned defeat.

Understandable.

He had heard they had even hired some clown private investigator in their desperation. A few token Federal agents had been combing the woods around their home and the lake in the few days that had passed. The local PD and Carl's outfit had to bring them in per protocol, but the case was still resting largely on his head. This was a county deal, therefore it remained his crime to solve.

That particular burden, unless you have lived it, is hard to wrap your head around. It kept you up nights. Old-dog cops didn't often live to old-dog ages. The stress was simply too high. Especially with this. No one wanted to touch a missing child case. Even these particular Feds, who weren't bad guys. But Carl thought they were wasting their time out there in the woods with their borrowed dogs and their fancy forensic team.

They simply couldn't believe that the girl had just. . . *vanished.* There was no trace. She might as well have been spirited away by some Irving-esque horseman or a witch in the night.

Carl pondered on that. Scratched his stubble. Tugged at his collar. And then Travis reappeared. Animated, and not just from the coffee. Their receptionist was right at his heels, pointing at the phone with her hot pink nails.

"Holy hell, Sheriff. Look at this!"

Travis came around his desk. Stood way too close. He set the phone down and tapped its screen frantically.

It was a picture of a young girl. She was about to go down a slide at a playground. A woman knelt at the bottom with arms outstretched. Her long, dark hair looked impeccable from behind. The kid at the top looked happy. Huge grin on her face. The sky above was crowded with clouds. A slate-gray overhang looming above the image. Between the photographer and the subjects, a chain link fence. An outsider looking in to a life she didn't possess. It was a distant shot. Zoomed all the way in to see everything she might see.

Travis flipped his thumb across the screen. Then he did it again. And again. And again.

Each scene in this mad flip-book depicted one commonality: Brittany Reynolds.

There she was walking out of school. There she was at her little league-soccer practice. There she was walking into a restaurant with her mom and dad. Sitting on a church's steps. Smiling. Blonde curls shining.

And then, there she was in her own backyard. Playing alone. From a distance.

Sheriff Scott stood from his chair. His mouth was slightly agape. He saw stars.

Travis took a few steps back. The air was palpable. His heart, too, was racing. The receptionist bit at her long nails nervously.

"Call the Feds. We might need them. Kate? Call the PD. We need everyone in on this."

They both nodded and scattered.

Carl picked up his own phone. He needed two things. First, he needed a warrant for the immediate arrest of Eliza

Stone. Second, he needed to get ahold of that certain set of brothers who owned Mountain Realty.

Daniel Spencer

It was early. No one else was inside the Mountain Realty office. Just Daniel and Bruce Spencer. They didn't always get along. They fought like– well, *brothers*.

They were practically whispering, despite their solitude. One of them had lit a Duraflame log in the wrap-around stack stone fireplace. It dismally awaited company as its lonely flame started to flicker anemically.

"Damn it, Bruce. I told you to stop being so hard on her. You can't talk like that to people, especially not *her*."

"This is a business, Dan. We're not a charity house. The woman needs help. Even you agree. She hasn't been to that therapist we recommended in God knows how long. She barely comes into the office anymore. I've told you about all the complaints we've received. . . And now – don't interrupt me – the fucking cops are coming in here like *we've* done something wrong!"

Bruce had his finger directed at Dan's chest like a dagger. Dan stood his ground.

"All right, fine. I'll find her. I take responsibility. I'm sure she's holed-up somewhere sleeping one off. She has access to basically all of our properties. . . And one of our cars. I have no idea where she might have gone, but I guess

I'll work a miracle so we can at least tell the sheriff she's alive and well. And alone."

"You do that. I have too much actual work to do to go play hide-and-seek with Eliza Stone. If you do find her, she's fired. This is ridiculous. I am beyond fed up with her."

Daniel sighed. Took a deep breath. He didn't know where to begin, but he was too proud to ask Bruce for any more help. Mountain Realty had almost one-hundred individual properties in the county. He walked over to his desk and slumped into the chair. Bruce did the same across the office.

Daniel pulled up his computer. Got out his notepad. Process of elimination. They knew she wasn't home. They had called countless times and he had gone by there every day for a week. He even walked inside at one point. The door was unlocked. What he saw there disturbed him, but Bruce didn't need to know anything about that.

He mentally took note of all the occupied apartments, condos, and homes they had available. Then – and fortunately there weren't all that many – he started listing unoccupied spaces that Eliza might have wandered off to for some serious alone time.

Why would she leave her home? What would she possibly be doing at one of their places? Bruce may be right. She could be dead in a ditch for all they knew. Or, and maybe worse than that, what if the sheriff was remotely right about that Reynolds kid? Was Eliza capable of that?

Daniel scribbled a few addresses down on his note pad, realized he had all this information available on his phone, and stopped his rapid writing.

Taking the car keys off his desk, he stood to leave. Donned his coat from the hook. He was always impeccably dressed, and almost looked the part of the private eye in his present attire. Missing persons were not his specialty. Far from it. He was simply concerned for a friend in need. Daniel Spencer always tried to see the best in people. He knew his optimism was slowing drying, like a dying creek bed, but he was willing to do what he could for someone who might need his help.

He briefly made eye contact with Bruce as he walked out the door. Both men were equally pissed at each other. Neither said a word as the door opened and then closed just as quickly with its usual creaks and clamor.

He was ultimately looking for that vehicle. Subaru Forester with the Mountain Realty logo and a reasonably well-crafted forest scene emblazoned all over the damn thing. Their agents were encouraged to take one of the cars out when showing properties, and he didn't mind if they took them around town otherwise, either. It was great advertisement. Even Bruce agreed.

These cars were also very easy to spot. Every apartment or resort complex Dan visited on his quest to find Eliza didn't have to be overly tedious. He had no intention of going door to door. He just needed to study the parking lots.

He just needed to find that car.

Unless, of course, she was driving her own? What was it? Some old gray beater? *I don't even know... Jesus. This is all too much.*

After a late-morning stop at one of the local coffee shops for a latte and a glazed donut, Dan sat with the heat running in his always-clean, white-pearl Mercedes A-Class. He was deep in thought as Duran Duran ruminated on a Monday new moon through his top-class stereo system. He tapped the steering wheel in time with the beat as he checked-off where he had been so far and where he still needed to go. He had basically hit all the spots in town. Now, it was time to venture out to the ski resorts.

If she wanted to be alone, she would go out there, for sure. *Somewhere near the top, I bet.*

As the caffeine and the New Wave radio stirred his molecules, he remembered a conversation he had one time with Eliza. It was after they had finished a showing together. It had been a done deal. They were arm in arm skipping into the parking lot after the clients had left. She was over the moon for the commission. Rich old couple from Atlanta wanting to retire in the mountains. Signed and sealed.

He remembered Eliza in that moment. Smiling. Carefree – or almost. Laughing with him as the spring cherry blossoms blew around like snowflakes in the crisp air.

They high-fived. They hugged. Eliza, knowing Dan well enough, kissed him on his cheek. They were friends. He couldn't help it. He knew he should keep a degree of separation with an employee, but he did care for her. He wanted her to always be as happy as she was in that moment. It was not meant to be, of course, but in that temporary snapshot of a second, she was positively brilliant.

She had said, "Dan. I swear to God, I'm going to live up here someday. I'm going to get the biggest damn house or condo or whatever I can afford, and I'm going to live on this mountain. As high up as I can get. I want to touch the clouds and look down on every little thing."

She pretended to soar like a bird in flight. He laughed. Encouraged her. She was serious, and he hoped that she would soon do just that.

But, less than a year later, Eliza Stone had been derailed by fate. Which brought Dan back to his current scavenger hunt. And a moral question that had been gnawing at him for several days. Biting his heels like an angry dog. Keeping him up at night.

Was Eliza capable of taking someone's child? No. . . Right? Surely not. The police were always wrong.

Not the Eliza he had once known. But maybe that woman was gone? Maybe she had succumbed to the waves and the weight of her personal anchor. Maybe she was lost, and maybe someone else was piloting her tiny ship?

Only one way to find out.

He put his latte back in the cup holder. He turned down the radio. The Smiths were not his jam, anyway. He backed his sleek car out of the parking lot and started driving up and up to the highest points in the county. The top of the world in these Southern States. As high as you could get, he drove.

Eliza Stone

The knock at the door echoed like a shot in the quiet space. Eliza jumped at the sudden sound. The girl was having a peanut-butter sandwich on stale bread in the kitchen and dropped it on her plate with a start, when the *thud thud thud* came unexpectedly. Their eyes locked, both unblinking. Brittany's gaze held an animal quality engulfed with both fear and excitement. Eliza's, meanwhile, flashed with rabid panic.

Who the hell is that?

As Eliza instinctively turned towards the knock at the door, Brittany hopped down from her bar stool like a cat leaving a perch. Eliza turned back just as quickly. Like a flash, she had Brittany by the collar of her T-shirt. A vein bulged in her tense neck, and she spat when she spoke. Her too long and dirty fingernail was less than an inch from the girl's face.

"Lily, don't you move a muscle. . . Not a sound, do you understand? I will take all of your toys away and make you sleep in the closet for a week. Not. . . A. . . Sound."

She led the girl roughly towards the pantry, opened the door, and pushed her inside. She had to crouch below the first shelf and whimpered like a neglected puppy when the door closed, leaving her in the dark.

Like all children, Brittany was afraid of the dark. Adults don't outgrow that fear, they just acclimatize to the absence of light. Adult minds won't allow themselves to wander into the corners and shadows where a child's mind will venture. Yet we all know, even as adults, that the dark can be very frightening.

Eliza walked cautiously through the kitchen into the vaulted living room of the large condo. The door was still yards away, and it might as well have been miles. When she made it to the small hallway that led to the door, she paused. Leaned against the wall despite the urgent, angered, knocks at the door. Its generic frame looked like a stoic gate to Hell, or perhaps a way out of the Abyss. The only way out of a suffocating pit was through: this was a fact she knew well. And, probably, there was in fact no way out of this at all. Not now, nor had there ever been.

Through the peephole, a man in an out-of-fashion but once expensive suit stood on the mat in front of her reverse-telescope vantage. It was her boss. Well, one of them. Before she could decide what to do, he reached into his overcoat for a set of master keys. He shuffled through them, found the one he needed, and reached towards the door's lock.

Eliza, panicked, instinctively opened the door before his key even made contact.

Shit...

"Dan. Hey."

He was in no mood for small talk. He pushed past her almost immediately. The door closed lazily behind them as he entered the hall. He had a look in his eye like she had never seen before. He was always so nice to her.

"Dan, I–"

"Stop. Just don't, Eliza. I mean, what the fuck? Really? How bad do you want to lose your job?"

Eliza was silent. She hadn't spoken to another adult in weeks.

Dan turned to face her, once he was squarely in the living room. He had been studying the floor, and the walls, now seemingly taken aback by every nuance of the woman's appearance. He had the look of a hawk narrowing its eyes at the sight of some foreign prey. Eliza, in another life, would have been made self-conscious by his gaze. But now, in her current state, there was next to nothing that would move her in that regard. She stood completely still, and eventually made eye contact with him.

Eliza's unwashed and unkempt hair hung in her face, all but concealing an off-putting pallor and too-dark eyes. The scar from the accident was unconcealed by any make-up and was clearer than ever. Her gray bathrobe had not been washed, and its neck hung loosely around her exposed collar bones. She wore nothing but underwear beneath its loose contour, and those were also unremarkable. Dan couldn't help but notice her untended bare feet, and unshaven legs beneath the bottom cusp of the dingy robe. And, she had this *smell*. . . Like a denned animal mixed with a strong but imprecise body odor.

"Eliza. . . I know you have. . . Been through a really tough time. But this. . . I mean, look at yourself. My god. You don't look, or *smell*, good at all, Eliza. What in the world are you doing up here, really? We're going to get you some help. Let me help you get some things together, and we'll just head down. . ."

Just then, a noise came from the kitchen. It was quiet, but just loud enough to get Dan's attention. A bump against the pantry door, and what sounded like a muffled whimper.

"What was that?"

Eliza couldn't respond. More rustling in the pantry, and then some very real crying.

"Eliza. . . Is there someone else in here with us? You just need to say yes or no, okay? We're going to get you some help, like I said, so you need to start talking. I can help you. Whatever it is."

Dan's voice was surprisingly calm. Even he was surprised at his composure. He had no idea who was in that kitchen pantry, but his intentions were sincere. He cared about Eliza and felt truly sorry for what had happened to her daughter. But, seeing her like this. . . This was not appropriate. Something was terribly wrong. Her mind, her movements, the whole thing just wasn't right. She was a broken toy, and he deeply hoped that she hadn't brought someone else into her private Hell up here on the side of a God-forsaken mountain.

Dan turned towards the kitchen. Without speaking, Eliza jumped in front of him. She implored him to stop in mumbled pleas and then rabidly pitched screams as he forced ahead. She pulled at his clothes and tried to grab his hands.

"Stop. You need to calm down. I mean it. . ."

Dan had his hands on Eliza's shoulders as she pushed against him with everything she had. For someone who was bordering on malnourishment and weighed practically half of what he did, she had some uncanny strength. Finally, when it was apparent that a *child* was crying in the kitchen pantry, Dan had to use more force. He tossed Eliza aside and she stumbled off balance into the closest wall, barely breaking her fall.

On the end table beside her, there was a heavy, ornate vase. Furnished apartment standard décor. Dan took two determined steps towards the kitchen entrance, but never fully crossed the threshold. Eliza, expelling a scream that bordered on banshee fervor, lifted the vase overhead and closed the few feet between them before Dan could respond.

When she hit him, the vase didn't break. It just made a dull noise with no echo. Not even off the vaulted ceilings.

There was a moment of punctuated silence as the realtor realized what had happened. His eyes were blank, his face grew instantly pale, and he shuddered like a man stepping out into the cold from the warmth of an inviting hearthside.

"She's *mine*! That is *my* daughter!"

Eliza's words echoed off the ceilings, but Dan didn't register. There was a concert of church bells and emergency sirens ringing between his ears that blocked all sound. His vision was blurred, and he felt more drunk than after his brother's fiftieth birthday party, a few years back. Walking down the street back to his quaint house on Laurel Lane with four gin martinis coursing through his bloodstream. The room was literally spinning, and an unwashed, black-haired figure was at the epicenter of his concussion.

Eliza's mouth moved repeatedly. She looked like a Fury. There was no logic in her movements. When she swung the vase a second time, Dan felt the corners of his impaired vision grow dark. He could taste copper in his mouth. The opposite wall looked both impossibly close and a million miles away as he tried to mobilize his limbs away from his attacker.

The glass coffee table, which he had ordered for all of these condominiums from a designer in High Point, was the last thing he remembered as his limp body tumbled forward. They cost $879 a piece: a splurge that his brother strongly disapproved of at the time. The thick-layered glass emanated a green hue, and the wrought-iron frame with its delicate swivels had further driven the price. Both materials greeted his head with the same shock that they had met Mountain Realty's budget. It was a fine centerpiece, and a shame to shatter under his relaxed weight.

Blinking slowly on the floor, Dan thought the blood pooling before him looked like a fine wine staining his hand-picked rug. The shards of glass glistened like a fabulous bouquet of diamonds in the tilted sunlight, and he felt no pain.

All was well in his dissolving mind as Eliza struck him twice more with the vase. She fell to the floor in a heap beside him when it was all finished. Her heavy breaths and sweat betrayed any sense of readiness for what she had just done. Her hands shook uncontrollably, and she felt ill. Despite the drugs, despite the medication, she had never felt any moment more strongly in her life. Not even when the news of Lily passing began to hit home.

All was in slow motion, instantly imprinting into her memory. She would remember the curtains blocking the feeble sunlight from entering the room. She would remember the vague smell of garbage coming from the kitchen. And she would remember the kid screaming in the pantry.

"I'm coming, baby! It's okay. It's all okay now. Don't open the door. . . Mommy is coming right now."

She spoke in sputtered gasps. She was unsure of everything but knew that she had to get rid of this burden quickly. No daughter of hers would have to process a sight such as this. Her mind was reeling. Her heart rate had never been higher. Adrenaline opened her veins like a big snort of powder.

The rug. . . The guest room. . . Easy fix. Roll him up and get him out of the way.

It took less than five minutes for Eliza to dispose of Dan Spencer in the downstairs guest bedroom. Door closed. Rug and body barely through the threshold to block it from opening, after she wrestled with the positioning.

Good. It was done. Besides the rush, she felt no apology or remorse for her actions. Dan had been good to her, but he should have left her alone. He had no business coming all the way up here to snoop or interfere.

Back in the kitchen, she opened the pantry door to find the little girl crying in a heap. Her fingers were plugged in her ears and she was screaming.

Eliza had an injection prepared for her. This would settle her down. She needed to sleep this one off, and Eliza needed to stop the hammer pounding between her ears.

In the guest bedroom, Daniel Spencer's blood stained the interior of the rug like spilled ink across a blank page. All that he had ever known floated briefly in the ether, passed through the bay window, and vaporized into the early spring air above the mountains and below the sky.

Daniel Spencer, and all that he ever would be, was simply *gone*.

No bugles, no drums, and Eliza's mind rattled and banged like all the clamor in the deepest layer of Hell. Infinite and black, even the bay windows could shed no light on the scene she directed on the stage of her creation.

Elsa

She had fallen asleep reading *Lord of the Flies*. It was violent, and she wasn't sure if she liked it or fully agreed with its premise.

Elsa Privette still tried to believe that people were ultimately good inside. This was hard to keep in faith, but she tried. Her grandmother would have insisted.

When Piggy got killed and the conch shell shattered, Elsa felt almost ill. She didn't like that. She had seen a bit of herself in Piggy, and his premature demise wasn't comforting in the least.

She amended her thoughts just as she was turning out the light.

People are probably good. At least when they are young. But their experiences can make them bad. Or, at least, both good and bad. Who knows?

And, avoid groups. Groups always. . . what's the word? Factionate. When they divide, people always fought. They would try to hurt each other for no real reason. They would probably be friends if not for the pull of the "group" or whatever their faction presumably represented.

With that, Elsa clicked the lamp and she was suddenly shrouded in familiar darkness. Sleep came quickly for her. Elsa's mind often wandered, but not when she was tired. Sleep was a welcome respite.

Unless she dreamed a *certain way*. And then, her dreams marauded through her slumber like a consumptive hoard. They often left her breathless and stressed. She knew those dreams well. Those were the ones that might come true.

Unfortunately, that night she dreamed a *certain way*.

Banner Lake. Shrouded in mist and fog. Almost dark, but she could still see.

She was standing on the bank of the lake. Or what looked like the lake. There was a canoe or ferry in front of her. Its pilot was robed and had his back to her. He waited in the gloom, and she boarded his craft with no reluctancy. It seemed what she was required to do.

The silent ferryman pushed away from the loamy soil with a long, black oar. Elsa took her seat behind him as they drifted across the dark lake.

Moonlight revealed the buried town below. She knew it was there, but she had never seen it. In her dream, Elsa could make out the shape of little buildings and stores and houses lost beneath the placid surface. In a dream within the dream, she envisioned the townspeople waving up to her. Their skin was blue-gray and they were nothing more than lost shades in the murky depths. Yet, they still waved, desperate for contact and connection like all the rest of us.

Their drowning done, all they had left was to wave. Elsa did not reciprocate in her dream. She would have in real life, but she, too, was different in this ancient and haunted place.

Older, colder, a friend of the darkness.

On, the ferryman took her. And then the scene was different. Cavernous and darker still.

A river, no longer a lake, and on its shore lay the littered bodies of the long-dead and the newly passed. They, too, were blue-gray, but they did not wave. No one greeted her in this special vision of Hell.

On their eyes, spectral golden coins kept the lids shut tight. A tax for the ferryman, but he had no use for coin nor gold nor light, so far up stream. Those things no longer mattered.

He rowed to shore and bid Elsa depart on the bank, amongst the dead. He gifted her two gold coins and motioned for her to take her place among the Lost. She did as she was told. The earth was cold and damp beneath her frail body as she lay down to rest. She applied the coins over her crystal-blue eyes, and a profound warmth overtook her. She knew this was the end, but then the eyelid movies began to dance before her like puppets performing in a shadow box.

She saw her house. Her mom. Waving goodbye without a kiss or a word. Thunder. Lightning. A calendar on the wall. A date in red marker. Clear as day. A feeling of helplessness like she had never felt before. A deep pain, and then she was absorbed into nothingness. All was gone. She was struck dumb and blind and deaf all at once.

But Elsa Privette wasn't ready to die. She still had things to do. In a fit, she removed the coins from her eyes. She couldn't wake herself from this awful dream, although she was rapidly becoming aware that she roamed in that other place hidden between her ears.

She sat up with a start, still on the shore of a blue-gray river. Still in the shadows. To her right, she suddenly recognized who lay beside her. There could be no doubt. Her sister lay naked on the bank, like all the rest of the blissfully dead. Sleeping, but not sleeping. Coins on her eyes. Cold as the icy water that careened before them.

And then she heard the laughter. The ferryman was still there. Watching and waiting. He finally turned on his ornate craft to face her and stepped from boat to shore. Joining the dead. Haunting amongst them. He removed his hood and shroud. It was a man. He smelled like liquor and aftershave. She could recognize his face. Fear overtook her. Her heart exploded within her chest.

And just as he reached for her, fighting with everything in her fragile frame, Elsa Privette awoke in her own familiar bed.

Her T-shirt was soaked in sweat. Her unruly hair hung in her eyes. She rocked back and forth in her night-light glow with quiet whimpers. Nothing else in the house moved.

Her dream, what she had seen, she knew it was a premonition of things to come. The ones she remembered almost always came true. She was certain of this one more than any other she had ever had. She had been having similar ones the last few weeks, but this one was the most powerful.

The most vivid dream she had ever endured.

Part of her young and innocent self still lingered in that Hades of her dreamworld. Her sister's broken and dead body resting on the coal-black bank. Randall's laughter echoing off the cavernous walls. Everything closing in around her. Claustrophobic and cold. No mother to save her. No grandmother to cry on her shoulder. The loneliest feeling she had ever felt.

She finally stopped sobbing and gathered her thoughts. She had to tell someone. Someone would believe her.

Only one person came to mind.

He might believe her. He might be able to help her.

Mr. Wilder had to know about her dream. His was the only face that came to mind. She prayed to it in the dark as she fought the pull of sleep.

If she didn't sleep, she couldn't dream. If she didn't dream, then nothing bad would come true.

Rylan

Lacy and I were watching a movie. It was called *A Ghost Story*, and I was really enjoying it. She was mostly exploring her phone, but that was okay. We were snuggled up on the couch. Sharing a whisky and a big cookie from the bakery. My mind was unraveling like the layered dimensions of the film, and I hoped time was indeed nonlinear, like in its plot.

I could live in and visit and explore this moment for a long time. Maybe forever. Her warm skin, the smell of her hair, the furrow of her brow. Every freckle, every pore of her skin, the twinkle in her emerald eyes was mine in that instant. On a cheap but comfortable couch. In an inexpensive yet cozy condo wrapped in the Mother's hills and captured in a snapshot that would haunt me and have me for years to come.

But then, she spoke. And turned to face me on the narrow surface of the couch. A concerned look appeared on her face like a mask.

"Pause that for a minute."

I obliged. She was staring at her phone screen. I could see the Tanawah News 5 logo on its surface illuminated in Blue light.

"What's up?"

"So, you heard about that kidnapping right? The little girl? Brittany Reynolds."

"Yes. We've talked about it."

"Well, they originally thought it was some weird ass pervert who took her or whatever. Now, they're thinking it's actually a *woman* who kidnapped her. Some realtor. Local chick, too. Apparently she lost her daughter in a car accident last winter, and the cops have reason to believe she was nuts enough to literally steal this little girl from her own backyard."

"Huh. Wow. Weird."

"That's it? That's all you have to say? 'Huh, wow, weird'?"

"Lacy, I mean, I'm trying to–"

"This doesn't bother you? Or at least *interest* you?"

"Yes. I am very worried about the girl. But I'm sure everything will work out fine."

"Really?"

She was getting pretty riled-up. I was feeling pretty sleepy. I didn't want to argue about something completely out of my control.

"No, you're right. I really do want to hear about this. It's awful."

"Yes. Obviously."

She was holding the phone screen very close to my face. Emphatically. A vaguely familiar face caught my eye on its pixelated surface. Right there under the News 5 header.

"Wait a minute. That was. . . That's the woman who rented my apartment! Holy shit!"

"This Elizabeth Stone person?"

"Yeah. She goes by Eliza. I knew there was something odd about her. Only met her once or twice. Her eyes. . . Demeanor. You know. Weird."

"Well, she's apparently missing. No one's seen her for a while. She hasn't been to work, and those brothers at Mountain Realty are a little concerned for *her* safety. They don't think she's taken anyone's kid. They think she might have fallen off the wagon or whatever. Here. Just read the damn article. There's a video interview, too."

I obliged. We read the words together and watched one of the Spencer brother's earnestly report that Eliza Stone was a good person who had just been through a lot. Rough life. The daughter who died and all that. I blinked slowly, watching the images unfold. I didn't know what to believe. I personally still thought some redneck perv had stolen her away. I didn't expect a happy ending and had to suppress the thought of 'where the hell were her parents when she was taken?'

I also knew that sometimes things were stranger than they seemed. More layered, deeper, and darker. I thought of another little girl I knew as I finished the news report and began to converse again with Lacy.

Some things couldn't be helped. Sex offenders and modern witches kidnapping kids by twilight.

But some things *could* be helped. Kids who could speak up and tell you that all was not well. Look you right in the eye. Ask for help. Beg for someone to care.

Kids just like Elsa Privette.

I had all but washed my hands of her situation after the winter break. That night at the gas station, right before Christmas, as soon as we got to my uncle's house, I fired-off an email to the counselor and texted Tony directly. I had CC'd Lacy as witness, just in case my opinion of things had *jumped to conclusions* as I had been told before.

I told them both everything we saw that night. I left out the tense details of my exchange with Randall, but did mention his *threatening* demeanor to both Lacy and me. I had been very clear that I felt Elsa and her sister were not safe. They were very much in danger of more than a few bumps and bruises around that maniac.

Tony's response: "I'll look into after the break. Thx."

Counselor Kathy's response: "Ho ho ho! I'm away for Christmas Break, but will respond to your email after Santa comes to visit."

There had been no response and no follow-up. I felt almost self-conscious about bringing the whole thing up to them. I knew that Lacy was right. Her view on compassion and empathy. They had to be more than clumsily offered sentiments. The other side of that so-called empathy was someone's reality. It was real life.

And that was often stranger than imagination. Odder than make-believe.

Surreal.

At lunch the next day, I sat with my co-teachers at our round, teacher table. It was frequently trespassed by kids needing to use the restroom, or needing an extra quarter for ice cream, or just wanting to stand awkwardly while I ate my customary sandwich and chips. They always came up to me first, as I was the one most likely to acquiesce to whatever request may came down the line. It appeared hyper-generous, but in reality I knew that it was the fastest way to regain peace and quiet.

I looked over at my class's table a few times during our twenty-five minute lunch period. My kids were always pretty well-behaved. My co-teachers were talking about what would be on their Easter menus, and I even contributed with a remembered recipe for an intricate deviled egg, to appear more social than I was liable to be. I complained about them a lot. Lots of eye-rolling and telling Lacythat I couldn't relate to their nineteen-kids-a-piece and church-three-times-a-week personalities. But, truth was, they were always nice to me. They had helped me adjust to a new school with grace. They were all good women.

I was the asshole, but they never treated me like that.

I looked over each of them quickly. They could have been sisters. All a little heavy. All a little red-faced. All very cheery and tired at the same time. They were like Dickensian carolers in the Scrooge piece. Well-meaning and perfectly harmless. Then, I felt eyes on me in return. I glanced across the noisy cafeteria and eventually caught a glance. Elsa Privette, staring a hole in me. Sitting about as alone as a kid could sit at the end of one of the long tables. Isolated and quietly sad. Swinging her feet beneath the table. Her dirty Converse sneakers rocking like a pendulum beneath her frail body.

She hadn't been in first period that morning. Rare for her. She was definitely looking right at me. And then I saw it. The side of her face bruised and scraped. Holy shit. That was a bad black eye. I could read her eyes as she stared at me. I felt guilty and dirty for some reason. She looked like she was trying to communicate to me through some primal means. Telepathic. An arrow shot from her kaleidoscopic blue eyes.

I had to look away.

"Hey, Cindy. What's up with Elsa? Look at her eye. She wasn't in first period this morning?"

I nudged the nearest Dickensian extra sitting beside me with my elbow. She put down her soup spoon for a moment after a hearty bite of microwaved Progresso with crushed Saltines. Glanced over at the elfin creature swinging her feet. Elsa dropped her head and her face turned red as soon as she deciphered that we were talking about her.

Cindy wiped her mouth neatly with a too-thin napkin.

"Ry, I tell you. They need to do something about that. That's about the fourth time I've seen a bruise on that child. Plain turns my stomach."

"Right? I've talked to whatshername and Tony about it. Nothing. Nothing has changed. Last fall, she had an obvious handprint on her arm and—"

One of the other teachers interrupted me.

"Ya'll, I'm not sayin' that we should call CPS or anything, but something has gotta give. Ever since that poor girl's grandmom died, she hasn't had a prayer. Her mom's trash. Useless. That stepdad is abusive, and worse – a drunk. And her sister, who I taught for three years, is heading down the wrong path. And that little girl tries so hard in school and somehow manages to keep it together. She has a hundred in my class. Literally. A hundred."

We all nodded. Elsa caught my eye again. She was staring a hole through me and me alone.

What is it with that girl? Why me?

Regardless of the *why*, Elsa Privette trusted me for some reason. That was clear. Some ethereal connection, an unseen bond that I couldn't decipher.

And a few hours later, during my long-awaited planning period where I had a moment's quiet, there was a gentle knock on the door. I didn't even need to look up from my computer. I knew who it was, and she came right inside without any expressed permission.

Her T-shirt of the day had a spattering of bleach stain on its black front and too-long sleeves. It advertised a local construction company where some relative of hers must have worked at some point. Her jeans looked reasonably new, but the Converse were definitely hand-me-downs from either the sister or the Goodwill. She wasn't smiling as she approached my desk. I felt no need to make small talk but did rise to pull her up a chair in front of my desk.

She sat without a word. Moved her wild hair back over her ear so I could clearly see the bruised side of her face. She gave me a look that was not timid. Nor was it youthful. It was a look of being very tired, and she suddenly had the intensity of an angered woman three times her age.

"Have you talked to the counselor about this?" I asked, my voice low. Technically, we should not have been having this conversation at all.

"She was busy when I went by the office this morning. I didn't get to talk to her."

"Have you talked to anyone else about your face?"

"No."

"What happened?"

She shook her head no, as if I was starting to cross a line.

"Elsa, look at me. I can't help you if you just sit there and shake your head. Was it your step-dad? Your mom? Someone else?"

"He's not my step-dad."

"I know that, but you know who I mean. Randall. Did he hit you?"

"He pushed me out of a bar stool. I fell backwards and hit the floor. He hurt my sister worse. I think her nose might be broken."

"Jesus. Elsa, you have to tell–"

"I'm telling *you*, Mr. Wilder. I don't trust many people. People aren't always nice to me. Even teachers. They give me weird looks. I understand *why* sometimes. I know I'm not the most *normal* kid, but I don't care. For whatever reason, I trust you. And I have something else to tell you, too."

"What's that?"

"You know that I sometimes have dreams? Things that tend to come true when I have the same dream a lot. Or one that's really vivid."

I ran a hand through my hair. Trying not to look frustrated at this sudden dump of bad news being poured onto my waiting plate.

I don't get paid enough for this...

I nodded in spite of myself.

"I have had these dreams lately. I'm usually standing in our kitchen. There is a bad storm outside. Like, really bad. I can hear this whir and roar right outside our house. The walls rattle like they may cave in at any minute. Like a tornado, but I know we don't usually have tornados in the mountains. It's also very dark.

"On the wall, I see our calendar with a date on there, circled in red. I can see it very clearly. I can also see our clock. No hands are moving, like it's frozen in place. I know that something really bad is happening behind me, but I feel frozen. Like I can't turn around. When I wake-up, I'm always shaking. My hands, and I feel very cold. But, I always think of two people when I wake up. Very clearly. One is my sister, and I can't *feel* her anymore. You know what I mean? It scares me really badly. I just know something awful has happened to her, but I never know exactly what because I always freeze in the dream. I usually go check on her in her room. To make sure she's okay. And the other person. . . I know how this sounds, Mr. Wilder. . . But the other person is always you. Like I'm *supposed* to tell you about this dream. So, I just did."

I paused for a long minute. I had no idea what this little creature was talking about. She believed whatever it was. Whatever dream she kept having, and somehow she thought that I was a part of it. I thought about the Cherokee boy and his grandmother. I thought about what she had said about her grandmother. I thought about that candle before Christmas. I don't think I believed in any of it, but I certainly believed that she did.

"Elsa, I don't know what you want me to say. I mean, I'm sure this is just a dream. I can tell that you're really worried, and I do want to help you. I'm going straight to the office in just a minute. I'm going to try to get you some help."

"Help? You're going to try to get me some help, Mr Wilder?"

She had a wild look in her eye. She laughed to herself. I felt embarrassed in her presence.

"People always *say* they want to help, but no one ever really does. You know something? I thought you might be different. I thought you might understand that I don't have much at home. I don't have good parents. I don't have anyone to fall back on, at all. That man, Randy – he's not the worst thing out there. I have had other dreams that were far worse. There's this woman in them, and. . . Well, never mind. What I'm trying to say is that I hope you won't let me down. I don't think you will, in the end. I don't expect anything of you, but I hope that I can be surprised. Just once. If it gets really bad, I hope someone will surprise me one day."

I was looking at the floor as she spoke. My not-especially-tall frame towering over her diminutive one. I glanced back at her. Her gaze never shifted. She motioned for me to lean close. She whispered something in my ear. It was a date. It was not far away. She whispered a time. It was not especially late, but late enough to be fully dark. I got goosebumps. I did not know why.

Without a goodbye, without her customary politeness, she left after she whispered her vague clue. Her vaporous truth. I felt empty. I felt angry. And I felt helpless. Frozen like the girl in a dream that I did not fully believe or understand.

I gathered myself. It took a long while. Thought about my next steps. Decided that I was pretty pissed, and that was often more than enough to move me out of whatever inertia life threw my way.

A part of me considered storming down to the counselor's office with Tony in tow and causing a scene. Slamming doors and raising voices and really letting her know what a pathetic job I thought she was doing at keeping these kids safe. That would be one way to handle this, but I knew deep down that me raising hell and embarrassing myself in the main office would ultimately do no good.

This system is badly broken. I had known this for some time. Shattered like stained glass sparkling in a dim light. Nothing more than a mirage to bind us from action. We trip over ourselves and our policies on a wrinkled rug of apathy. Despite our best intentions as teachers, and parents, and policemen, and so-called citizens, we only *think* we want to help. When it comes right down to it, like in that moment, I, too, felt frozen in place, like all good intentions suspended in the human ether.

I was a real *hero*. Let me tell you. Unless I chose to act on this myself, I was just as immaterial and feckless as the counselor sitting in a cushy chair filing her nails and wondering what's for dinner.

I didn't know if I had that kind of courage. The courage to actually do something for that elfin little girl. I doubted it, but maybe courage, too, is just phony posturing. Everything is simply situational. An occasion to either act or be still.

I did not know what to do. My years on the Earth were not yet vast enough to prepare me for this kind of decision.

An hour later, I was flying down the road at a breakneck pace. Running myself into the ground. I was apparently only capable of fighting with myself. Fighting with a coward. Fighting with the mirage of a man.

Shadow-boxing in a dark room.

―

"Uncle Ray, can I ask you something?"

It was just us two. Out on his back porch, overlooking the river. The trees hung with a spring-green that was hypnotically beautiful, after long months of their absence. Lost in the snow, but now renewed.

Ray sat on one side of a picnic table and I sat on a nearby rocker. He had brought some papers out to grade, just as I was liable to do at this time of evening. They fluttered gently in the almost-warm breeze. Windchimes kissed and separated in their constant dance, somewhere in the distance. It was a perfect night, and it was a perfect place to speak with an older man with whom I had so much in common.

We both sipped his good whiskey. A bourbon tonight, as it was getting too warm to fully enjoy his usual Scotch. I felt warm and relaxed, despite my racing mind and stressed countenance. I sat in such paradox as he glanced my way and capped his red pen.

He took a deep sigh. Raised his eyebrows dramatically.

"This is some bad writing, Ry. Jesus, I don't know how some of these kids passed high school."

"I'm sure."

"What did you want to ask me?"

His voice was soft and calm as always. It was just what I needed. Even more than Lacy. Even more than being alone.

"It's a long story, but I guess I'll get right to the point."

"We have all the time in the world if you want to divulge, young sir."

I chuckled. He smiled at me.

"No, it's probably better that I don't. I just wanted to ask... Well, have you ever been in position where you've been asked to help someone, but you didn't really know *how* to help? Like, maybe with a student or something. Where there was an obvious degree of separation between your lives, and that creates a natural boundary. Am I making any sense?"

Ray took a swig of his drink. Shook the spherical ice cube in his glass around a bit, and then finished it off with a click of his lips. Somewhere, up on the mountain, a lonely songbird sang for a mate. Maybe it was a nightingale; maybe it didn't matter, but his song resonated nonetheless.

"Making sense... You don't have to make sense to know what you are trying to say, Ry. I think I understand. Sure, I guess. I've been asked to help people, even when I didn't think I could do much for them. Want to share some context here?"

"Let's just say it's someone I would really like to help if I could. They don't deserve their situation. Not at all. I just don't know what I can do to help them except... Without – you know – really crossing a line."

"Uh-huh. I think I know where your head is at with this. Look, I've been teaching a long time. Never high school or middle school like you, but I've worked with plenty of young people. It's a hazard of our job choice, after all. You think you're going to just get to sit and read and write and publish and all that, but in reality you are more akin to a sculptor of unformed shapes than what you think you are as an academic.

"I've had a girl, nineteen-years old, come to me pregnant and bawling her eyes out. First boyfriend, first time... Huh. Why me, right? I've had a young guy come out to me in a too-quiet classroom because they thought it was a safe space. It was another time, mind you, but not that long ago. I've had to talk about family shit, break-ups, the Big Game, erectile dysfunction, and everything else under the sun at one point or another, doing what we do. It's never easy. It's always made me uncomfortable, and I don't know if I ever *really* helped anyone. But, I think I helped by simply existing in those moments. You know? Being there when someone needed to talk, whether I wanted to or not. It wasn't my cup of tea, the emotional stuff and the tears, but I tried to show that I cared. Yeah, I did that pretty well, I guess."

I was nodding as he spoke. This is what I needed to hear.

"That all makes sense, Uncle Ray. I can relate, for sure. This one case I'm talking about... Man, it's bad. I feel so sorry for this girl. What she's going through at home. I feel kind of trapped. I *can* help her. I can, but I don't know if I'm capable of what she's really asking of me. It scares me. Being on the cusp of something like this, you know? One step forward, and you're a hero for someone who really needs it. One step back, and you're a fucking coward. I don't know which is worse. I just know what is easiest."

Ray's gray blues eyes narrowed as I spoke. He seemed almost perturbed. I couldn't put my finger on the intention of his gaze.

"Huh. That's interesting, Rylan. I don't know exactly what you're talking about, but I do know *you*. You're my nephew, for Christ's sakes. I would be very disappointed to think you were afraid to act on something that you thought was important. That's not you. Your dad wouldn't like that, either. We didn't raise a coward. The way you act, the way you take things by the horns. . . Hell, the way you run and the athlete you always were. Damn fierce. That's not the stuff of cowards. Whatever it is you're talking about, my Rylan is always the hero. At least, in my mind."

He poured another finger of whiskey into his glass, its deep brown muddling with the icy straw of its devoured kin.

He spoke again.

"This is part of becoming a man, Rylan. We all have little choices along the way. Some pull us back into boyhood. We can't always help it. Some propel us forward, and some are dead-ends entirely. You've had a tough year. No doubt. That will help you grow. Anything bad that happens to us. . . We grow as a result. We move on and we're stronger for it. Remember that."

His voice was almost shaking as he finished. I could see tiny tears welling in his eyes, but they never fell. Never cascaded down his bearded cheek. No little rain for one of my own heroes.

I felt almost embarrassed. I looked away. Studied an ancient spruce across the river. Averted my gaze for a long moment. I had nothing to add to the wisdom I had sought.

"Rylan?"

"Yeah, Uncle Ray?"

"I'm so fucking proud of you."

And then, little springs formed in my own deep-set eyes. I fought them back the best as I could. My throat tightened. I clenched my hands. I won the battle, but barely.

I knew what I had to do. There would be no escaping this. I was fated to lose myself in the world of another.

Randall Lightner

The skating rink was busy. He had to park his truck on the far end of the gravel lot. Girl was supposed to be outside by now. It was already after nine.

He texted Jenny's phone.

"Hurry up. I'm here."

No response. On the radio, Willie and Merle sang about Pancho Villa and some Pat Garrett fuck named "Lefty". Randall liked that song. He wished ill on Lefty. He hoped Cleveland was very cold. He smiled at the thought of Villa and his sombrero and the hot Mexican sun on his tanned face. Double pistols. Bandoliers and too much tequila.

He nodded and mouthed along to the tune. Took a swig of his own poison. Bottle of the Bird 101 wrapped in a paper sack. The neon lights and sign of the skating rink danced as his vision slowly started to move in time. Someone brought their kids outside and into the car beside him. Nice-looking couple. They all touched like a daisy chain as they walked across the parking lot.

He wondered what that was like. Gave them a sneer as they boarded their family van. Spit out the window in their general direction.

He didn't know why. Most days, Randall Lightner hated himself. He knew he was ugly. He knew he was mean. Why not own it?

He was just about to call Jenny, when he saw her silhouette appear at the door. Some boy hanging off her like a vine. She play-pushed him away. He stole his little nervous kiss. She pushed him again. He could hear her laugh through the night air. He felt angry. Jealous even. He didn't know why.

Well, he kind of did.

She walked towards his truck slowly. Her young shape, coursing through the darkness, illuminated in purples and pinks. He swigged his whiskey. His mouth watered. His eyes wandered as she neared his truck. Too tight top and those ripped jeans. Limber little thing pulling her waif form up and into the cabin. She smelled like bubble gum and scentless, sweet-girl sweat.

They didn't greet. He just started to drive.

Finally.

"Who was that boy all over you?"

"Nobody."

"He looked like *somebody*."

"What's it to *you*, old man?"

She giggled. He could feel her eyes on him.

"You know you ought not make an old man jealous like that. I used to clean-up at the skating rink when I was your age."

He gave her a look.

"I knew you was jealous of me."

She hit his arm. It was their usual game.

He glanced back over. Her nose still had a little bandage on it from where he had. . . lost his temper. Her eyes looked better. Easy to pass-off as an accident. He didn't feel any guilt. Not really. But he reached across to take her chin gently in his rough hand.

"Damn, sis. Sorry about that the other day. I mean it. I shouldn't have done that."

"Ass." He half-smiled. So did she. "It's okay, Randy. I was being a bitch."

They both smiled to themselves in the gentle glow of the radio lights.

A mile passed. The headlights illuminated yellow lines and farmhouses. They slowed for a family of deer crossing the road. Randall made a pistol with his hand and let the hammer fall as the mama passed.

They both laughed.

"You eat anything?"

"Naw. I ain't hungry, though."

"You sure? I can get us something."

"Naw. I'm good."

"You ready to go home or do you want a ride around for a bit?"

"Ride."

"Here."

He passed her the bottle wearing its brown bag disguise. She sipped it. Made a face. Opened her mouth in a 'wow' expression. Sipped it again and kept it in her hand. Randall smiled as he drove. She tried to change the radio station. He protested. They compromised on a channel playing 'Hotel California'.

That song was older than both of them. It didn't matter. It spoke of Escape and Death to two souls who needed the former and weren't particular afraid of the latter. Both were, essentially, a vacation from their mundane days.

He parked up at the Harris Knob overlook. The sky was crystal clear. The stars strained to see them as they clearly made out each one of their audience. You could see town below. You could see Johnson City to the west. And that tiny glow way far down the mountain – that was probably Charlotte.

She didn't seem to care as Randy pointed these things out to her. Just making conversation. They sat on his tailgate and she shivered every now and then in the night air. He gave her his coat. The stiff denim pitched around her like a little tent. She leaned against him. The bottle was less than half-full, as the optimist would say.

"Randy?"

"Yeah."

"I wish I wasn't your step-daughter."

"You ain't really my step-daughter, dummy."

"You get me. You ain't like them other boys. They is so stupid. God damn. That boy tonight, he ain't shit, you know?"

"Yep, little sis."

Jenny looked down. She put her hand on his knee. They made eye contact.

"Randy, I ain't been with no boy yet. I know I act all big, but I ain't never done nothing but kissed 'em and let 'em touch me. I just wanted you to know that."

He laughed. She didn't. Her pouty, embarrassed look was almost too much for him.

"Shit, girl. You had me and your mama both fooled. We thought you'd be out to here by the time you turned sixteen."

He motioned to illustrate an exaggerated pregnancy. Sixteen was only a few months away.

She hit him on the arm. Then again on the chest.

"That ain't funny, you ass."

He caught her fist before she could hit him again. Squeezed it to the point it started to hurt her. Then, he kissed it. Opened her palm. Studied her tiny hand with the terrible, teenage nail job. Pulled her closer, and they kissed. He touched her. She let out a little sigh. She had never been this drunk. Whatever was in that bottle hit harder than the Bud Light she sipped and shared at her friends' houses. She couldn't even feel her face as he caressed it.

He laid her back on the cold tailgate. She trembled. She shook like a leaf as he touched her. She knew this wasn't right. Alarms were ringing like tornado sirens in her young brain. The tiny, tiny portion of her that might have actually wanted this no longer spoke. In its stead, her whole being protested whatever they were doing. This was no longer fun. This was no longer some harmless fantasy.

They were alone, and he was getting riled-up like all the other boys.

"Randy, don't."

"Hmm?"

He kissed her belly. Inching lower.

"Please. This ain't... Mama would kill us... Please."

He wasn't listening. The reptile nesting between his ears was starting to take over his every movement.

Then, like sudden lightning on a summer afternoon, headlights. Pulling up beside them on that overlook at Harris Knob. Another couple trying to get lucky.

They both sat up. The man, frustrated. The girl, relieved.

"Well, damn. We better get going home."

Jenny immediately hopped-off the tail gate and was in the cabin of the old truck before Randy could gather his thoughts. He needed a moment, as men do. He nodded at the young couple pulled up beside them.

Enjoy it, kids. You don't know how quickly it passes. You think you do, but damn if you don't.

They were both silent on the way home. Not a word was exchanged. There was nothing to say.

Jenny got sick in that yard when they finally arrived. She pulled away from Randall when he tried to help her. He just walked inside like nothing had happened. Left her to it.

That had been the longest drive of her young life. Her hands shook violently and she tremored herself to sleep with muted sobs into a suffocating pillow that smelled like her shampoo. She felt polluted despite the clean scent ricocheting back at her.

She was deeply afraid, and there was no one for her to talk to and no one to listen.

Alone was just a word, but it was also the most intense emotion she had never known.

The next day.

"How long you going to be gone again, April?"

"Just the weekend. Concert's Saturday night. I'll be back Sunday."

"And I have to stay here and watch your fucking kids? Can't wait."

She gave him a sideways glance as he sat on the bed. She was half-dressed, half-not. He was in his boxers. The room smelled like sweat, cheap aftershave, and cigarette smoke. The girls were at school.

"Come on, babe. I never get to do nothin'. Watch 'em for me those few days, try not to get completely shit faced while I'm gone. You know, Elsa'll tell on you if you do."

They both half-laughed, but the woman was serious.

"Really, Randy. You gotta stop being so rough with them. You damn near broke Jenny's nose last time you pitched a fit. Somebody's bound to get wise and throw you in jail. I heard about that old cock sheriff coming up here. Told you. Elsa tells all."

Randall reclined back on the bed. Reached for a Winston. Lit it skillfully and a ghastly plume filled the room after a few deep puffs.

Elsa... The fucking bane of my existence.

"You oughta send that girl off to some weirdo school. I told you, she gives me the creeps. I look at her sometimes, and... Hell, I don't know. I can't read her at all. And I'm pretty good at reading people."

"She is weird, ain't she?"

They both chuckled again. It was equally strained, whether they admitted it or not. Both of them were a little waryof the younger girl. Something about her was intimidating. Like she was from another time or place. She was smart, despite her momma's tenth-grade education. She was disciplined without being taught what that even meant. She was polite, despite their eternal rudeness.

She was mysterious. She was detached from them. She knew she was better than them. They knew it, too.

And Randall couldn't shake this feeling he got around her. It was basically all the time. Every glance. Every gentle smile. Every bite of cereal in the morning. Every greeting.

In everything she did, Randall saw his own death. She filled him with a special dread like some elfin Reaper. He didn't have a conscience. He had done some terrible things in his life and hoped to keep doing them.

But when he accidentally made the mistake of looking into those crystal-blue kaleidoscopes she called eyes, he somehow saw his end staring back at him. A reflective pool. An enchanted well, prognosticating a hard stop for his heart and lungs.

Surely, it had to all be in his head. She was just a child, after all.

Randall Lightner puffed his cigarette. The woman rubbed his legs as she climbed back onto the bed like a pale and dirty feline. He could see her backbone and the crease of her hips in the stained mirror on the dresser. He grabbed her coarse, peroxided hair as she started to do her thing.

Something told him he better enjoy moments like this. Simple and fleeting as they were. He briefly studied the trashed bedroom. He stared up at the ceiling fan, spinning on a forever loop. He glanced out the window into the unkept yard. The mountains rising off in all directions like sentinels coming to call.

Putting his cigarette out in the overfilled ash tray and relaxing deeper into his pillow, Randall Lightner knew he better enjoy the hell out of everything he could for as long as he was allowed.

Time was a placid river. Flowing slowly. Imperceptible as the Earth's mad spiral in some depressed corner of space. Time was nothing more than a horizon, a marker to count our days.

Beyond that horizon on the placid river of time, there was bound to be some awful waterfall. Pulling you down violently to the surge and the rocks below. Shattering your little canoe, often when you least expect it.

Even time has an eventual expiration date; at least, for ants crawling on a rock spiraling in deep depressing space. Randall mused on that as he closed his eyes.

Time: the slowest, fastest killer come to call.

He did not smile at this thought.

Time, like Elsa's glass grenade eyes, could all explode at any minute.

Eliza Stone

It was getting dark outside. Almost too dark to see. Eliza's eyes dilated in the gloom as she stared out the bay windows of the condo on the mountain. Below, nothing and everything stretched out before her like the black plains of Hell. She felt like she was floating over the landscape like a night raven. No wind could reach her through the thick glass, yet she could feel the breeze caressing her pale and frail skin.

Something strong opened the doors of her perception to the fullest. She had never been this high. She was flying. Floating over the ground like a black angel.

Why save a drop? Why save a single pill?

She figured this was it. This would be the night. Daniel would be missing now. Brittany was *still* missing. Surely the cops would be on their way. She had known this wouldn't last forever. She hadn't wanted it to last forever. Even eternity has its bordered frame like a dull portrait of some forgotten time. A still-frame clip. An Impressionist view of the Afterlife that you can only see if you're dead.

And the champagne toasts and all the red-painted walls in the Ever-After Mansion lure you inside. God's dull friends wait for you. They're dead, too. And the other

Lord. . . Well, he welcomes some special guests in a back room where the wine is as red as the walls and his company keeps you coming back for more every time you die and are born and again and round it goes.

And you die. And that's tonight.

Eliza laughed maniacally to herself. She couldn't tell if it was aloud or held inside. The fading light outside gave her goosebumps. The rising moon brought electricity to her limbs and reanimated her fragile frame in necromancer jerks. Her mind was shattered like the glass strewn all over the floor. Brittany Reynolds lay on the sofa. Mostly asleep. Eliza had made sure of that. She no longer cared about the dosage of any potions she prescribed, for her cauldron over-floweth.

After tonight, we won't have to worry about anything, Baby Girl. We can just be together. I'll protect you. I'll always be here for you. We just have to go to sleep first. That's all. Just go to sleep and nothing bad can happen after that.

Eliza's paranoia had been at its peak right before a gift had recently fallen into her lap. That gift had been her friend. Her best friend, if she was honest.

Daniel Spencer.

Dan.

With his sacrifice, she knew the hounds would be fully unleashed. They would come hungry, but she hoped by then they would find their prey already drifting in the Styx. Away and laughing. Gone, save for the coins on their eyes.

If they came early, tried to catch her off-guard, then she only hoped that they would not spare her life. She would give them every reason *not to* if that were the case. She feared nothing. The End, especially, was no stranger to her. They were good friends, too. They commiserated like an old couple having shared innumerable years of sorrow and triumph together. They rocked on porch chairs and sipped their lemonade. Eliza's hair blew in the breeze. His baritone voice boomed off into the hills.

And they laughed at everything and all the time yet to come. The End is but an asterisk.

Eliza was ready to face that unknown. She was finished here. She had her moment with her surrogate Lily. She got to be a mother again, albeit briefly and with much reserve. In a moment, she would carry her new daughter upstairs with her. She would sing her a lullaby. She would tell her a story. She would push something strong into her system. And that would be that. And she would do the same favor to herself, once her deed was done.

After a moment or two, Eternity would open its arms to them both. She would meet its embrace and drift upon its placid waves. Peace would eventually come to her.

A release like she had never known.

Please, she begged.

Sheriff Scott

The old sheriff drove with fervor up the mountain. Night had fallen, and the trees seemed to groan and beckon him forward as the headlights revealed their sinister outline. His palms were sweating against the steering wheel, but his grip was tight. His heart raced with a sick kind of adrenaline that he had experienced only on the worst days of his life.

Mountain Realty had eleven properties on Winter Ridge. The ski resort wasn't the biggest in the region, but it did have the best views and these rentals were always booked in the winter. Now, they would mostly all be unoccupied. Only four currently housed guests. The rest were empty, vacant shells. Perfect for hiding something. His only lead was intuitive.

I'd pick one near the top. . .

Bruce had phoned less than an hour before. Told him Dan was missing. Said that he was very worried. He wouldn't return his calls or texts. They had a spat a few days back, but nothing major. Nothing worse than their usual quarrels. He said he knew deep down that Eliza was involved. Even he could *feel* it, whatever that meant.

He asked the sheriff to please go look for him. He had tried all the obvious places, and even some less obvious ones. This was very unlike his brother...

Bruce's stern voice had been shaking from the moment he called the sheriff. He was deeply concerned. There could be no hiding that fact.

And so Carl drove to the very peak of the mountain. Up towards the black sky, an impenetrable umbrella in the dark. The stars were taciturn reminders that he was as close to heaven as even the most honest of men would ever be. In the day light, it was beautiful up here. The deep greens would just have begun their march towards summer blossoms. The views, spectacular. Top of the world. He noticed familiar street signs, little shops, and eventually the ski slopes themselves in his periphery. His mind was a million miles away, however.

Eyes fixed on the yellow double-line drawing a divide on the narrow road, he thought only of the little girl. The sheriff and his wife had never been able to have children. Fitting for his profession, it had worn on them both when they were younger and still able to conceive a healthy boy or girl. Failing in that, he always held a soft spot for kids. They were a happy mystery to him, and he always doted on his deputies' children, whenever given the chance. He even played Santa for the Christmas parties at the station. Even Ansley and Wykes County came to their big holiday gatherings. These parties were a hit.

How could you hurt a child?

A refrain he had muttered too many times in his career. There was no answer. Human nature was a dark forest with many spiraling paths of possibility. Most roads were easily understood. Many were not. Some were inexplicable, the things we were capable of doing.

Sheriff Scott reached the last cul de sac of condos at the very top of the mountain. There was only the main road in and out of the parking area. The three buildings up here had been a source of great discontent among the town council. They were eye sores on the ridge. Profitability had won, as commerce usurped serenity ten times out of ten.

He pulled out the map of Winter Ridge Resort that the younger brother at Mountain Realty had given him, less than an hour before. The property was expansive, but their rentals were circled in red. There were only three possibilities up here at Day's End Retreat. The buildings looked at him, in the gloom, with austere disinterest. The residual streetlights offered little to abate the dark, and there were only a few cars sharing the spaces with his truck. He scoured the lot for anything resembling the missing Mountain Realty SUV. Nothing in sight, which didn't surprise him.

She had gone on this long without being caught. . . Why make such a simple mistake?

He turned and reached into the glove compartment for his Maglite. It weighted heavy in his hand, loaded down with three D batteries that produced quite the modern torch. Scanning the buildings and walkways constantly, nothing seemed to move. The world was still, as if in mourning for some undisclosed tragedy. At his hip, he removed the big revolver that had become a familiar weight over the years. A comfort, if nothing else. Like a child's security blanket. He opened the cylinder on the stainless Colt to reveal six dull-eyed .357 cartridges looking back at him. Same as it always was, but he felt that checking one more time was always prudent. The cylinder closed with a tight metallic click, and he returned the pistol to the smooth-worn holster at his side. His radio had been silent ever since he called in to the station last. He knew that back-up would be on the way, but it was over a half-hour drive from town up to the very top of Winter Ridge. He had requested a search warrant for all eleven properties, but there was no word on that.

He was alone, and perhaps it was better that way.

The sheriff's stomach made a churning sound as he exited his truck and stepped out into the night. He gave one more cursory look at the map and then folded it back into his pocket. Managing more than a trot across the parking area, he headed to the furthest building on the right, where Mountain Realty had one condo: Number 1152, 'Dreamscape', door code 5995#. He arrived at the door under the dim light of the entryway, took a breath, and knocked assertively.

"Sheriff's Department. Open up!"

No answer. His heart started to race.

"I have a warrant to search the property. Open up or I'm coming inside!"

He lied. Or maybe not. Probable cause was cause enough for him tonight.

Just then a door opened up behind him on the landing. The sheriff spun with hand on pistol grip.

"Woah, woah! I'm just seeing what's going on. Sorry, officer."

A short, studious-looking man stood with only his face and a raised hand exposed in the doorway of the condo opposite 1152.

"Go back inside. Lock the door."

"What's– uh, why. . . Should we be worried?"

"No, you're fine. Just doing a routine search."

"Uh, okay. Sorry, officer."

Just as he was about to close the door, Sheriff Scott stopped him.

"Hey, fella. You seen anybody going in or out of this one? Anyone at all?"

The sheriff heard an inquisitive woman's voice calling out to see what was the matter from inside the other condo.

"It's okay, honey! Just speaking with a policeman. No, sir. We thought we were pretty much alone up here. Been staying since last Tuesday. Haven't heard a peep."

"You're sure? Nothing? Seen anybody go in or out of the other buildings?"

"Well, yeah. There have been a few other overnight guests. The cleaning service has been up a few times. And the Mountain Realty folks have been–"

"Mountain Realty? Where? Which building?"

"Well, I haven't seen the car since. . . I don't know, but the building over there. All the way across the lot."

The officer's heart sank. There was relief in such validation, but then there was also the looming thought of *actually having to act* in such cases. It's always easy to find the door but walking through it tests one's limit. Every single time, he had found. He didn't take the time to thank the man and left him standing bewildered with his beak-like nose peering out from the door.

The sheriff did his best to sprint back across the shadowed lot to the opposing building. The dark entry way yawned like a grave. There was no light in the landing on this side, and he felt like he was approaching the mouth of a tomb as he neared the steps. There were two Mountain Realty condos in this building. One on the first floor and one on the top, the third. He dismissed the first floor altogether and climbed the stairs as quickly as possible.

His breath was short at the top, but he didn't take any time to compose himself. He looked left and right at the top of the stairs. Three condos up here, no light. He clicked the button on his Maglite and all was illuminated. Leaving him feeling exposed. The still air, though warm, gave him goosebumps as his light rested on the unit in question.

Number 516, "Dreamcatcher", door code 5342#. His vision began to tunnel, like the beam of light he wielded, as he approached the door.

He did not knock or announce himself. He swapped the light into his left hand, turned it off, and pressed the buttons slowly on the door box. When he hit pound, the device glowed green and made a brief musical chime. It couldn't have lasted more than a second, but the noise seemed to hang in the air like the final crescendo of an opera. He heard the lock disengage within the door frame, and even his weathered hand trembled as he reached to turn the knob.

The air inside the condo seemed to inhale as the door was breached. He quickly pulled his revolver as soon as there was a crack between door and frame, and nudged the door open just enough to pass through with his boot. All was dark inside the hollow foyer, and he quietly closed the door behind him. One exit. No way out.

The sheriff entered, peering into the black as his eyes took their time to adjust. His pistol was raised at nothing, and he was afraid to turn on the flashlight. Then, as he skirted the wall and tried to quiet his breathing, two strong smells hit him with such force that his already queasy stomach almost vacated its contents. Nerves and disgust, something vile in the air.

Was that... sage?

And something putrid. A sick, sweet smell lurked behind the odor of burnt herbs. Poorly disguised, and now overpowering his nostrils and eyes. The stale air burned with each shallow breath. Taking a knee against what he perceived to be a corner, the sheriff turned on the flashlight and the room was narrowly illuminated with a blue-white glow.

He was apparently looking into the den from the angle where he knelt. The condo was unexpectedly large. At least three bedrooms, he guessed. He was leaning against the base of a stairway, so there was also a lofted space above. The room before him was big and open with vaulted ceilings. The rental's furnishings were sparse and unwelcoming in the shadows. A coffee table had been pushed aside near the opposite corner. The couch and two chairs sat at odd angles, unused, and his light scanned the room eagerly for a sign of why that was.

Where's the rug?

He could see an indentation in the beige carpet where a large rug had rested under the furniture, but it was no longer there; then his eyes paused on the coffee table. The glass face was shattered and there appeared to be shards littering the floor all over the room. The sheriff stood slowly to get a better look.

A brick-red stain colored one of the transparent fragments his light settled on, and then another. And another. His heart pitched one more leap and he could feel its desperate beating echo in his chest. He yelled into the open space, his voice more frightened than he would ever admit, if this story were to be retold.

"Eliza Stone? This is the Sheriff's department. I need you to show yourself. I know you are in here."

A long and hollow pause. No sound. Nothing moved in the dark.

"Eliza, I am not fucking around! It's time to go now! Come on out!"

He found a light switch behind him on the wall and reached for it. Nothing. He assumed some of these units had the power turned-off in the down season to save money. This must have been one of them. Or, someone had flipped the breaker to preserve the dark.

His eyes rested again on the blood-stained glass littering the floor. The beam bounced and shook to the irregular rhythm of his frantic heartbeat. He scanned the room for entry points. One, two. Maybe a kitchen, and then a bedroom off to the other side. He forced himself to move and began to low-shuffle across the room. He stepped gingerly, foot over foot, trying to avoid the scattered glass. He was almost successful until he was about to peer into the kitchen and dining space.

A sickeningly loud *crunch* under his boot seemed to echo like a voice through a canyon, just as he rounded the kitchen's corner. Pistol and light raised, a new room appeared before him. Another scent of rot and garbage. There was trash on the floor and counter. Old food. Dishes left where they had last been used. He looked closer. A gallon of milk, children's cereal, Little Debbie boxes, bags of candy, frozen pizzas and those kids' meals with the penguin on the box.

The sheriff's stomach dropped again as his light exposed a legion of maggots crawling over a spilled bag of garbage, halfway scattered across the floor. Someone had been living here. Someone had given up on any kind of domestic decency.

Someone had been feeding a child. . .

Never fully exposing his back to the open den behind him, the sheriff spun around and entered the larger space again. He had to get out of that kitchen before he wretched. Bolder now, almost convinced he was alone, he moved to the bedroom door across the den. Glass crunched and cracked under foot as he walked. He stood beside the door and twisted the knob underhanded to clear the room properly upon entry. The door swung a few inches, and then bumped something at floor level. He pushed it again, firmer this time with the palm of his hand. The air that wafted out of the room knocked him back like a blow. He stepped back and had to take a knee. His throat quivered and heaved as he brought his sleeve to his mouth and nose.

What the–

The sheriff managed to shine the light into the bedroom, holding the door open with his boot. There appeared to be a rolled rug blocking the door. It was folded clumsily in a heap with something obviously stuffed inside.

The missing rug from the den.

The sheriff knelt to peer inside the open end of the rug. In the darkness, dancing particles of dust frolicked like spectral orbs in the air. When he saw the soles of two Italian loafers almost protruding from the frayed roll of carpet, he let out a deep, guttural, animal sound and immediately closed the door. His back to the wall, chest rising and falling, the panic overtaking him in a wave. Then, it grew far worse.

The staircase across the room beckoned upward like the Reaper's dark cloak. The sheriff's light illuminated its base as he tried to compose what was left of his nerves. He wanted to be out of this room, out of this place. He should be home having dinner with his wife. This was a younger man's game, and where was his backup?

As these thoughts raced through the sheriff's frazzling mind, his blood began to freeze in his veins. His heart paused, he held his breath in the shade of the big room.

That can't be? I'm hearing things...

Above him, up the stairway, the inklings of a raspy voice floated down and began to flood into the very caverns of his being. The silence in the room, only disturbed by crunching glass, his breathing, and the slamming of a door since he arrived, was now taking a new shape in song.

A nursery rhyme? What is that?

It was clear that he was no longer alone. A woman was upstairs. She was singing a child's song into the dark. Very low, almost a whisper, but the sound penetrated the blackness like bleak sunlight peering through thick clouds. The sheriff's hands shook lightly. Would he be able to move or speak?

Just move, Carl. Damn it. It's only a woman. You know that... There's a little girl in here, for god's sake. You should have checked up there first. What are you thinking... Do something!

He managed to move his leaden legs across the room towards the bottom of the staircase. The light and the barrel of his pistol followed each other simultaneously to the top of the stairs as he rounded the filled banister. The height of the stairs seemed to reach upwards forever, but it couldn't have been more than twenty feet. Along the wall, someone had drawn picture after picture in crayon and finger paint. Some were low, and some were high. A child and an adult, drawing together. There were suns, and moons, and stick people. A spider. And a large dog that was hardly more than an animal shade.

A dog? No, the shape was wrong. He knew the shape, though.

A coyote.

At the very top, his light paused on a name. . . Lily. Written in a deep purple.

At the top of the stairs, once his eyes adjusted, what looked like the concealed flicker of candles broke the sheer darkness of the landing. Another room at the top. Maybe more?

How could you have not gone up here first. . .

The singing grew louder as he took the first step. Then a second. He could barely feel his feet as he slowly navigated the carpeted stairs. The adrenaline tore through him like a shot of epinephrine. Everything was numb and tingling.

It took three tries for his choked croaking to become an actual sentence. He had never seen anything like this before. He didn't know what he was supposed to do. All protocol had long left.

"Eliza Stone! I'm coming up there! I need you to lie down on the floor. Face down, with your hands behind your head. I know you hear me! This is your last warning, Eliza!"

The singing didn't stop immediately. It gently trailed off as the woman finished her nursey rhyme. Something old, maybe even a hymn. The creak of a door echoed off the vaulted ceiling above, and more candlelight illuminated the upstairs. Shadows danced like puppets in their flicker.

When she began to laugh, almost a low growl at first, all the hair on the back of Sheriff Scott's neck began to stand on end. There was no reason in the sound. Hysterical menace, a banshee cry. Static ran through his nervous system like a train. He rounded the corner at the top of the stairs and peered down a narrow hallway. His flashlight revealed a partially open door at the end of the slender passage. It was streaked with little handprints in purple paint. Something was streaked along the hallway wall on one side, and what appeared to be a giant raven was drawn on the other.

And then, movement in the room beyond. The laughing stopped. A figure appeared in the doorway. Wild hair and all black. A woman's silhouette, but not a woman any longer. Something else. The most frightening image the sheriff had ever seen. His light exposed her frame, but it also fragmented the image in an unholy glow.

She seemed to be looking in the room behind her. Fixated on something. She mumbled a few words in the shadows. He could see her breathing, but that was the only evidence that he was not looking on at something ethereal.

When she pushed the door open all the way, and he could clearly see the big knife in her hand, his stomach dropped like an elevator's sudden halt. The shriek she made when she began to charge reverberated off the walls, the ceilings, everything... It would haunt every dream he would ever have. There could be no peace.

Fuck...

The flashlight hit the floor as the sheriff brought both hands to his revolver. Its beam was useless and unwelcome anymore. There was no hope for light in this place and moment. The woman moved irregularly. The angles weren't right; the mechanics inhuman. He focused first on the knife raised back and over her head as she ran. Time froze. Even her sprint slowed to the point where he could see each foot fall, rise, and touch the ground and rise again as if she was floating. His sight picture narrowed until all he saw was the dark of her robe. He could pick out singular fibers in the dark, his senses reeled to the point of tasting the air around him.

The hammer rocked back as he squeezed the trigger. It then thrusted forward like a boxer's punch. Light and sound and fire exploded into the hallway. A flashbulb bursting in the night. The figure before him was unphased by the shock of it all, but a dense dark spray spattered the wall behind her as she attacked. The sheriff retreated several steps before firing again, and then again. His ears were bleeding from the percussion, but he wouldn't notice that for several more minutes.

The third shot was at point-blank range. The impact hit the woman with such force that even her madness could not counter or ignore. She slammed into the wall behind her and bounced off like a pinball. Three or four stumbling steps backward and then her footing was gone. She seemed to hover impossibly long in the air before finally collapsing in a crooked heap on the carpeted floor.

She writhed like a snake, curling and hissing and trying in vain to stand. The sheriff kept the pistol on her, but he didn't have the stomach to fire again. She was finished, and eventually her impossible stillness made that very clear.

He stepped forward a few paces until he stood over the woman in black. The woman who used to be Eliza Stone, the realtor and mother who had tried to put a new life together. That was not the tortured shell of a person that now lay before him, and the old man felt like he had just put down a rabid animal rather than a human being. The butcher's knife lay some feet away, but he slid it even further with his boot as he studied the corpse at his feet for any signs of life. There were none, and perhaps there hadn't been for quite some time.

He kneeled down beside her and put two trained fingers to her neck. Her skin was cold, reptilian. Blood ran from her mouth onto the carpet when he turned her head. Her jaw fell slack.

That was that. No doubt that she was gone.

He stood from her side. Down the hallway, candles continued to flicker and dance like demons around some ancient pyre. Older and darker than any Christian depiction, he could almost hear their serpent tongues luring him into the shadowed bedroom beyond. Words were useless, and rational thought was long abandoned as he approached the doorway. He experienced his movements from afar as if he was watching a live performance on stage. A cult horror or Faustian play.

Entering the room with his pistol lowered, he instinctively knew there was no longer a threat in this place. He managed to whisper the girl's name. Her *real* name. There was no echo or reverberation. Only silence. He called again, and then the silence pressed down on him like scattered earth onto a casket. One glance around the room was all he needed.

There was no hope for her. That time had passed. Sheriff Scott and the whole feckless world were all too late. They had failed. She looked like she was sleeping among the stuffed animals on the bed. Like a doll, or the archaic impression of an angel. It was all too horrible. There was only nothingness in that haunted room. Ghosts were real, and so were demons. Every terrible thing was real. Monsters and witches. And, worst of all, the people who invented them into existence.

When his deputies arrived, they found the old man sitting against the wall in the upstairs bedroom. He was crying like a child, his face covered in his hands, and paid them no mind. This would be his last night on the job. His badge would rest on the desk of the mayor by noon the following day.

The papers would call him a hero, but all he felt was emptiness.

Rylan

"Rylan! Come in here. Hurry!"

Lacy and I were at my place. It was early, a little after six. I had just finished shaving and getting ready for work. She was in the kitchen watching the news while she made our sandwiches for lunch. I messed with an unruly curl with my fingers one more time in the mirror, and she called again. Urgently.

"Coming!"

Jesus... What's the rush?

I walked into the living room. She had paused mid-Mayo swipe behind the counter, her face terse and stiff. She motioned without moving to the TV set. I followed her gaze. A reporter stood outside what looked like a condominium complex. Maybe up at one of the ski resorts. It was too foggy to tell for sure. Blue lights flickered like disco balls in the distance, and caution tape swayed in the breeze like prayer flags. The reporter was mid-recount when I walked into the room, but I got the gist. Her words came in waves as my mind focused on what was happening.

'Officers are saying this is one of the most gruesome crime scenes they have ever encountered... Heinous...

Like something out of a horror movie. . . The woman, Elizabeth Stone. . . Kidnapped little Brittany Reynolds and kept her in one of the condos behind me now. . . Killed local real estate agent and co-owner of Mountain Realty Daniel Spencer in the same unit. . . Sheriff Carlton Scott responded on scene last night and made this shocking discovery. . . Excellent police work. . . Remarkable that he was able to locate the condo among Mountain Realty's many properties on Winter Ridge. . . He was attacked by Ms. Stone sometime around ten p.m. after entering the unit and was able to take the perpetrator down without incurring any bodily harm. . . Brittany Reynolds, age six, was found dead in the upstairs bedroom. . . Extremely strange behavior. . . Drawings on the wall. . . Almost like a lair. . .'

I looked back at Lacy. Tears were streaming down her face as she watched the scene unfold on my 36-inch television screen. The media's callous and too excited telling of the story was vulgar as always, but the fact remained that the little girl for whom police had searched for the last week or more and the papers had railed over was quite dead. Everyone was too late. Like most anything, we had all failed. Despicable and flawed, our best intentions.

And Elizabeth Stone? She had stood in this very room. She *sold* me this apartment, for god's sake. . . I remembered her eyes. Her aura. The stark presence of *something not quite* right with her.

I walked into the kitchen. Lacy laid down her butter knife and bread. We hugged for what felt like forever. She was sobbing on my shoulder, and I felt a million miles away. My mind raced and traced back to the conversation I had with Elsa Privette a few days earlier. She was asking me for help. She had sounded desperate, and I did not believe her panic was validated in the least.

But, a *dream*? Really? Was I supposed to believe that? I had told the school all along. They should pass that along. I had done what anyone else would do when a young person comes to you with bruises and asks for help.

And, to that point, I had also done precisely nothing.

Nothing at all.

Nothing more than a PC abstraction and deferment. Playing by the rules. Pass it up the ladder. I had been a fucking coward. After seeing this news report, I felt dirty and polluted. I felt weak and apathetic.

Was there time to change something? Time to save a life or two? I thought of the sheriff. What would he have done had he known the truth all this time? About the Reynolds girl, I mean.

I had the luxury of truth from the mouth of a babe. She had chosen me to ask for help. If I didn't do something, after this newsreel, after her full confessional, then whatever came next rested on my shoulders.

I just didn't know what I was expected to do.

What did Elsa Privette really need from me?

Randall Lightner

Randall had just cracked open a fresh beer when the phone rang. The woman had left for her trip a few hours earlier. Elsa had made them Hamburger Helper for dinner, and the empty bowl sat derelict in his lap.

"Elsa? Jenny? Somebody grab me that phone!"

No answer from either, but a few seconds later Elsa pressed the portable phone gently against his shoulder.

"There you go."

Her voice was too soft. She made no sound approaching his chair. It had almost startled him.

Little bitch could have slit my throat if she wanted. . . I would have never heard her coming.

The Stone woman had promised him the same thing. He had been afraid that she was serious. He had dreamed about her a lot in recent weeks. The news about the girl and all that came as no surprise to him. Even the old sheriff had called to say he had been right. It was an underhanded thank you, sure, but Randall had at least appreciated the minor effort.

He answered the phone as Elsa scurried back to her room.

"What?"

"Hey, boss. I gots some news."

It was one of his guys.

"What?"

"Well, you are about to get a call. It ain't gonna be good. Um, we just lost a house. Fire department and police is all over the place out in Cave Creek. Fuckin' Jimmy and Dane is dead, too. I was at the convenient store when it happened. Whole place blew up. They was in the basement. You know what I's getting at. All the product's gone. We had made the full month's batch. . ."

Randall's mind was spinning like a jacks ball. He owned a lot of shitty property. He had a few piss-poor tenants, but most of his ramshackle roach motels were exclusively used for cooking. If he was hearing this correctly, apparently one of them had gone up in flames. If it was the one in Cave Creek, it was about to cost him a lot of money and a hell of a lot of trouble.

The law dog would be calling. The voice on the other end of the line was right about that. Meth lab explosions were fairly common and very easy to source. They didn't take an arson investigator to figure out, exactly.

He mumbled something to the voice. The man said something back and was still in midsentence when Randall hit END on the receiver. He needed no further explanation from him. News received. A shot of white rage rushed through him like a bolt. This was familiar to him. The quick heat of an anger so sharp it rang like ice in his blood. He could go to jail for this one. House was in his brother's name, but his brother was in jail. It was paid for ten times over, but still. . . He was the owner of record. He might lie his way out of it. Claim total ignorance and blame the departed gentlemen cooks who politely blew themselves to smithereens.

The cops would obviously come a'calling soon. Only buffer might be all this noise with the dead little girl. In a place where nothing ever happened, that might just keep the dogs at bay for a day or two while they sorted everything out in Cave Creek. He could concoct a grand story by then, for sure.

He thought on all this for a long while. Finished a beer, crushed the can out of some juvenile habit. Realized beer wouldn't do tonight. He needed liquor to think straight. Clear his thoughts.

"Elsa!!"

He screamed her name this time. In her bedroom, Elsa had just reclined back on her beanbag chair, reading Conrad and thinking about the tropics. She used to jump out of her skin when he would yell her name like that. Her hands would start shaking and she would feel a little sick. Now, it was commonplace. She was numb to it. No big deal.

She sighed. Closed her book, quickly stood, and hurried down the narrow hall. She peeked inside Jenny's room as she passed. Made eye contact with her. She looked like a frightened animal. She had been acting really weird at home the last few weeks. Elsa didn't know why, nor did she ask. Their relationship had become a shallow pool reflecting only a common biology, and it hurt her feelings. They barely talked anymore.

She missed her sister, and she somehow felt Randall was to blame. She made tight fists as she entered the dingy living room. Felt her fingernails dig into her palms.

There he sat with his back to her. Three beer cans on the table beside him. The dinner she had cooked was eaten and the bowl discarded on the floor. The TV screen in front of him advertised a local car dealer attempting to sell the same two trucks she had seen him waving at for the last month on that station. The volume was too low to hear it, but she could recite every line of his pitch at this point.

Elsa didn't like television. Everything was too repetitious and dull for her tastes. There was no creativity that she could discern dancing across that bulging screen, except for maybe a few good movies that she had seen. They had been okay. Her grandmom had liked movies a lot.

She spoke, still standing behind him. He couldn't hit or push her this way. It was for the best.

"Yes, Randy?"

"What took you so long? Pour me a drink, will ya?"

"Yes, sir. What would you like?"

"Just the Jack, or the Wild Turkey. Whatever the hell is on the counter in there."

Elsa nodded and marched into the kitchen to fulfil his request.

"Ice?"

"A little."

She filled his usual glass with three ice cubes popped from the plastic tray. It had a NASCAR logo on it and was never entirely clean. She tried to remember which one of these bottles made him mean, and which one made him fall asleep. She thought the Turkey one was stronger since it had '50.5%' on the label, so that might knock him out faster after a few glasses. She opened that one with a little difficulty and poured it about halfway full, like he had taught her. He got mad if it was too full or not enough. A dull-eyed turkey stared back at her when she set the bottle down on the counter. It looked as dead as the poor deer mounted on the wall in the living room, and about as numb as she felt interacting with this imposter sitting in her real daddy's chair.

She handed him the drink to no thanks. He asked her to bring the bottle. She obediently brought it back to him. He tucked it into the crook between the La-Z-Boy and his side.

"Who was that on the phone?"

He took a deep breath. Pointed to the couch. She guessed that she was supposed to sit. This was unusual. 'Walking on eggshells' was just an old saying to most people, but to Elsa it implied the acrobatic maneuvers she had learned to use around Randy. Especially when he was drinking, which was a good portion of the time.

"Typical bullshit. Could be bad. I know how much you'd hate it if I got locked up."

He winked at her sarcastically as she sat down across from him. Her soft gaze conveyed neither agreement nor disagreement.

"What's up?"

"You know I have a lot of property. All over the damn county, and out towards Newberry. Well, one of my old houses just burned to the ground with two guys inside."

"Oh my gosh..."

He held his hand up. She paused on cue. Hand instinctively covering her mouth in surprise.

"It's fine. No need for any sentiment. The men inside– well, they weren't exactly good guys. But they *were* loose business associates of mine. What they were doing in the house... Well, that wasn't exactly legal either."

Elsa nodded slowly. Randall hated that her face demonstrated no semblance of judgment or condescension.

"Look, reason I sat you down to tell you this is because I trust you. I don't trust your damn mama, and I don't trust that cat-in-heat sitting eavesdropping in her room!"

He yelled this last bit. It sounded oddly personal. There was a shuffling inside Jenny's room and something fell with a thud. The elder sister mumbled something through the walls that didn't sound very polite. Elsa cringed and scrunched her face. Randy finished off his drink, and rapidly poured himself another before the ice could melt, even a little.

Randy sighed deeply with the next sip. He motioned to the heirloom desk in the corner of the room, then spoke very slowly. He looked Elsa right in the eye. She stared right back.

"Anyway, I was saying. If this gets bad, and it might, I'm going to give you some information. You're smart enough to know what to do with it. I ain't got a proper will or nothing, but I got my intentions in there. Manilla envelope and lots of paperwork. You need to get this over to Jason Bridges, the lawyer, and let him sort it out if something happens to me. Your mama is too dumb and lazy to get everything together, but proof of everything I own is in that old roll-top desk over yonder. Secret compartment underneath the bottom drawer. It's got everything you need. I'm leaving everything to you girls for whatever fool reason. I ain't got nobody else but my brother, and he's in prison. There's a note for ten grand cash in there for when he gets out. Make sure he gets it if you get the chance, or at least tell Bridges. He's gotten me out of a few binds, the fat son-of-a-bitch."

Elsa was puzzled, but oddly understood his position. She assumed he was talking about one of his drug houses that she had heard him brag about. She knew that was basically how he made a living. She was a naturally grateful person, and he did buy everything they needed around the house. Her grandmom had told her to never judge anyone. She guessed that also applied to Randy, but it was very hard for her.

"Well? What you got on your mind?"

Elsa suddenly returned to the moment from the vastness of her racing thoughts.

"Randy, I. . . I don't know what you want me to do with this stuff. Shouldn't Mama–?"

"Damn it, girl, I just told you. Even if I spelled it out to that woman, all she'd do is go drain my bank account and the rest would go to waste. Or she'd smoke it or shoot it and leave y'all to damn rot. She has no idea about my holdings, and she don't know shit from Shinola. Take everything in that drawer to the lawyer. If I get locked up or killed over this mess, you're in charge. Just get it to Bridges. I don't know, have that Indian woman you love so much take you down to his office. Let him handle everything, and don't you dare tell your mama or sister. They'll get plenty out of the deal in time. You hear me?"

Elsa sighed. She nodded. Looked down at the floor.

"Okay, Randy. I hope nothing bad happens to you, though. I'll do what you need me to do."

He took a long swig of fire water. His mouthed danced briefly with hot vanilla and toffee and numbness. It was a pity he couldn't fuck and marry a bottle of liquor. It was all he really loved, beside the occasional flash of anger where he got to break someone's head. See blood explode out of a nose or a mouth.

He finished his glass again. Stared Elsa down. She was still staring back. He felt his body relax. He saw Death in her eyes. Some not-too-distant fate swam in those blue pools. He was drowning in its arms. A vision of Release, clear as day.

Fuck it. Death has gotta be better than prison.

He had just given his last intentions to an elf. Jesus Christ. Life was ridiculous and Death was a cruel joke. Both happened while you blinked. One kept the light on, the other turned it off. Simple as that.

Randy motioned for her to leave him alone. Let him drink in peace. Let him find an old Western on the television. Let him fall asleep and dream of nothing. Tomorrow, or on the notion thereof, he planned to do more of the same. Wait and drink, and drink and wait. He felt a flicker of deep rage rising in him with each breath. A whisper of vulnerability. When the hounds finally came, he hoped he'd at least take a few down with him.

A wild dog can't abide the kennel.

Rylan

On the day Elsa had proclaimed *it* would happen, whatever that might be, I felt nothing but numbness. I felt like a death-row prisoner awaiting the chair. Like a novice understudy being thrust onto stage of Broadway's biggest premier. I was too nervous for nerves and too paranoid for jitters.

I was ill-prepared for whatever may await me. All I had was the word born from a child's frightened dream, my two hands, a sharp mind, and a body trained to hopefully take a few licks.

Hell, I still wasn't convinced that I was *really going to do anything*. I just couldn't quite go there in my mind. I had yet to commit to anything but a quick jaunt up the mountain and a look around the house. If anything went south, I would call the cops or try to intervene in some minor way.

God, that sounds about pathetic. . .

Somewhere deep in my very core, though, I knew she was right. I knew Elsa Privette had some– I don't know the exact word. . . *talent*. Maybe that was close enough. I did believe that something really bad was going to happen to her or her sister or whoever on the night she had foretold.

I wished to God she hadn't told me, because now I felt obliged to do something.

I pictured that evil son-of-a-bitch she had to contend with each day. I pictured him when he was drunk. Mean, loud, sloppy and looking for a punching bag. I thought about our two brief interactions. I felt the intimidation again that he had imposed on me, and I'm a grown man. I couldn't imagine being a kid living in the special Hell he could create.

It made me angry. It made me clench my fists. It made me hate him and every half-man just like him.

I can erase him.

And I knew that I could. Somehow, I felt as confident in that fact as Elsa did in her premonition. It might kill me, too. It might land me in prison for a very long time, but I knew that when it came right down to it. . . With the element of surprise and the youthful benefit of not fearing my limits, I might just win the upper hand if it came down to that.

Maybe.

It was a Saturday. Elsa said her mom would be gone, that much was clear. That was a fact. I knew that I needed my evening free to complete whatever fool's errand I was supposedly planning, so I needed to dispatch any plans.

Lunch. I would have lunch with Lacy, say that my uncle wanted me to grab dinner with a few of his coworkers or something, and then I would have the night to myself.

"How's your salad?" I asked, between slow and steady mouthfuls of a habanero cheeseburger at one of our favorite haunts. It was my favorite thing on the menu, but today it tasted like melted plastic. I had no appetite. Dread filled the empty space in my stomach. I ate only to give the guise of normalcy. I dipped each French fry with disgust. The ketchup looked like theatrical blood on the crispy potato underneath.

"It's good. I love this blue cheese dressing. Want a bite?"

Lacy held her fork out to me with some green apple-romaine-bacon bit-dressing combo pierced upon it. I probably turned a shade of green.

"No, I'm good with my burger. Thanks, though."

"You okay, Ry? You seem a thousand miles away today."

Damn this woman. She knew me too well. It was weird sometimes.

"Yeah. I'm good! My knee's bothering me today. Had a rough run this morning."

I lied, but it was something familiar to rest a false truth upon. In truth, my body was a hundred percent. I felt like I could run through a brick wall and rip old oaks from their very roots.

"You run too much. Of course your knee's going to hurt."

She waved her now-empty fork at me to prove her point. She summoned the waiter. She ordered another glass of Chardonnay. It was just after noon. She impressed me to no end.

"Why aren't you drinking? It's the weekend! Come on! Catch-up!"

Peace. She had left a few minutes ago. I was alone in my apartment. It was very quiet.

I felt very alone, indeed.

I opened the big trunk at the foot of my bed. It had traveled up here with me, almost nine months ago, when the world as I knew it seemed in shambles. It had traveled with me to college, had witnessed my young life unfold in bedrooms and closets. It held all sorts of memorabilia. I dug through the layers of my life so far looking for what I needed. Family photographs. My dad in the Army. My mom on prom night. They both looked so beautiful, and so young.

I moved aside race medals and trophies. Plaques from high school and college awarding me all manner of academic and athletic accolades. I stacked a few books that were special to me. That had perhaps shaped me in some way. *1984* and *Dorian Gray*. *The Wind-Up Bird Chronicle* and some Paulo Coelho. I finally found what I needed near the bottom of it all. A time capsule, of sorts.

I found my old hunting knife. I found a black ski mask from one of our first wintry trips to these mountains.

The knife was surprisingly sharp as I removed it from its sheath. Examined the blade, carefully moved my thumb across its surface, returned it to the leather casing. The mask looked empty and plain. It mirrored my state of mind. We were kindred spirits. I just needed it to cover my face and remove my identity for a short while. Disguise the scared boy who knelt beside an old trunk in a minimally decorated room. Make him look more like a man.

Make him brave. Make him be less selfish. Make him do something for someone in need.

I knew it would take more than a mask and a knife, but it was a start. It was the best that I knew how to do.

It would have to be enough.

It had all come to this, and though my hands shook as I donned my gloves and ski mask, I felt decided and unanimous in what I was about to do.

My intentions were noble enough, at least to my young and naïve way of thinking. I would sneak through the woods, get within ear shot of the house, check things out for a while, and if anything was going sideways in there... I would try to do something to stop it. The mask and the knife felt silly, but it was all I had to go on at the moment. If Randall Lightner saw me on his property, I'd be dead anyway.

I had parked just out of sight of the meandering dirt road that led up the mountain. It was getting dark, and there was little residual sunshine in these deep woods. Not at this hour. Nowhere the shine of a security light, a warm house's interior glow, no moon yet to abate the gloaming. I had brought a flashlight, but I wouldn't need it. I had been up here on foot enough to find my way even through the dark. I was no longer a stranger to these trees and this mountain. I had become as a nocturnal animal best adept in the blackness.

I took the hunting knife out of its scabbard one more time. It looked dangerous, sharp, eager. I hoped that I would be the same if I had occasion to use it. I gave it gently, lovingly, back to its leather lover resting at my hip.

I opened the door to my car and stepped out into the gloom. I eased it shut and proceeded into the woods. I felt that I was moving automatically. A wind-up toy posturing at the hands of some unpredictable fate.

My breathing was audible in my ears alone and the mask further obscured my sight. Every step brought me closer to full dark. Thunder rumbled in the distance like some cryptic beast awakening from deep sleep. Somewhere in a cavern below the earth, possibly only in my mind.

Though it had been less than a half-hour, it seemed like I walked for days in the thick woods. I lifted my feet carefully with each step, setting them down just as cautiously. Still, the leaves and sticks on the ground creaked and cracked. Practically silent to the observer, I felt like I might as well be setting off fireworks in the trees.

King Lear in the fog came to mind. My stomach clenched with nerves every few seconds. I took deep breaths that didn't soothe. My chest tightened, and I had to take pause several times as I made my way to the small house. As it came into view, looking like a derelict ice sculpture emerging from the void, I had to take a knee.

Then, I fully laid down on my back.

I studied the sky as I gathered myself yet again. The clouds above, or the idea of them, reached for me with long dark arms. Taciturn beggars calling for blood. Begging the ground to surrender. And then, not being satisfied, began to cry tears of resignation. Rain drops fell slowly around as another clap of thunder rang through the statuesque trees. This time, it was closer and unimagined. I blinked away a drop or two, saw the leaves around me begin to glisten. It was warm, at least, and a part of me wished that I would simply pass away and fade into the soft earth on which I lay.

I may have even nodded off. Stress and strain and nerves almost shutting me down. I may have even dreamed. When I awoke, I was surrounded by the deep impenetrable darkness of these night woods. Then, like a flashbulb in a bunker, lightning crashed through the black. The sky was now in full cacophony with a strong spring storm. I jolted awake when I began to process a different sound apart from the rain, wind, and thunder. Maybe it had drifted into my dream, and I was just now processing the noise.

Screaming and yelling inside the tiny house. A man's voice overpowering a woman's, like a boxer's sudden attack on his opponent. A young girl was crying uncontrollably somewhere behind the noise.

I rolled over from my temporary respite and waited on hands and knees. I stared at the house as if I might develop x-ray vision. My eyes studied every corner of the space. One window was visible on the far left, but the room within was dark. A screen door on the opposing side showed just a touch of flickering light. The kitchen, maybe? It seemed like the shouting was coming from that side of the house, but the weather was pitching sounds in all directions.

I lay low as the fighting grew louder. The little girl's crying had stopped. I assumed that was probably Elsa. The other girl, the sister, was still shouting in fever pitch. The man's voice was replaced by the sound of animal fervor and breaking glass. And then, a second of silence. Like the sudden close of an opera, but with no crescendo of applause to abate the still.

Like a shotgun blast, the screen door suddenly burst open. The clamor startled me more than any bolt of lightning. A figure appeared briefly, and then was retracted back into the house as if attached to a bungee cord. Shouting, screaming. . . The door opened again, the sister appeared – Jenny, this time on the ground crawling to escape some unseen presence. And then he appeared.

Just silhouettes in the dark, but very much present. He grabbed her by the hair as she kicked and protested.

At that, I rose slowly to my feet. My legs protested and briefly buckled, but I regained my balance after a moment. Shielded by the dark and pouring rain, I moved low and quickly across the back yard. I took cover briefly behind what remained of an old car and determined that the window of the left was my best bet to get inside the house. Adrenaline surged through my limbs. My heart pounded in my chest, pulsing blood rapidly into my ear drums.

The man was obviously preoccupied with the screaming elder daughter, but I didn't want to risk the side door. Getting blown away by this homicidal madman like a common home invader would not be a great legacy. I waited for a passing flicker of lightning to fade, and then sprinted to the side of the house. At the window, I peered inside as best as I could.

Dark, maybe I could make out a child's bedroom? I didn't see anyone inside, regardless. I put three clumsy, gloved fingers on the edge of the window and pushed upward. No budge. Four fingers. . . Nothing.

If this thing is painted shut, I'm so fucked.

Kneeling below the window, I positioned what I could of both hands on the seal and put my back into opening it. Finally, it gave way. There was the slightest creak as it opened, but the sound was quickly swallowed by a roll of thunder. At its widest, I thought I could narrowly fit through the opening and get inside the house.

I shimmied through as quickly and quietly as I could. Fortunately, the only thing below the window in the room was a child's plastic table that I moved back, just a bit, with my foot as I entered the room.

The heavy smell of old smoke and damp staleness met me as soon as I settled in the room. All the lights were off, but I made out a flicker coming from down the hall. A television it looked like, and the volume had to be a full blast. I didn't hear anyone screaming or yelling or fighting anymore. I didn't know what that meant.

Resting on one knee at the window, I carefully thumbed the button on the sheath at my side and removed the hunting knife. It felt like it weighed ten pounds in my hand. They were no longer shaking, but I felt every fiber of my being was electrified and humming like live wire.

I suddenly remembered my very first boyhood scrap. Summer going into seventh grade. Hormones and first crushes. Growing like weeds in all directions. Tension had built between me and this kid all baseball season, and he just wouldn't drop whatever our initial issue had been. He wasn't particularly big or anything, but he was the singular most annoying kid in our grade; popular, he already had a girlfriend, was the star player on the team, highlights in his surfer blond hair, and got away with bloody murder all the time. Name calling, ganging-up after practice with his idiot cronies, and eventually a shoving match in the dugout during a scrimmage game had all led to a decisive moment.

When I say a shoving match, I mean that I pushed him first, far too irresolutely. He pushed me back, much harder, and I stumbled backwards onto the ground. As I lay momentarily on the gritty concrete floor of the dugout, with all the guys oohing and pointing at me, surrounded by the shells of derelict sunflower seeds and plastic Gatorade caps, I felt a heat run through me not dissimilar to what I was feeling now.

My chest heaved up and down in my 'Kinnett Dairy Kings' uniform. The kid was both doubled-over laughing at me and yelling "What? You want some?" And, "Get up, pussy!" for added effect in my general direction as his goons stood by. I remember this clearly. The hot rage, the hands shaking and the weak knees all at once. Our vacant head coach, who was some sort of youth pastor, seemed to be studying the formation of clouds in the sky near third base. A few kids in the field were looking in our direction to see what the commotion was about. And then, I saw my dad looking right at me from outside the chain-link fence. Dismay and worry spread across his face like a wine stain.

My mom and all the patient mothers of boyhood youth were chatting like magpies and had not seen a thing. All the grandparents and the folding chairs and the family dog or two all seemed to sit placidly without concern. But no, there he was. My dad. Staring right at me. Silently begging me to get up and do something. Pleading even. This look strengthened my resolve enough to get off the ground, but then I would also need to do something to remove the horrified look on his face, I supposed.

"Billy," I said, brushing off my permanently red-dirt stained baseball pants and rising to my full summergrowth-spurt height, "I'm about to kick your ass."

At school, I was known as the smart kid, the quiet student; perhaps a little weird, but no one viewed me as particularly weak. I also played football every year. As a result, I apparently spoke with an exaggerated resolve, when I called him out, that caused the whole team to grow quiet. This, of course, beguiled my nerves and fit-throwing inner rage, but it did give me a little more courage. That, and the fact that I now had more of an audience than just my dad staring into my soul from the sidelines. Everything moved in slow motion after that, as things do in such an excited state. Play stopped on the infield, my mom struggled to rise out of her camping chair, mouths opened and closed like guppies from the parental crowd. Our "aw-shucks" ol' coach was initiating what looked to be a slow trot to the dugout on stiff legs.

When I hit him, the punch was almost too clean. Impossible to duplicate. Hand of God stuff, really. His dumb purple and green braces immediately severed his upper lip. I felt the metal scrape across my knuckles as my fist traveled from chin to nose in a driving blow. His hat brim went from forehead to right ear. He started to back-peddle clumsily into his two or three boyfriends who stood with dumbfounded expressions. They scattered into each other rather than catching him, and soon enough he lay flat on his back amid the sunflower shells. In a panic, like a trapped animal, he wiggled frantically from side to side trying to regain his feet. I took a few steps closer and yelled with pointed finger, "Don't! Don't even think about getting up."

He paused for a moment, considered briefly his next move, licking his lip frantically as salty blood covered his soon-to-be straight teeth, and then they came: the tears of embarrassment and the fear only a bully can know when he is bested. This was the first time he had ever fallen victim to retaliation of any kind. He seemed to have never known physical discomfort, either. His reign was over. In youth, there is no regaining grace in this regard.

Laughter and Roman bloodlust erupted from the full team as the tears streamed down his cheeks. Coach shuffled past the boys and helped young Billy to his feet, admonishing me as he did. Telling me that I was "finished for the day", and to "get out of here!" That was fine. I would gladly take the fall for this. I turned to find my team bag amid its twins hanging on hooks against the back wall of the dugout. Boys cleared out of my way as I rummaged through them. I walked out of the dugout with adrenaline navigating my blood stream like a mad Italian in the Formula One.

My parents were packing up and silent when I reached them, "appalled" parents mumbled all around. It didn't matter what they said. I didn't hear it.

When we reached the parking lot after a silent Forever, and were well out of sight of all the simple, well-meaning characters of my youth, my mom started on about being embarrassed and disappointed at me while she searched for the car keys in her purse. The adrenaline was rapidly being replaced by a weird nausea. My head hurt.

Just then, though, I felt my dad's hand on my shoulder. I turned to look up at him. He mouthed, "I'm very proud of you," so Mom wouldn't hear. He smiled, and I began to feel better.

I began to feel the slow burn of childhood simmering into manhood that day, as well. Eventually, my mom acquiesced and we had a good laugh about the whole ordeal in the car on the way home. I even got to pick my favorite steak restaurant for dinner that night. All was well, and another sunset of my youth moved me one step closer to the present.

Now, the quiet boy who had loved books was replaced by a grown man. Strong, fast, smart. Powerful... Yet I was still cowering in a child's bedroom. In the dark of a stranger's house. I faced another bully, but one magnified from mild sadism into something truly terrible. I could hear him breathing and grumbling down the hall. Furniture was moving violently. An earthquake in the shadow of a flickering TV. A monster expanding and filled with hate. The boyhood fear gripped me, the urge to flee was overpowering, but I remembered lying there in the dirt that day. My father's face. Growing rage, and then– the sound of Elsa's voice sounding down the hall and the monster's roar back to silence her.

With knife in hand, I forced my body into motion. Water dripped off my clothes from the torrential storm, growing ever louder, outside. Droplets fell silently onto the old carpet, and I moved in slow motion into the hallway. My eyes adjusting, I could make out another bedroom just ahead. Further down, there seemed to be a door leading into the kitchen and then an opening into the living room just beyond that. That's where the scuffling and fighting was coming from, still brimming, but now desperate.

The length of the hall was less than twenty feet, but it felt like an eternal ribbon. The carpet felt soft under my boots, like I might sink into it at any moment. I pressed against the left wall when I passed the other bedroom. Creeping inch by inch. Inch by inch. Coming just into sight of the kitchen, there she was.

Elsa sat on the dingy floor against the little kitchen table, hugging her knees so tightly I thought her spindly legs might break. In one hand, she clutched her pillow. It's red surface visibly moist from tears. Strands of disheveled hair hung in her face, and she wept with silent heaves of her chest. The dim shadow of blood streamed from her mouth in tiny streams as she shook.

I knelt and leaned into her field of vision. Was I trying to get her attention? I must have, but God only knows why. She eventually sensed me there, and her eyes widened like a frightened animal. A concealed squeal was all she could muster, and she covered her mouth to prevent a scream with her free hand. In my ridiculous ski mask and black attire, she had no idea who I was or why I was there. I wanted so badly to pull up the mask and reassure her that it was me, but that might only scare her worse than she already was. Instead, I just put a finger to my nearly covered lips and made a "keep it down" motion with my other hand, brandishing the knife as I gestured. She seemed to calm down just a bit, maybe.

Once I was relatively confident that she wasn't going to let out a blood-curdling, pre-teen girl shriek at my presence in the house, I ever so carefully looked around the corner behind me and into the living room.

Fuck...

There he was, standing with his back to me. The other daughter at his feet, her hair in a bundle around his fist. He had turned the TV volume up to maximum level, attempting to drown out a sound despite the storm raging outside and the house residing in the middle of nowhere. I could see his spit with every shout and insult filling the air in the glow of the television. The poor girl's nose and brow were bleeding profusely.

How could she have possibly known it would get this bad tonight?

I glanced back into the kitchen, and she was staring right back at me. Anxious, waiting, expectant. Pleading with her crystal blue eyes for me to do *something* or get out of their house. Just then he slammed the girl against the coffee table in the living room. She was barely moving. He slapped her in the back of the head and pressed his boot into her back. He was yelling, but the opus crescendo in my head was allowing no words to filter. This snapshot will forever keep me awake at night. A dirty living room with beer cans, whiskey bottles, and Dr Enufs scattered all about. A petrified deer head mounted on the faux wooden panel wall. A disgusting old couch and chair illuminated in the blue-purple glow of the TV. A rerun of *All in the Family* flickering across the screen of the old set. Archie Bunker's voice. . . I could never hear it again without my chest tightening and a wave of nausea overcoming me.

And, him. With his back perfectly turned to me. A white T-shirt with lightly stained armpits sitting atop an old pair of blue jeans. A camo hat. His arms and neck and back musculature all looked sinuous and striking just under the surface. His movements were unstable. He was utterly lit, clumsy-drunk, but still alert enough to retain his strength.

At least in a room full of children. . .

He knelt beside the girl and began to whisper something into her ear. She seemed to go limp at whatever he said. He reached his hand around to her breast and gave a visible, hard squeeze. She covered her chest in vain. He then traced a line along the back of her jeans, over her ass, and then moved to the inside of her thigh. The girl was frozen. She was no longer moving, but I could see the panicked breaths becoming shallower with each passing second. He roughly positioned her on the table.

He stood to his full height, almost a head taller than me. I took one last deep breath as he began to undo his belt. His head down and voice still mocking. I turned the blade underhanded, the serrations pointed upward. My grip was vice-tight. The distance between us closed faster than I imagined; I might have let out a primal grunt as I lunged forward.

The knife moved swiftly back and thrust forward in my hand as if guided by a puppeteer. He was just turning to face me when the blade struck his broad back. I felt it hit with more force than expected, right into his shoulder blade. The knife deflected to the side, doing little more than ripping his shirt and fecklessly jabbing into him. The impact, however, knocked him off balance and sent him tumbling forward over the girl on the table. He tripped over his own feet after hitting that impediment and fell loudly at the foot of the old armchair. Somewhere behind me, dishes rattled from the fall and a picture fell off the wall.

The girl turned over on the table and slid onto the floor. She saw me but was not registering anything. Shock. Semi-conscious. The man flipped onto his back and used the armchair to pull himself up.

"The fuck?" he sputtered.

He reached his left hand across his body to feel the stab wound on his back. When he looked, oily blood glistened in the flutter of the TV images. Then he focused his gaze on me. Rage and confusion.

"Who the fuck–?"

He didn't finish his sentence, but instead plowed forward in my direction. I froze. When he tackled me, the knife went flying and I felt the slat wall slam into my back as his weight knocked the wind out of me. Surprisingly, coherent thoughts entered my mind as we struggled against the wall.

I had not prepared for this. I should have brought a gun and made this quick if I had to do anything. What had I been thinking? A knife? Who would have heard a gunshot out here, anyway? What was I doing out here in the first place? He was going to kill me. The police would ID me. This was be the culmination of my life's pursuit. Nothing more than a common house burglar, robbing a dirt-poor family. Ironies would abound. Questions would abound.

He grunted and strained to take me to the floor, but I realized that I was standing my ground. I could smell whisky and stress sweat as he pressed against me. His motions were awkward and decidedly slower than I expected. He was used to scrapping with scarecrows and bullying yokels that had always known him, that had always feared him.

I was neither of those. Maybe, just maybe, *he was not prepared for me*. Not the other way around.

A red stain was spreading further across his back as we wrestled. I tried to get a grip on his shirt, or obtain some leverage at all, but then the punches came. I felt the first one hit me in the lower rib cage, and any wind that I had recovered quickly left me again. I let out a groan, and he pulled away just long enough to land a glancing blow on the side of my face. His hand around my throat now, airway immediately blocked, he reared back for the second punch.

No. . . This wasn't going to be how I went out. . . *Not here. . . Not by you.*

I grabbed his shoulders and instinctively kicked off the wall with my trail leg. He tripped over the coffee table again and I went flying towards the kitchen door. I heard the TV fall and go silent behind me. He had landed against the stand and knocked the whole set over. More dishes rattled, something else fell off the wall. We were creating earthquakes like marching Titans in the tiny house. My mask had shifted on my face, leaving me in momentary blackness until I could adjust it. I quickly regained my feet and caught a glimpse of Elsa peering out from under the kitchen table. I cannot describe the look on her face. It was phantom and haunted and surreal.

Now, there was even less light than before. The TV volume was replaced by the rock-concert roar in my head. Elsa's whimpers. The almost-dead girl's shallow breaths.

The man was barely moving in the corner of the room. His head was twisted against the fallen TV set, and he was rubbing his neck and temples spastically. I scanned the floor for the knife, but it was too dark to see. Thunder rolled off in the distance, but the lightning had begun to subside. We were surrounded by shadows. Shades were the only witnesses to this strange and violent scene.

As he was trying to stand, groping in the dimness for any piece of furniture to aid his balance, I looked at the battered sister on the floor. Her frame was all I could see, but I thought about her pain. She looked pitiful. I turned once more to Elsa in the kitchen. The sweet girl from my class. The girl who liked books and wanted to write them one day. Who wanted to leave this squalor behind and move to Paris. Whose absent mother and the maniac now stumbling around the room would do all they could to keep her buried in this place.

Real empathy overwhelmed me, and I don't know if I had ever truly felt that before. I had always been selfish. Perhaps even Narcissistic at times. When Teresa left me, I thought only of my anger and my loss. I had been cruel, and it had been deserved, but it was misdirected. I hated myself for being too cowardly to truly confront the situation.

Instead, I just left. I disappeared into the hills like a specter. I hid my head in the snow. I was not noble, and I was broken. Graceless. But the same place that was tearing so many people apart was working to put me back together. Another irony.

As he stood on stumbling legs where the TV had been, his back to me again, I decided that I would not let him continue. This was where he would stop. Another part of me was about to die, of that I was sure, but perhaps these girls could live a better life as a result. Not in fear or forever paralyzed, but as normal people do. The sacrificial lamb would not be me or Elsa or the sister in this house tonight.

In the dark, our shades would continue to haunt the world. They would wander on, but his was about to exit forever.

I walked across the room without thinking further. He turned to face me briefly, but I hit him just as quickly with a straight punch. He didn't fall, but it didn't matter. It gave me the one chance I needed. My forearm was around his throat and my opposite hand gripped his sweat-slick hair from behind. A kind of dance ensued before we both were on the ground once again. He grumbled and struggled with everything he had. Legs and arms flailed around me. I'm sure that I was hit and scratched and bit in the fray, but I felt nothing. I focused on the blank wall in front of me. A mirror in the dark to reflect everything back to me. All the hard miles, all the pain, all the work, all the good, all the bad, all the love, and all the hate I had ever felt poured out of me as my grip got ever tighter.

I was screaming at the top of my voice before I realized that I was making a sound. My yell dissolved into a growl. The growl dissolved into tears. Streaming down my face like little waterfalls, absorbing into the mask I wore. A mask had always hidden my true feelings, so this was suitable. My strength was frightening. My resolve was terrifying, even to me. His jerking became desperate, and then calmed as if he was coming to peace with his fate. An animal being put to sleep. Only his left leg twitched as I gave one last infinitely tight squeeze.

I realized then that my back was arching off the floor, my heels dug in deep, and now the wall was replaced with the ceiling above me. The eventual crack of his neck as I tugged and twisted startled me back to the reality of the room.

A stillness came over everything. Everything was quiet now.

I lay for a minute longer before rolling him off of me. A fan spun overhead making a sleepy whirring sound. The mounted deer still stared into the dark room, vacant, the glassy marbles in its stuffed head forever unblinking.

I finally stood. Jenny lay unmoving on the floor, but she was breathing. I could make out Elsa's shadowy silhouette standing in the narrow kitchen doorway. Her pillow hung limply by her side, and she held something in her opposite hand. I walked towards her slowly with my hands extended as a sign of peace, just like one would approach a stray dog.

As I neared, she slowly extended my knife up to me, handle first. I took it as gently as I could so as not to accidentally cut her. It must have bounced into the kitchen during our fight.

I knelt beside her. She was still crying and trembling, but the violence of her previous state was subdued. I smoothed her hair back from her face with my gloved hand. She did not seem afraid. In spite of it all, she looked right back at me.

Did she know who I was? Could she possibly know?

I purposefully tried to alter my voice, but my words ultimately came out like a cracked record spinning on a phonograph. My throat was impossibly dry, and it took great effort to speak.

"Do you see that clock on the wall?"

She nodded.

"In ten minutes, I want you to call 911. Do you understand?"

She nodded again, faster this time.

"I think your sister will be okay, but she needs an ambulance. Okay? I just need ten minutes to get out of here."

She seemed to understand without my needing to explain.

"Is he. . . Is he dead?"

I turned around to face the living room, as if I needed to confirm who she was talking about. When I did, a part deep inside of me half-expected him to be standing again and ready to kill me. But, no. . . He still lay on his stomach where I had flipped him over. His head was at an unnatural angle and an arm was tucked awkwardly under his body, but I supposed he could just be sleeping off a serious bender lying there like that.

I nodded yes to answer her question. Her mood didn't change. She didn't seem surprised or frightened at the prospect of his dead body lying on the living room floor.

"Will you be okay here by yourself? You can try to wake your sister up as soon as I leave. She's just in shock. As for him, just tell the police exactly what happened. He got very drunk. He got very mean, then someone broke in as he was hurting you and your sister. There was a bad fight, and then the intruder left."

She nodded one final time. She looked dazed, as if awakening from a dream.

I asked again. "Are you okay?"

She spoke slowly. "I think. . . I think I will be okay now."

I wanted to hug her, to tell her how sorry I was, but I couldn't. If she hadn't recognized me by now, that would surely give me away. So, with that, I stood to leave. She was so small beside me, but her eyes followed mine as I rose.

The screen door closed with no sound as I walked out into the night. The storm had passed, but thunder still rumbled off in the invisible distance. Before me, the blackness of the woods beckoned me forward into whatever eventual void awaited us all. Oblivion rested in the shadowed trees, and I required no light to find my way.

Epilogue

Rylan

My face was hurting. My ribs were sore, but I was okay. I got home late. Every passing car had been the police in my mind. Waiting to arrest me over and over again for what I had done. Right or wrong, justifiable or not, murder in the first degree bore a high penalty in these so-called United States.

I went inside. My dark apartment welcomed me with familiar smells. Familiar shapes when I flicked on the lamp. I wanted to disappear into my own walls. Fall through the floor of my space and be gone forever. But I didn't. I made my way into my bedroom. Removed the dark clothes I wore. Put them in the dirty laundry for a thorough wash. Took my hunting knife into the bathroom. Ran it under the sink. Coated it in Dial and scrubbed the dangerous blade for an eternity.

My hands shook as I did this. I felt nauseated in intermittent bursts. Adrenaline leaving my system and nervous energy all coalescing deep inside me. Blood ran from the knife's point and edge into the sink, then it was gone. DNA down the drain. The evidence disappearing like spat toothpaste. I dried it thoroughly afterward. Returned it to its sheath and put it back in the trunk where it, too, could rest.

I showered. Rinsing my own sins down the drain. The hot water burned my skin. I scrubbed myself vigorously. I wanted to be clean again. I wanted to erase this night forever. I laughed out loud at some point. Endorphins rushing through me like so many illicit drugs.

I would never be clean again. I would never erase this night, but I could live with impurity. My bottled-up anger and rage had been exorcised. I had sacrificed the proverbial sacred deer. I had helped someone in need, and I would be fine.

I was cold and chilled when I lay down in bed that night. I pulled every blanket up around me. My mind swirled with how to explain the deepening bruises on the left side of my face. With where I was that night when asked. Answers came. Lies were abundant. None were expressly unprovable.

Maybe I had been out helping a friend? Maybe I was out doing something good with my time? Disprove that, if you can. Call me a liar. I didn't care.

I checked my phone. I had left it behind, and it rested quietly on my dresser. Lacy had texted me several times. She told me that she missed me tonight. She said that she loved me before she had gone to sleep. I texted her back. I reciprocated her sentiments, and what's odd. . . I truly felt them. Not a selfish love. Not a desperate need for affection. But a familiar, sincere, *I love you.*

And, funny thing is, once the adrenaline fully wore-off and I quieted my mind, when police boots didn't kick down my door and news helicopters didn't fly overhead, I slept like a baby.

I had made my peace with own demons. They weren't too bad. They were just part and parcel of *me*, after all, and I could live with that.

They had not consumed me. I had not condemned them. We got along just fine in the end.

We worked well together, these demons and I. I didn't have many friends, so they would have to do.

Elsa did not come to school for almost two weeks. Her sister had been in the hospital for most of that time. Broken ribs and shock symptoms. The mother made a scene over the dead boyfriend and demanded a thorough police investigation. She gave name after name of possible culprits, hicks and dealers and anyone he had ever disagreed with about anything. There was something about one of his properties literally exploding due to one malfeasance or another. Surely the two events were related, they thought. I had just nodded and agreed.

My name never came up, and why should it? Only one brief story was written in the paper about the incident atop Holloway Knob. It vanished like distant woodsmoke into an autumn breeze. Insignificant in the scheme of things.

Rabid dogs often killed each other. Nature's natural erasure had simply taken its course.

The missing girl who wound up dead at the hands of a tormented realtor had stolen the headlines, as it should have, and the press was exhausted with violence by the time this came to print. Ironies and paradoxes abound, as it were.

I arrived early to work on the day Elsa returned to school. There had been whispers and murmurs about the girl the whole week prior. My colleagues had her staying with a foster family, in a group home, transferring to Charlotte, and whatever other stories one could concoct to delve into the plight of a young girl following a particularly damaging incident.

None of these hypotheses were true, and I had been sure that jaws would drop when she did, in fact, return to school. Dropped off by her mother, who had seemed to come into some money at the passing of her suitor. Homemade drugs were a profitable business, after all. Probably found a buried coffee can or two with some serious cash after his passing. Who knows?

I was in the library for some time that morning, helping Lacy with her end-of-year displays. The paper maché butterflies and flowers of spring gave way to graduation hats and giant sunshines of summer. We were taping a beach umbrella onto an empty wall when I saw her through the media center glass. She was in the front office, speaking with Tony and the counselor, and there was much nodding and sympathizing and posturing. Deep relief at seeing her in a familiar environment, in new, clean clothes, and smiling filled me with a warmth that I would not have expected.

"Hey, look who's back."

Lacy turned to see.

"Little Elsa. . . They say she saw the whole thing happen right in front of her."

I shrugged after a moment, after her small form had passed the window.

"She seems okay to me. At first glance, I mean."

"Oh, I bet she's going to be so messed up after this. My God, she's had such a terrible time."

"Well, she's a tough kid. Probably tougher than we know. I'm sure she'll be fine in time."

Our eyes met briefly. Lacy gave me a curious smile. That was it. Nothing more.

———

It was about ten minutes before the bell rang and my classroom would be filled with the cacophony of pre-teen chatter and laughter. I sat at my computer downloading a few video clips for my lessons that day, and an almost imperceptible knock came at the door.

"Come in!" I yelled, as I always did.

A small figure appeared as the door opened. It was her. She looked bright and light as air, entering the room.

"Mr. Wilder?"

Her voice was meek and soft, as it always was.

I stood by my desk as she entered the room, the door closing behind her. She wasn't carrying her pillow, and I hadn't seen it with her through the glass in the library, either. She walked slowly to my desk before I replied. I had not thought about how I might feel or how I would behave when I saw her again. I stood silent in the back of the room, uncharacteristic of me. She didn't seem to notice my strange behavior, but her eyes stared right at me. Bluer than ever. Little elfin crystals.

She stood right before me. I still could not speak. I had no idea what to say. When I saw her eyes fill with tears, a lump began to form somewhere deep in my chest. It traveled up to my throat, and it brought me to my knees. We were face to face, then.

"Mr. Wilder?"

"Yes?" I managed.

Her arms wrapped around me so tightly that I could hardly breathe. Her head rested on my shoulder, and I hesitantly hugged her back. I held back my own tears as she cried quietly. The room became overwhelmingly bright in the fluorescent glow; my eyes ached as the light reflected off the empty desks.

After a long moment, she stepped gently away to face me. She wiped her tears, the redness under her eyes only more apparent blemishes on her fair skin.

"Thank you, Mr. Wilder."

I swallowed deeply. I could no longer speak.

Her voice trembled ever so lightly, but her words came out clear and steady.

"I know. . . I know what you did for me. And I wanted to say thank you."

I wanted to disappear, but I could not. I wanted to turn away, but I was unable to move. Emotion upon emotion stirred inside me like a storm. I was cast about in its wake and waves, the salt spray of the sea now streaming down my face. Now it was her turn to wipe *my* tears. Her hand felt so small and fragile on my face, but she looked stronger than I had ever seen her, staring right back into my eyes.

"Don't cry, Mr. Wilder. I think it will all be okay now. You made it all okay."

The morning bell sounded to break the overwhelming silence that had filled the room. I continued to kneel for a moment as she slowly turned to take her seat. She removed her backpack, sat it on the floor beside her desk, and took out a handful of supplies to begin her day.

Just like any day before, and for many days to come, she began to hum softly to herself and swung her feet playfully beneath her seat.

Elsa turned to me one last time before the door opened and full life returned to the quiet room. I managed to stand and compose myself as best as I could. She smiled and seemed to emanate a radiance that bore all the warmth and hope of a spring day. Her spring would evolve to summer, as all springs do, and life would run its course with us hapless travelers like leaves down the river. All destined to rest where we may, our fates eternally undefined.

Day would always fade to evening. The eventide would pass into the shadows of night. Through such darkness, and even in its deepest shade, there will always be enough light to abate the void.

I really hoped this was true.

The End.